DEB ON AIR—LIVE AT FIVE

OTHER FIVE STAR TITLES BY LAURIE MOORE:

A DEBUTANTE DETECTIVE MYSTERY

DEB ON AIR—LIVE AT FIVE

LAURIE MOORE

FIVE STAR
A part of Gale, Cengage Learning

GALE
CENGAGE Learning®

Detroit • New York • San Francisco • New Haven, Conn • Waterville, Maine • London

LIBRARY OF CONGRESS CATALOGING-IN-PUBLICATION DATA

Moore, Laurie.
    Deb on air live at five : a debutante detective mystery / Laurie
Moore. — First Edition.
      pages cm
    ISBN 978-1-4328-2725-0 (hardcover) — ISBN 1-4328-2725-1
(hardcover)
      1. Debutantes—Texas—Fiction. I. Title.
PS3613.O564D43 2013
813'.6—dc23   2013008275

First Edition. First Printing: July 2013
Find us on Facebook– https://www.facebook.com/FiveStarCengage
Visit our website– http://www.gale.cengage.com/fivestar/
Contact Five Star™ Publishing at FiveStar@cengage.com

Printed in Mexico
1 2 3 4 5 6 7 17 16 15 14 13

For Laura

ACKNOWLEDGMENTS

Many thanks to Five Star editor, Tiffany Schofield, for years of unflagging support, and my daughter, Laura, for being such an inspiration to me.

CHAPTER ONE

Dear Diary,

The inescapable truth my wicked stepmother, Nerissa Fascett Prescott, couldn't get past is that, even though she did a monstrous thing by murdering my mother and attempting to kill my father in order to raid the Prescott family fortune, she was still a human being who required food and water. She probably never dreamed that a Fort Worth debutante would spend almost two weeks pursuing her from the U.S.A. across the Mexican border after she took refuge at a wealthy banker's hacienda in the Chihuahua Desert; or that I'd eventually track her movements through the minions delivering groceries to his house. Most of all, I'm virtually certain that, in her wildest dreams, she never expected to wake up to the feel of the heel of my shoe on her throat as I spit into her face and pointed my trusty-rusty little Llama .380 caliber at her frontal lobe. But, down in beautiful, enchanted Meh-hee-co, I turned into a hopeless romantic.

Then again, maybe I felt testy after camping out atop a plateau overlooking the hacienda after teaming up with a ragtag team of Mexican miscreants and crazy white ex-patriots, living a primitive lifestyle without my Harkman Beemis charge card and regular lunches at the sushi restaurant where everyone shouted, "Dainty— Dainty Prescott—over here!" each time I glided in dressed to the nines.

Heavy footfalls sheared my concentration. With my pen

hovering above the page in my journal, I looked up in time to see a couple of bruisers from the El Paso Police Department hauling in a weather-beaten man with his hands cuffed behind his back. He smelled like a cascading torrent of rotting flesh and urine, and wore all black. The only thing missing was a rusty machete and big floppy sombrero to pull his whole outfit together. When I arrived at the El Paso County Jail an hour ago, I commandeered a seat near the booking desk where I could stretch out my legs; now, I quickly pulled them in as the officers approached. Their prisoner dripped blood from a head wound that, from its size and damage, looked like it'd made contact with the business end of a big metal flashlight, and I didn't want my new shoes ruined.

As they marched this desperado past me, I whiffed the air around him. He smelled like the devil's toenails, and looked like he hadn't bathed in a year. He skewered me with a crazed stare, and I went back to making entries in my journal.

At times when I didn't think I could take any more of Mexico's hostile conditions, I daydreamed of Jim Bruckman, a detective with the Fort Worth Police Department, and tried to fall asleep. It was the only way I could be with him whenever I wanted out in no-man's-land; and I'd invent scenarios that would encourage his forgiveness for returning to Mexico over his objections. There was still a two-million-dollar bounty on my head from when I rescued my sister, Teensy, from this swill pit a few weeks before, after men in a gypsy cab beat her unconscious and left her on a dirty, Ciudad Juárez back street to die. When I told him I had no choice but to hunt down Nerissa, he dumped me.

A tattoo-covered woman of indeterminate age and ancestry sheared my concentration when she slid into one of the chairs across from me. She had on a man's wife-beater and skintight leggings that'd been cut off to make shorts. I tried to ignore her, but each time I glanced up, I caught her looking me up and down.

"Excuse me, but what're you staring at? Is there a problem?"

"You look like my first prison bitch."

Speechless, I returned my attention to my journal. I could feel her beady snake-eyes boring a hole through me.

I tried to avoid making eye contact, but after a few minutes, I gave in to the urge. Sure enough, she was still giving me the visual once-over.

She leaned in conspiratorially. "Know what I'm thinkin'?" She didn't wait for an answer. "I'm thinkin' I should wait to kill you until after all these people are gone."

I slammed my journal shut and moved closer to police personnel at the opposite end of the room. Once I was reasonably sure she wouldn't bother me anymore, I resumed writing.

Back in Fort Worth, Texas, my name's being dragged through the mud. Even though I worked at WBFD-TV in Fort Worth, I hoped viewers would turn off their TV sets and stop believing what the newspapers wrote about moi, Dainty Prescott. The stories being disseminated about me around the Metroplex have been largely untrue, and they keep using that same scary picture of me that Border Patrol took when I allegedly re-entered the country illegally. Call it tabloid sensationalism, designed to sell newspapers or beef-up ratings, like publishing photographs of movie stars, face-down in the gutter, after a night of booze, drugs, and debauchery. As documented proof that I'm a classy and impeccably dressed blue-eyed blonde, I had Amanda Vásquez, the pygmy interpreter and guide that I'd used a few weeks before when I went to Ciudad Juárez to hunt for my sister, take my picture with my camera phone. At least if things went badly and I ended up on the front page of the local newspaper again—or on television, before a viewing audience of millions—the deranged-looking image of me dragging Nerissa across the shallow part of the Rio Bravo and back into Texas wouldn't be the last one branded in the public's memory.

Believe it or not, I didn't go off on this expedition half-cocked; I actually had this exploit under control. Sometimes you have to go to Hell to put the Devil in prison, and I went to Mexico to hunt down Nerissa like the evil, murderous vamp she is. I survived the metallic pings of bullet-scored metal, and I did what I came to do—

"Miss Prescott? Excuse me. Sorry, ma'am, I didn't mean to startle you. But the Tarrant County Sheriff's Department's extradition unit's here to transport your stepmother back to Fort Worth, and you said you wanted to talk to the deputies before we pulled the prisoner out of lockup and turned her over to them."

I glanced up from my journal and blinked several times. My concentration had become so focused that I must've appeared autistic with indifference.

The El Paso sheriff's deputy doing the talking had a calm demeanor, a face like a geometry problem, and the density of a cinderblock. With his eagle-beak nose, high cheekbones, and a brass name plate pinned to his shirt that read J. SILVERLEAF, I figured Deputy Silverleaf had to be of Native American descent. He knew how badly I wanted to be on the next flight out to Love Field, but he also knew I wouldn't leave until I saw Nerissa being hauled off in a squad car wearing handcuffs and leg irons.

"Yes, please. I need to speak to them. It's a long drive back to Fort Worth, and they need to know what they're dealing with."

I heard a faraway feminine laugh that drew me in its direction.

Amanda, dressed like a fashion emergency of Chernobyl proportions, sauntered up from a trip to the vending machine holding a cellophane wrapper pulled back from a three-pack of chocolate cakes—the ones in the shape of rifle cartridges with the white marshmallow cream filling inside. When she opened her mouth to shove the first of the cakes in like a wood chipper, everyone in the room who looked our way could see she had a big enough gap between her teeth to insert a rotisserie chicken into it.

She spoke with chocolate mortared between her teeth. "Did you tell Captain Sensitive your stepmother's family might try to waylay the deputies while they're on the road? You know that's a pretty desolate drive." Amanda has a love-hate relationship with peace officers.

I wished she hadn't said that. I already wanted to dry-heave into the hedges outside the building because I had enough hor- ror shows going on in my head without worrying about one of Nerissa's kin ambushing the two deputies and taking her from their custody.

I closed my journal. We accompanied Deputy Silverleaf to a controlled-access area where the deputies waited for jailers to bring my stepmother down. Amanda saw them first. Then I caught sight of them out of the corner of my eye.

When we came within thirty feet of the Tarrant County law- dogs, the El Paso deputy made serious eye contact with me and said, "Nice website, by the way. Impressive video."

"Thanks." I assumed he meant the WBFD website my boss, station manager J. Gordon Pfeiffer, provided for each of the "blow-dries"—which is what Gordon's assistant, Rochelle LeDuc, calls the on-air talent. Since I'm a paid extern with an undergraduate degree in broadcast journalism, I have my own page because I occasionally fill in as a sub for the blow-dries by delivering the morning drive-time, noon report, the *Live at Five* report, or the *News at Ten* broadcasts.

Then Deputy Silverleaf winked. My thanks may've been a bit too reflexive; in the Metroplex, I've become used to people recognizing me in public and fawning over my celebrity, but in

El Paso, I should've been yesterday's news. I wanted to ask him more about the video comment, but the three of us had come even with the Tarrant deputies, so Silverleaf made introductions and then left us to our conversation.

The county had sent a male-female team to transport my stepmother, I supposed so that the female could accompany Nerissa to the restroom on the long way back, should bathroom breaks become necessary. The calm cadence of their respiration should've settled me but it didn't. It didn't matter if they were seasoned officers or not. I intended to fill them in on exactly what they needed to know, and planned to furnish every bit of information I knew about the diabolical woman before they made the journey back.

Death can be disarming. Safety first.

This room had developed a personality rife with sterility and desolation. Waiting cast a pall of apprehension over me, which prompted my warning. "I'm not telling you how to run your business, but you need to know exactly what you're dealing with."

The male, who looked sixty-ish and balding but also physically fit, assured me they'd read over the four arrest warrants for murder, attempted murder, and two counts of endangering the lives of my sister and her friend, as well as the accompanying paperwork for each charge. Which was just another way of telling me, "You'll need intensive therapy after this and will probably be locked up in a psychiatric facility so long your driver's license will expire."

The female, a forty-something, blockbuster of a woman with processed blonde hair, spoke in a calm, capable voice. "We'll take it from here."

Then her partner piped up in an "I'm a big dog" kind of way; and the lady deputy chuckled in an "I'm pretty high-strung myself" kind of way; and I'm all "What the hell am I even doing here?" in a kind of "These cockroaches are the size of my Porsche" kind of way.

Urgency gripped me. "You don't understand." I filled them in on how I came home one day to find my mother dead on her bedroom floor, and how Daddy remarried shortly thereafter. I explained that I'd found a book called *The Ladies' Guide to Homicide* among Nerissa's belongings, and I told them how she'd tried to murder my father. Then I informed them about Nerissa's people, and how Gus Quintanilla, a former Texas Ranger and acquaintance of Daddy's, had warned me that word on the street had it that her family planned to intercept the patrol car and physically remove her from the custody of extraditing officers. "You have to get DPS involved." By DPS, I meant the Department of Public Safety, better known as the highway patrol.

In Texas, there's a saying: *You don't run from a red patch.* What it means is that you don't mess with Texas highway patrol officers. Tall and imposing in their Stetson hats and taupe-colored uniforms with blue epaulets on the shoulders and red patches on their sleeves, our troopers spend long hours alone in their cruisers, sometimes without a backup around for miles. They don't take guff off anybody, and it'd be a huge mistake to misinterpret their professionalism and cordial demeanor as weakness.

"Please—*listen to me.*" My eyes widened like those of a coed in the sudden shadow of a slasher. "Ask DPS to escort you from county to county until you get her back to Fort Worth." I was thinking in terms of a relay race, where a trooper could fall in and relieve the previous trooper at each county line.

The clink of shackles alerted me. I looked over to see my stepmother being escorted down the corridor. I realized that I'd stumbled into "I want to sew your skin into a bustier" territory when her mouth widened into a grin, as if she'd been waiting to kill me for a very long time. A serpent of nausea coiled in my gut.

"Please take this seriously." My voice dissolved to a whisper. My eyes shifted to Amanda. "I can't do this again. I can't go back into Mexico. They'll kill me next time."

Nerissa saw me and smirked. Then she made eye contact with the male deputy, and—*train, meet wreck*—what I predicted would become an ongoing flirtation with law enforcement began. I backed away to give them a wide berth, and Amanda followed my lead. We trailed the deputies to the transport vehicle, a police package sedan equipped with a caged area and computer, also called an MDT, or mobile data transmitter. As we waited for them to seat Nerissa inside the caged area, invasive red and blue emergency lights from incoming cruisers lit up the sally port. I wished my camera phone had been charged so I could send pictures to show Bruckman what he missed while he went to the Indian casino, played blackjack, and ate chateaubriand with his cohorts. I'd managed to pull off what even professional recovery specialists and the U.S. government wouldn't touch with a ten-foot pole. That's when it flashed into my mind about all those breaking news stories of shootouts, snipers, and standoffs, and I started to hallucinate the next hillbilly gun battle.

Nerissa tuned up like a howler monkey.

Before they closed off my stepmother from view, she burst into crocodile tears that were anything but convincing. "Dainty, please. You have to talk to your father for me. I didn't do it. I didn't hurt your mom, and I didn't try to kill your dad. You have to believe me."

But I didn't. "Flight is a sign of guilt."

Since the last time I'd seen her, I was pretty sure she had Botox. Which only made her look like everything anyone said to her came as a surprise.

When her protests lost effect, she gave me a slitty-eyed look, and left me with an ominous warning. "Just remember, Dainty, I'm back. Watch yours."

The dead air felt so thick I wanted to claw my way right through it.

The door to the sally port rolled open for an incoming patrol car. Swallows took flight from the sidewalk in a flap of wings so severe that my ears shivered. Nerissa's eyes cut to the exit. In the gray light of early morning, the fronds of a decorative palm tree in the distance hung as dreary and limp as channeled cast iron skillets. In that exact moment, our eyes locked, and I could almost see freedom vibrating off the top of her head.

Then she lunged at me. The senior deputy pushed her aside so hard he nearly toppled her back into the seat.

While he closed my stepmother in, the female deputy opened the front passenger door. For a few seconds, I glimpsed myself in the side mirror. My reflection appeared as diaphanous and spectral as a ghost. My expression looked especially disturbing. It was as though I were peering into the huge blue doll-eyes of a dead person.

I shifted my eyes to Amanda. Her nose had lifted as if to catch a scent. As the door opened and the deputies drove out of the sally port with their taillights receding, I said, "They're not going to listen to me, are they?"

We didn't need to be telepathic to know we shared the same thought. I knew her so well that her tone of voice told me exactly what I'd suspected.

"You can't help people who won't help themselves, diva."

And that's when she fist-bumped me. Because events such as this get branded in your mind and haunt you for the rest of your life. The entire experience ended up being bewilderingly frightening.

17

CHAPTER TWO

After I'd ramrodded Nerissa across the Mexican border and turned her over to the local authorities, I arranged for a flight back to Fort Worth. Teensy and Gran picked me up at Love Field Airport close to midnight.

And Amanda.

Apparently, Amanda finds Fort Worth charming, and Dallas, even more so because of the smorgasbord of alternative lifestyles Big-D has to choose from. She'd flown back with me, too, although I'm not sure how she got past Homeland Security. I'd calmly walked past airport security, but they stopped Amanda and led her into a holding area where they conducted a full-body search. Probably because she was acting all jittery and suspicious, with her nostrils flared, and her neck veins plumped up like garden hoses. When traveling with Amanda, you can pretty much count on some kind of screwed-up mess happening; you just don't know what it's going to be, or how bad, until it happens. You figure things might get a little weird, or that you might get messed up, but you never expect to be escorted out of the terminal wearing surgeon's booties, with your clothes folded in a neat little stack, and your combat boots on top.

With her eyes cast downward, Amanda gave a slow head-shake. "That was *so* not my fault."

"Really? Have you met you? Because that's totally something you'd do." I wasn't off base, either. It was so weird people moved to give us room on the sidewalk.

I spotted my blue-haired grandmother's circa sixties Cadillac idling at the far end of the arrival lane as we exited the terminal, and pointed the car out to Amanda. Airport Police were directing traffic, forcing slow-moving cars to keep going, and Amanda and I picked up our pace so my grandmother wouldn't have to make another loop around. As we closed in, I gave a big friendly wave and trotted toward them. I'd missed Gran. Like when you stub your toe and the throbbing finally subsides.

You'd have thought twenty-one-year-old Teensy would've been driving, now, wouldn't you, given the fact that Gran can barely keep her turquoise Cadillac between the lanes during the daytime, let alone at night . . . but no. Then I saw it—Teensy'd dyed her hair pink.

This convinced me they'd both gone off the deep end.

Amanda said, "Your sister has pink hair."

"Thank you so much for pointing this out." Amanda was rapidly approaching my rubber shoe rule—you know, where once a month everyone should be able to slap someone with a rubber shoe, like a bedroom slipper? It's almost like a victimless crime, so long as you keep in mind that someday you could be someone's rubber shoe person. Exasperated, I said, "Don't say anything. Pretend it's normal. Maybe it just looks pink because of the fluorescents. Maybe it's strawberry blonde."

"You really believe that, diva?"

"Of course not."

I opened the back passenger door and greeted my sister and Gran with a chipper "Bonjour" in a daring French accent, then encouraged Amanda into the car with a nudge. I climbed in after her and we were peeling away from the curb even before I pulled my other foot inside.

I was so exhausted I didn't know whether I'd found a rope or lost a horse. The need for sleep had invaded every fiber of my being, and all I wanted was to curl up on the original brocade upholstery in the back seat of this classic automobile like a tortellini, and drift into slumber. I didn't dare.

Gran sailed this barge through two consecutive red lights at about twenty-five miles per hour to Teensy's and my screams. Amanda just sat there, making going to the hospital look easy, and studying us like we were specimens under a microscope.

I've had issues with Gran's driving before, and once, when I had too much to drink—which almost never happens since I'm the designated driver for the world—I almost drunk-dialed the DPS to tell them to yank her license. By the time I sobered up, I had such a headache I convinced myself I'd dreamed it.

At an intersection along Harry Hines Boulevard, where prostitutes strut their stuff, Amanda sat erect.

She said, "What's this?" like she found it alluring. I shot her a warning glare.

"It's where hookers go to make a living," I answered mechanically.

Gran admonished me sharply. "Dainty, you need to tone down your choice of words."

"It's true."

"I don't care if it's true or not. We don't talk like that. If you're going to refer to them, you should use the term 'ladies of the evening.' "

Amanda smirked. Teensy let out a horse laugh.

Then Amanda chided me. "Really, Dainty, listen to your grandmother."

Gran's eyes darted to the rearview mirror. As she sailed through another red light, I could tell from her slitty-eyed glare that Amanda's feeble attempt to curry favor had fallen on deaf ears. I hadn't yet suggested to my grandmother that Amanda should stay at the Preston Hollow estate, and anticipated the request would go over like a reptile at a tea party. Then, Teensy remembered to scream at the traffic signal, and I promptly forgot about anything other than arriving at Gran's in one piece.

"So where shall we drop you?" Gran locked eyes with Amanda in the mirror.

Amanda shot me one of those, *You didn't tell her?* looks. After my heart jump-started itself, I mustered up a bit of practiced innocence. "Oh, didn't I tell you, Gran? I'm sure I mentioned it. She's coming to the house with us."

"No, you didn't tell me." Gran's tone went instantly icy. She'd huffed so much at every comment she found irritating that it sounded like she was deflating. "I'm afraid we don't have room."

"Is it because I'm black?" Amanda said.

"It's because you're . . . short."

"Dainty's short." Teensy and Amanda, in stereo.

"I'm a pygmy," Amanda said. Unnecessarily, I might add.

"Not the same thing," Gran said coolly, with her hands positioned on the big steering wheel at the ten and two positions.

"Why can't I stay over? I can sleep in Dainty's room."

Gran's eyelids fluttered in astonishment. "I don't bloody think so," she said, as I thought *Who among us is speaking in an un-Rubanbleu manner now?* The Rubanbleu is the premier ladies social group in Fort Worth. Gran's a member. So was our mother and Gran's mother. As legacies, Teensy and I each made our debut into society as debutantes at The Rubanbleu ball. Otherwise, to be invited to join this exclusive woman's club, you'd need a sponsor. Even after spending a minimum of five years on a waiting list, getting voted-in is a one-shot deal. As hard as it is to get accepted into The Rubanbleu, it's easy to get kicked out. While no Prescott women have ever been asked to leave, Gran thinks Teensy and I have the dubious potential to become the first outcasts.

And just like that, I smacked Gran. But only in my head, because violence would get me kicked out of The Rubanbleu, and, these days, The Rubanbleu happens to be my umbilical cord to sanity. And because I didn't like to think which bridge abutment I'd have to live under if I socked my grandmother.

Amanda would've realized how my grandmother is if she'd been around when Gran updated her will. Previously, it denied inheritance to family members with non-white spouses, and any mixed-race children. Now it does the same with politically correct terminology, except that it includes Swedish people because she got it in her head that Bruckman is of Swedish descent— probably because of his light blonde hair and cornflower blue eyes. She's still bitter over the fact that the Swedes remained neutral during WWII and failed to do anything to impede the Nazis. When we met Bruckman and his family for dinner at Opiala's, a five-star French-themed restaurant in Dallas, she bragged about how accepting she is of all nationalities. She did this in front of Bruckman and his mother, who's German. The Bruckmans are actually of English descent, with a long family history as Lords of the Manor in Britain.

Of course, by that time, the damage had been done.

No small wonder that same night, when I met Bruckman's sophisticated grandparents, the first words out of his grandmother's mouth were, "If anything happens to our Jimmy, you won't get one crying dime of the insurance money."

Amanda was about to smart off, but I grabbed her wrist and tightened my fingers around it painfully. No need to throw gasoline on the flames by mentioning that Amanda and I had shared the same dreadful bed at Hotel Malamuerte down in Ciudad Juárez while looking for Teensy. I didn't want Gran to kill us all by bouncing the Cadillac over the curb and into a telephone pole from the shock of it. Or maybe she'd do it to restore the family honor.

Whatever.

I motioned her over and whispered out of Gran's earshot. "If you say one damned word about . . ." Amanda fanned away the rest of my sentence as if it were a pesky gnat. ". . . I'll find a good taxidermist and stand you out in Gran's front yard like a lantern boy."

"You're a very angry person," Amanda challenged. "I'm only coming home with you because I like your sister."

Teensy, the resident people-pleaser, beamed.

I can't recall whether this was the first time a non-white person had ever been inside this Cadillac other than to detail it—except for the time I caught Moses, Gran's gardener, behind the wheel, taking a break from the noonday sun. He'd positioned himself on the brocade seat with the car door opened and his feet on the bricks, eating a huge chicken fried steak his wife, Lydia, made for his lunch. He bribed me with a piece, including a share of the mashed potatoes and white cream gravy Lydia made to go with it. Best chicken fried steak I ever had in my whole life, and I've never had anything remotely close since. That Lydia sure knew how to cook.

Gran's corrosive voice cut short my reverie with an observation about Nerissa.

"That nincompoop spent over five thousand dollars to fly in a Feng shui master, and house him in a five-star hotel. She had him walk around the house you grew up in with a compass, moving things around to help improve the 'energy flow.' All that's left of your Barbie-pink bedroom is a yoga mat and a lamp. He thinks he's coming back tomorrow to finish the job. So unless you want to be there to tell him 'Job's over,' and get caught up in the fallout when he learns he's not getting paid, you'll come home with me. Besides," she said with an aristocratic sniff, "I'm not driving all the way over to Fort Worth at this time of night.

"Plus, it's safer at my house. You don't know whether that ninny's family members are watching the Rivercrest house. They could kill you in your sleep."

"Well, we wouldn't want that." *Moi.*

"Don't get smart with me, young lady." Gran, snappish and on edge.

"Don't get smart with Gran." Amanda, animated and mocking.

"Don't call me Gran. I'm not your grandmother."

"No, Mrs. Prescott, you're definitely not my grandmother. You look nothing like her. She wore big hoop earrings the size of horseshoes, made out of elephant hair, and had a bone threaded through her nose."

"Really?" Teensy twisted in the seat, totally taken in. What can I say? Teensy's still brain damaged from the beating she took in Ciudad Juárez. The chemicals penetrating her scalp from her pink "do" aren't helping, either.

Gran's eyes flickered to the rearview mirror. She locked me in her blue gaze. "I don't understand how these things happen to you, Dainty. They don't happen to anyone else."

She was referring to Amanda glomming onto me.

"She means I'm a trouble magnet." I tried to pass Gran's comment off as a total disconnect, but Amanda knew this wasn't what Gran meant at all. Nice save. *Not.*

Teensy let out another horse bray at Gran's expense. She slapped her knee, and I swear, if she'd been drinking a soda pop, it would've spewed from her nose and splattered the dashboard.

Gran slammed on the brakes one car-length from the painted white line below the hanging amber traffic light. This had nothing to do with following the law; it had to do with putting an end to the discussion, which had become moderately uncomfortable. The light turned red, and, there we were, everyone bickering.

Crazy Amanda fit right in.

I went quiet and sunk into my own thoughts, mostly about how to get Jim Bruckman back, while the conversation between Teensy and Amanda turned into background noise.

A dark, shadowy blur moved at the limits of my vision. On instinct, I turned to my left and gasped at the sight of a man rushing the Cadillac. He yanked open Gran's door and unleashed a string of profanity, hurling vulgar insults at us and debasing the entire female gender. My heart beat like a savage fist, but for Teensy, it was déjà vu all over again. She'd realized we were being carjacked before he'd even yanked Gran out from behind the wheel.

My sister curled into a fetal position, covered her head defensively, and whimpered, "Don't hurt me, don't hurt me. I'll do anything you say . . ." She seemed to be slipping into shock, and I wondered where to get a Mylar blanket to wrap her in.

For the next minute or so, everything moved in slow motion.

From the back seat window, I viewed Gran from the waist down as he lifted her by the shoulders and slammed her feet hard onto the street.

Then, for no good reason, a fireball exploded from my grandmother's hand. The blast of a gunshot echoed through the night. Dazzled by an inner vision of orange and blue fireworks, I took cover.

I don't know how long we cowered, frozen, screaming at the top of our lungs—Teensy and Amanda and me—but my ears were still ringing when Gran jumped back inside the car, gunned the engine, and sped through the intersection.

Wait . . . what?

I admit it. I was hypnotized. But this unfortunate event cast a pall of apprehension over the rest of the people inside the car.

No one spoke for five blocks as Gran sailed through one red light after another.

"So as I was saying, Dainty, that nitwit your father married brought in a decorator and you don't even have a bed at the Rivercrest house." Gran spoke in the same birdlike warble, as if carjackings were *de rigueur,* as opposed to a life-threatening event. Or a routine exercise calculated to improve her response time—like those pop-up targets you find at the gun range.

Soft cries coming from the front passenger seat replaced Teensy's whimpers. She still lay on her side, twisted like a curly fry. With her hands and arms shielding her head, she chanted to the car's interior, "I'm okay, I'm okay, I'm okay . . ."

I blinked. I looked at Amanda, who was looking back, slack-jawed, with one of those, contorted, *What the hell just happened?* grimaces on her face. About that time, I realized my ears were ringing. Amanda's must've been ringing, too, because she hit the heel of her hand against her head several times, yawned, winced, and did a little wet-dog headshake.

I recovered my voice. "Gran—did you just shoot that guy?" When she didn't answer, I said, "Did it hit him? If you did, we have to call an ambulance."

Still nothing.

"Gran." I patted her shoulder. It felt bony and small against the flat of my hand. "Are you carrying a gun?" Stupid question, since my eyes slewed to the seat where a handgun rested comfortably against her thigh. "Do you have a permit to carry?"

Gran snapped, "Your sister's having a nervous breakdown, and *that's* what's bothering you? Whether I have a gun permit?"

Teensy came out of her psychotic break, and reached for the revolver. "Cool." Amanda and I hit the floorboard—déjà vu—all over again, only this time Amanda tried to burrow under me instead of on top of me.

My sister hasn't been right since the kidnapping in Mexico.

"I don't need a permit," Gran said. "It's my God-given right to carry a gun if I want to—the United States Constitution gives me the right to bear arms."

I pulled out my cell phone and stabbed out 911. When the Dallas PD dispatcher answered, I told her she might want to have a patrol car drive through that intersection to check out a "man down." I told her this as my grandmother yelled at me to "hang up the damned phone."

I'm pretty sure this is the first time my grandmother has ever cursed. Good breeding had prevented un-Rubanbleu behavior of any sort, and my grandmother's manners are impeccable.

Without providing my name, I did just that.

CHAPTER THREE

After we left the scene of the crime, Gran didn't voice any more snide remarks about me dragging Amanda home with us. Shooting a man acts as a kind of bucket of ice water to the face. I wondered what Amanda must think of us as the old Caddy slumped heavily down the road and slowed at the mouth of Gran's red brick driveway. She pressed her key remote and the solenoids on the iron gate started clicking as the gate yawned open.

I watched Amanda's reaction carefully. Instead of gaping in awe at my grandmother's breathtaking estate, or gazing admiringly upon the architecturally and historically significant red brick Georgian two-story, she gave an almost imperceptible nod and said, "So this is what's wrong with you."

Even the trees were spotlighted. Majestic oaks looked like a convention of kindly old grandparents stretching their limbs for a welcome-home hug. After Gran parked in the matching brick carriage house at the back of the property, next to the pavilion near the swimming pool, Amanda got out of the car. Startled by the life-size bronze sculpture as she looked over the manor, she reflexively hopped back and assumed a martial arts pose.

"Hey, karate kid—at ease—it's yard art," I said, as Amanda grudgingly relaxed.

"It could happen to anyone." Teensy leaned in and spoke in a conspiratorial whisper. "Forgot to mention . . . Gran's getting senile. Last night as she was getting ready for bed, she spotted a man in the neighbor's yard staring at her through the bedroom window. Ten minutes later, he was still there. She freaked out and called the cops. The creeper turned out to be the neighbor's new marble David statue." She turned to Amanda. "C'mon, Mandy, I'll show you around the house."

Mandy?

I questioned whether Amanda should get palsy-walsy with Teensy during her visit. After all, I'm the only one who's aware of Amanda's deepest, darkest secret. And while I've known of people like her before, Gran would make her leave if she found out about the skeleton in Amanda's closet.

As Teensy began the grand tour, I watched them enter the house and wondered what Amanda thought of the place.

Gran's beautiful Georgian mansion has many fireplaces, high ceilings, beautiful plank floors, plenty of crown molding, and staircases. It even has a mezzanine that overlooks the informal living room from three sides. The furnishings are mostly period pieces and the majority of the upholstered pieces are done in white silk damask. It's not a kid-friendly place.

Gran called out, "Stay out of the formal living room." Followed by, "And the formal dining room." Followed by, "Don't go into the library. Or the den. Or downstairs."

I suppose she expected us to catapult onto the second floor. And me, into the attic, which had been transformed into my bedroom last summer when I moved in with her temporarily while my sorority sisters and I waited to move into our new apartment. Which never happened. Anyway, the attic's furnished with all the boxed-up Madame Alexander dolls that I wasn't allowed to play with as a child, as well as cast-off antiques that made their way up here whenever the antique dealers Gran patronized found suitable upgrades to replace pieces downstairs. I painted the walls in the same restful aqua as the informal living room, and there are a couple of fireside chairs next to a trompe l'oeil fireplace my friend and recovering sorority sister, Venice Hanover, painted over an accent wall one summer after we went off to college.

I miss Venice. We used to do everything together. But until she figures out how to get home, she's stuck in Africa. Venice agreed to relocate to a city with little to no electricity and poor-quality water for three times the amount of money she was making at her current job in Fort Worth, and arrived for her new job while I was down in Mexico rescuing Teensy. Unfortunately, she didn't realize until after she got halfway across the globe that she and her boss had negotiated her salary in two different currencies, and now she's in a Third World country making about one-third of what she made here.

Back to my room.

I didn't have curtains for this small, converted space because I needed the light to brighten my digs. When the moonlight slants in through the little windowpanes, I often gaze up and wonder if my mother ever looks down on Teensy and me, and whether she's proud of my accomplishments. I think we can all breathe a sigh of relief that I didn't embarrass the family this time, and that the two-million-dollar bounty on my head stops at the border. Maybe.

From the moment I was a tiny girl, I loved my Jenny Lind bed frame, even though the twin mattress was lumpy. But that's what gel pads and Waterford linens are for—to keep it dressed and to make it prettier and more comfortable.

For now, I only wanted sleep to suspend my worries. Tomorrow I could ponder what Nerissa meant about watching my back, or that crack Deputy Silverleaf made about liking my video. I'm absolutely certain he was smarting-off because there aren't any videos of me on the WBFD website. Nevertheless, like Scarlett O'Hara, I wouldn't think about that now; I'd think about it tomorrow.

But sleep eluded me. For no good reason, the hair stood up on the back of my neck. I had the irrational fear that someone was watching me. I crept to the window and flattened myself against the wall. Carefully, I peeked out. The only thing that seemed out of place was a small, dark car parked along the curb, just beyond the wrought iron gate. On a public street. It could've easily belonged to one of the neighbors, or their guests. Whatever. For the moment, I was at Gran's, inside a house with a three-tiered burglar alarm system that ultimately connected to a panel at the police department. I felt as safe as I could, considering people I didn't know and had never formally met had been trying to kill me for the past month.

I crawled back into bed and tried to fill my head with good thoughts until I drifted off to sleep—like how to win my boyfriend back, and how tomorrow we'd celebrate Thanksgiving.

CHAPTER FOUR

It isn't Thanksgiving at the Prescott compound until somebody cries.

Gran awakened me early. She wanted me to drive to Fort Worth to pick up Daddy and bring him back to Dallas for breakfast so he could spend the day and have Thanksgiving dinner with us. Which would've been fine except for the part where she dropped the keys to the Cadillac into my hand and told me to use her car. When I asked why, she gave me a crash course in shock and awe.

I think this was the first time I ever heard "Happy Thanksgiving," and "We sold your Porsche," in the same sentence.

"What do you mean y'all sold my Porsche?" I shrieked.

"Keep your voice down. Others are trying to sleep."

"What do you mean y'all sold my Porsche?" I shrilled.

"Calm down. It was for the best. We didn't know if you'd actually come back alive from Mexico and we decided—well, your father came up with the idea—but I thought he made a good point. We decided it'd be a lot easier to sell it while you were gone than to have it tied up in probate if you didn't make it back. It takes years to declare someone dead, and you know how impatient your father is." She delivered this kick-in-the-gut in a warbling, singsong, old-lady bird voice, as if someone had phoned for a treasured, family recipe and she'd left out a secret ingredient. Accidentally. On purpose.

"You people thought I wouldn't come back? *Hello,* I'm stand-

32

ing right in front of you." With a great flourish of outstretched arms, mind you. I watched, incredulous, as Gran touched a finger to each ear. "What're you doing? You're tuning me out?"

"No, but if you insist on yelling, I can hear you without having them on."

This further confirmed my suspicion that my grandmother had turned off her new hearing aids. She picked them up a week or so before I went to Mexico the first time to rescue Teensy, and didn't bother to mention it in order to see if anyone in the family would notice. Hers are the tiny, flesh-toned kind that fit into the ear canal, and are all but invisible. Later, she informed us she'd rewritten her will—three times.

"I want my car back." My jaw dropped open. "Have you people lost your minds?"

Gran bristled. "I'm just as sane as the next person."

I seriously doubted that. My family's coming unraveled at the seams. I dressed quickly, eager to take up the matter with Daddy.

Driving Gran's Cadillac is like floating a huge turquoise barge down an asphalt canal. It's unwieldy and embarrassing, and I'm pretty sure the shock absorbers needed replacing thirty years ago since Gran never met a pothole she didn't try to conquer. I'm not sure if it's an eyesight problem, or pure defiance, but this car bobs like the cork on a baited hook. I'd rather not be seen in this circa sixties Caddy, even if it did survive the years to become a classic auto, so I dug through the cardboard box of charitable donations I'd set aside and pulled out a ball cap to use as part of my disguise. For the record, ball caps and debutantes do not go together; however, this gimme-cap came from the Colonial golf tournament, and I saved it thinking someone might be able to use it. Today, that "someone" was me.

The hospital staff at Our Lady of Perpetual Suffering arranged for Daddy to be transferred to Tranquility Villas, a nursing home and rehab center, where he'll stay a few more weeks until he's well enough to go back home to the Rivercrest estate. Aspen Wicklow, the newest anchor at WBFD-TV, put her parents in Tranquility Villas. Her mother has a closed-head injury, and her father has Alzheimer's, so even though they're there for different reasons, Tranquility Villas seems to be the place to be when you need rehab, or get old and senile.

Note to Self: See whether they'll take Gran.

According to Gran, it's not Thanksgiving unless the family's together, so at her insistence (read: badgering), the rehab director agreed Daddy could come to Dallas for the day if we promised to keep the stress level to a minimum (read: no tabloid TV-style Thanksgiving debacle). That's like telling a camel not to spit. But we all agreed—except Amanda—to do our best and that's why I struck out at dawn from Gran's house, in her big bloated Cadillac. She planned to prepare a nice breakfast for Daddy, spoil him rotten, and fuss over him like she did when he was a boy—a smothered boy whose Selective Service number during the Vietnam draft lottery turned out to be 359, yet he still felt compelled to put some real estate between him and my grandmother by enlisting in the military.

On the drive to Tranquility Villas, I tuned Gran's radio to a news station. Even though there were no breaking news announcements confirming that Nerissa's redneck, recidivist relatives had ambushed the extradition officers, I didn't know any jail personnel who I could charm into telling me whether she'd arrived at her new digs. As much as I wanted to ask Bruckman to find out for me, I couldn't bring myself to call him. By the time I reached the outskirts of Fort Worth, I'd worked myself into a panic. Not knowing was making me neurotic. What if she'd gotten away? What if she came after me? It's not like I could turn into the invisible debutante behind the wheel of Gran's car.

No telling what she'd do if she caught me alone. There were so many levels to Nerissa's craziness that nobody should've been surprised that the marriage didn't work. She couldn't cook, and when she got riled up she looked like a serial killer. And just when you thought you'd excavated to the bottom floor of her craziness, you discovered a crazy basement; and a crazy underground garage; and after that, a crazy fallout shelter. With every mile closer to Fort Worth, I felt my neurosis ratcheting up. It occurred to me to get a gun. Venice's mother carried a pink one. But at this point, I'd probably end up shooting myself in the foot. Or capping an innocent bystander—that'd get me spit-roasted in Hell for sure. For no good reason, I realized that all the times I'd checked behind the shower curtain before getting in didn't prepare me for what to do if I actually encountered a slasher. That's when I decided not to let thoughts of Nerissa move, rent-free, into my own crazy attic.

I swung by the rehab place and glimpsed my father through the front windows. He was already headed out the door with spring in his step and a nurse hot on his heels by the time I bounced onto the circular drive and rolled up under the portico. Seated behind the wheel of Gran's bloated car, I stretched across the seat and manually unlocked the door. Then I popped the latch and pushed it open.

As he wrangled inside of the vintage Cadillac, my soon-to-be-single, undiagnosed alcoholic, out-of-touch father promptly presented me with a bill for $1,996,854.78.

"Why?"

"For having to raise your selfish, pampered ass."

The nurse shot me a warning look. "Try not to upset Mr. Prescott."

Me? Upset *him?* I wanted to tell her it was the other way around. Instead, I flashed a smile, *Okay*. And why would I do that? I mean, after all, this is the man who cut me off financially, which began the domino effect of cut-up credit cards, and recently ended with the sale of my beloved Porsche.

"Well, I hate to be the bearer of bad news, Daddy—" the nurse was still within earshot, and I was trying my best to modulate the hysteria building within me "—but I don't have the money to pay you back."

"I'm taking it out of your trust fund."

"As a reminder, I didn't ask to be born."

Daddy meditated on this idea for about two seconds while the nurse assisted him into the car. "Technically, you weren't born. Your mother had a C-section so you were surgically excised—like a tumor."

"You're comparing me to a tumor?"

"I didn't say you were malignant. You're benign. Non-threatening. But you're still there."

While waiting for Florence Nightingale to help seat-belt him in, I reached into my handbag and tore a piece of paper from a spiral notebook, and poised my pen to write. Once she closed the door and gave him one of those little *toodle-oo* finger waves good-bye, I handed him the paper.

"What's this?"

"It's a bill for bringing Nerissa back from Mexico." I'd invoiced him for two million, even. "It's okay, you can owe me the rest. Your credit's good here." Said with an enthusiasm I didn't feel.

"I'm not paying you one crying dime."

Adjust sunglasses. Exude confidence. Don't make eye contact.

"Sure you are. I'll send a separate invoice to the house for rescuing Teensy. That one's going to run you a lot more."

"How's that?"

"Because she's worth a lot more than Nerissa." I started the car and pulled out onto the street. "I realize you may have to sell some stock to pay the tab," I said airily, as if we'd just met and I didn't have a clue what kind of oil baron, wheeler-dealer I was dealing with, "but I'll be happy to take the Rivercrest house as payment in full if you'd rather deed it over to me instead of paying cash."

He torqued his jaw. And that's pretty much how the drive to Dallas went—cold, gelid, and frostily silent.

At Gran's house, I reintroduced Daddy to Amanda. They'd met while he was still in ICU at the hospital, but I'm pretty sure the doctors had him heavily medicated because he acted like he didn't recognize her when he walked through the front door and saw her standing next to Gran's Christmas tree, studying a three-foot-tall collection of elves. The flocked Scotch pine blazed with colorful lights, and the elves had been plugged into an extension cord. Grinding motor noises came in cadence with their jerky hand and arm movements. I decided to find it amusing when Amanda pretended to be part of the display, and launched into a few robotic movements of her own.

As Daddy gave her the visual once-over, his eyes thinned into a squint.

Teensy'd loaned her a pair of black leggings and a green pullover sweater, and Amanda had belted it at the waist. Our clothes are out of proportion for Amanda, so I thought Teensy did the best she could, considering what she had to work with. Until we could get to a kid's shop, Amanda would either have to wear her freshly laundered camouflage fatigues, or make do with our clothes. Unfortunately, the little boots she'd worn in Mexico, which turned out to be a salesman's sample of a standard combat boot, didn't work with her ensemble inside Gran's house, so Teensy provided her with a pair of black ballet slippers from a box of childhood keepsakes Gran had boxed and stored in the attic. I use the term "unfortunately" because these shoes were so old and dried out that they turned up at the tips.

I could almost read Daddy's mind. *Where'd the black elf come from?*

"You remember Amanda," I prompted. "She's the one I hired to take me into Mexico to find Teensy." I emphasized the words "Mexico" and "Teensy" to help jog his memory, even though this had already been explained to him in the hospital. Again, unfortunately, Daddy was hell-bent on "whipping Bruckman's ass" at the time for not keeping me from crossing the border, and had apparently forgotten all about Amanda's role in the family drama.

For a minute, they stood staring at each other and making quiet assessments.

"What?" Daddy finally said. "You couldn't spend the holiday with the rest of your people in the Emerald City?"

"I'm a pygmy." Her eyes cut to me, then back to Daddy. "And we already met. Dainty introduced us at the hospital."

"Well, no wonder I don't remember you. I was practically in a coma. So, did Mother hire you to wait on us today?"

Amanda stiffened. She stood inert and slitty-eyed. "I'm a guest."

"A guest?" He chuckled without humor. "Are you kidding? You must have acquired some dark and sinister dirt on my mother."

I stood on lead feet, thunderstruck, while Amanda resorted to honesty. "That's right. I'm blackmailing her."

I shouldn't have been worried. Most people would've been offended, but not Amanda. Even though Daddy was having a rollicking good time at her expense, she'd never storm out of the house when she had a tapeworm needing to be fed and there was a kitchen full of food waiting to be placed on the table.

"Be nice, Daddy, Amanda's our guest."

"Tell the truth." He backhanded me, good-naturedly, on the arm. "What kind of dirt did she dig up on the old bird?"

I shrugged it off. It didn't seem wise to start the day by telling him that Amanda could pretty much do anything she wanted to around here now that she'd witnessed Gran shoot a man.

He continued to study her with cold scrutiny. "There's something funny about you. I just can't seem to put my finger on it."

This was probably due, in part, to the testosterone-laden air.

My eyelids fluttered. Then Gran called us all into the informal dining room, and that's when our Thanksgiving breakfast turned *très* bizarre, beginning when Gran brought in the special plate she'd fixed for Daddy. And by special, I mean "different."

According to Daddy's doctor, he's supposed to eat bland cuisine until his stomach lining gets back to normal, so the plate Gran brought him from the kitchen arrived in various shades of beige—which is even less glamorous than it sounds. She stood beside his chair, pointedly waiting for him to unfurl the cloth napkin so she could set the plate in front of him.

He didn't budge. "I'm not eating that. Give me something with butter on it."

"You'll live longer." Gran, already on edge as a result of the interloper at the table, apparently planned to wait him out.

"Why would I want to live longer? Just give me what I want to eat and leave me alone. So what if I kick the bucket a few years before I'm supposed to? Big deal." Then he looked over at me. "By the way, I took a reverse mortgage on the house so there's no money in it when I die, just 'FYI.' "

"Doctor's orders," Gran protested.

"To hell with that quack. Don't fix me dry toast and oatmeal and pretend it's breakfast. If I'd wanted bland food, I'd have stayed at Tranquility Villas. What're you serving the rest of these people?"

"These people"—like we'd never met and had no familial connection. I glanced at Amanda's smirking face.

"They're getting chili-cheese grits, scrambled eggs with sausage, homemade cinnamon rolls, and buttered sourdough toast," Gran said as she removed the cloche covering her made-from-scratch biscuits and red-eye gravy. "Along with the rest of the trimmings." Which meant regular bacon, and thin-sliced, pan-fried pork chops.

"Don't drag me over here and trick me into thinking you're treating me to a holiday meal. And, Dainty, get off your duff and get me some hot sauce. And don't act like you don't know where it is."

"I've got you covered like dew on Dixie." I pushed back from the table, and that's where we might've left it if Gran hadn't threatened me with a *Don't you dare* look.

"Ha-ha," Teensy piped up. "Daddy told you to get off your duff . . ."

I glowered. "What are you . . . twelve?"

Amanda's shoulders heaved with silent laughter.

"You heard me, now, get cracking," Daddy said.

Appropriately cowed, I kept a watchful eye on Gran. Nobody crosses Gran. I suspected Daddy enjoyed this business of having her fuss over him. After all, my mother used to do the same thing—make a big deal over him—and now that she was gone, he missed it.

"Love these Paula Deen recipes," he said, eyeballing the food. "The broad can cook. We should fly her in next Thanksgiving."

"She wouldn't accept." Teensy, in the know. "She's got her own family."

"We'll fly them in, too," he said, with a cavalier hand-swat through the air, until Teensy reminded him that Paula Deen has grandchildren. Daddy's not big on kids. Teensy and I are seventh-generation Texans, but if we'd been born back when Texas was a Republic, we'd have been expected to work alongside of our pioneer ancestors. "Relax. I was making a joke. Are these her grits?"

"These are my recipes," Gran snapped. "You've been eating the same breakfast ever since you were in a high chair. Lord, I hope you're not getting senile."

Ditto. Because that would mean that the mental illnesses of half of the people seated around this table could be found in the *Diagnostic and Statistical Manual,* otherwise known as the DSM V.

Gran handed Daddy's plate of beige food to Teensy. "Take this to the kitchen and give it to the dog."

Teensy and I exchanged awkward looks. We don't have a dog. Then we both looked at Daddy, but his gaze kept flitting between Amanda and the elf decorations. Teensy cocked an eyebrow in confusion, but she excused herself from the table and ferried the plate to the kitchen without any back-talk.

"Teensy—hot sauce," Daddy yelled, followed by Gran's low-voltage challenge, "Don't you dare, little missy."

Gran slid into the chair at the head of the table, opposite from Daddy, whom she'd seated at the far end. This worked as a diabolical setup since it allowed the rest of us to be bullied from both ends.

As soon as Teensy disappeared from view, Daddy's fascination with the elves ended.

He shot me a wicked glare. "Why the hell did you let your sister dye her hair pink? You're the oldest; you're supposed to have better sense."

Amanda smiled at me from across the table—not a compassionate smile, a devious one.

"Hey, don't look at me." I shook out my napkin and placed it in my lap. Amanda followed my lead. I suspected her hesitation to select from the forks next to her plate stemmed from not knowing which to use. I picked up the big one from my own place setting, and noticed that Amanda copied me. I returned my attention to Daddy. "I've been gone for two weeks. Besides, Daddy, she's a grown-up."

"She's an idiot. Never thought I'd see the day when you'd turn out to be smarter than your sister."

This put a new twist on an old theme. The last time we were together as a family, Daddy decided Teensy had better sense than me. I defended myself by saying I thought we were pretty evenly matched in intelligence—that Teensy's grades might indicate she was book smart, but I'd made the Dean's List, and I had more common sense. After all, I wouldn't have fallen for anything Nerissa cooked up, such as going down to Mexico to kick up my heels.

Daddy said, "Ask yourself this: Has Teensy ever walked out of a restaurant restroom with the back of her skirt caught in her pantyhose?" To emphasize the point, he licked his index finger and marked the air in front of him. "Teensy . . . one. You . . . zero."

"In my defense," I reminded anybody at the table who actually gave a damn, "I scored high enough to get into Columbia."

"So, you scored high enough to get in. Big deal. They didn't accept you," Daddy pointed out.

"Well, that statement's not exactly accurate," Gran said absentmindedly. She suddenly checked herself, as if she'd opened Pandora's box and inadvertently released a nasty secret.

"Wait—what?" I twisted in my seat. My blue-haired grandmother tried to pretend she didn't hear me and fumbled with her napkin. My voice shrilled. "What'd you just say?" I slapped my napkin onto the empty plate. "What'd you mean, 'That statement's not exactly accurate'?"

Gran went into her *What? Who, me?* act. "Did you say something? Sorry, I didn't hear you."

"Yes, you did. You heard me. And I heard you. What'd you mean?"

To my shock and dismay, Gran admitted I'd been accepted to my dream university four years ago. She'd thrown this acceptance letter out because she didn't want me to move away.

"You what?" I shrieked. "You trashed my letter? What kind of person does that?" But I knew. The veil of selfishness hung so thick over this room I wanted to claw my way right through it. "You altered my destiny."

"Inside voice, Dainty. Use your inside voice," Gran said.

About that time, Teensy danced back into the room with a jar of peanut butter in her hand, and a big smile on her face. "What'd I miss?"

"Are you kidding me? How could you?" I looked over at my sister as my voice spiraled upward. "They threw out my acceptance letter to Columbia University."

"Oh, yeah . . . that." Teensy unfurled her napkin. "Bummer."

"You knew?" I shrilled. "Why didn't you tell me?"

Teensy blew out a heavy sigh. "Remember the time Gran took me to Harkman Beemis to pick out a dress to wear to the junior-senior prom with Maximilian Van Winkle?"

"You got hush money not to tell me?"

"It was baby blue taffeta, Dainty, and you know that's my favorite color," she singsonged. "What was I supposed to do? I was a freshman. Max was a senior. Have you forgotten what a huge deal it was to be asked out by an upperclassman?"

"Yeah." I could feel a cavity starting from all Teensy's sugar.

Daddy lifted his tea glass and let it hover near his lips. "Get a grip, Dainty. It happened four years ago."

Realization dawned, and not in a good way.

"You were in on it?" My eyes slewed to Amanda who was

soaking up the ambience like a sponge.

If they'd just informed me that a friend died, and expected me to get over it because it happened four years ago, the shock of the death would've still been fresh to me whether it was something they'd known for years or not. Same thing with the death of my bright future, my casually discarded acceptance letter to Columbia. No, no—the *murder* of my acceptance letter to my dream university. These people didn't treat me very well back then; you'd think they'd be tickled as pink as Teensy's hair if I went to undergraduate school out of state, wouldn't you?

"It's over, Dainty. Let it go." The biscuits had made it halfway around the table, and Daddy ladled red-eye gravy over his. "Here—have a biscuit."

I love Gran's homemade biscuits and red-eye gravy. And for just that reason, I passed them up. Teensy, on the other hand, helped herself to the food like she had a full-blown marijuana addiction.

My blood boiled. "Is that all you have to say for yourself?"

Amanda picked up her fork and inspected it. "What a nice silver pattern," she announced with forced enthusiasm. "What's it called?"

Ignoring her, I tried to keep the tremble out of my voice. "You knew how much I wanted to go to Columbia. I could've probably had an anchor job in the national market right now if I'd gone there." Words poured out in a hyperventilating rush.

Gran pooh-poohed the idea and changed the subject—which made me wonder what else my family'd been holding out on. Did they tear up the winning Powerball ticket because Gran thought it was a sin to gamble? Did they delete the phone message off the answering machine telling me I'd won a million-dollar sweepstakes . . . or trash a letter inviting me to compete on a popular game show with money prizes?

Tears blistered behind my eyeballs.

Daddy said, "If you're going to act like a big baby, then leave the table."

"Develop a backbone, not a wishbone. Don't be such a crybaby, Dainty," Teensy added. Meaning two minutes into her jaw-dropping treachery, I had to physically restrain myself from slapping her out of her chair.

A tear spilled over one cheek and splashed onto my empty plate. I pushed back from the luxurious tablescape. With as much dignity as I could muster, I lamely excused myself from the dining room with, "A fleck of mascara got into my eye."

On my brisk walk toward the staircase, I glimpsed Amanda cramming a cinnamon roll into her mouth, and heard her muted announcement, "I'll handle this."

A few minutes later, I heard a tap on the door of the second-floor guest bathroom.

"*Ocupada.*" Apparently, my brain was experiencing some sort of Mexican jet lag. It surprised me that I'd resorted to Spanish, the way I'd done in the airport restroom in El Paso when a lady tried the door handle to the stall I was in—not that I'd learned much Spanish during my two awful jaunts to Mexico—but it fell into place like a missing puzzle piece.

I'd tried to infuse cheer into my voice, but thinking about my family of dream killers just made it worse. Now, I'd have to reapply my mascara, and in order to do that, I'd have to get to my room in the attic.

"Let me in," Amanda said.

"No." There was nothing she could do to make me feel better, and I didn't want her to see me cry.

"Don't make me bust down this door, diva."

The thought of Amanda's little pigmy foot kicking in the door brought out a chuckle. Then again, she might do it. Then I'd have to contend with Gran. I unlatched the door and it swung open.

"Why are you crying?"

"Didn't you hear them? They conspired to ruin my life. My life could've been completely different—me, with my own talk show, or anchoring at CNN, or—"

"Yeah, and I could've been born Dainty Prescott, living with the crazy white people. But I wasn't. You were. I'd say you have a pretty good life, diva."

"Shouldn't you be downstairs feeding your tapeworm?"

"Hey, this is fun. At my house, when we have company sitting around the dinner table, we talk about who died, who's dying, and who should be killed." She drew in a deep breath. "Ah . . . holidays with the white people. This is exciting. Can't wait to tell my friends about it."

I sniffled. Then the contours of her face hardened. "Snap out of it. I'm not going back to the table without you."

"Why not? Gran's a good cook," I conceded. "You should eat with them."

"Because you're my friend. And because there's safety in numbers. And because you don't want to let these people beat you. Underneath it all, I think you're a nice person."

It took a few minutes to reapply my makeup, but Amanda waited. We got back to the table in time to participate in a conversation that had to do with procuring a new girlfriend for my father.

Teensy said, "You should scope out the country club. Pick somebody who likes tennis; then she can play tennis while you golf."

"I've seen some of those women, and I'm onto them. They're not members of the club—they just take lessons there so they can scout out the rich old men."

"What about Tandy Westlake's mother?" Teensy, again. Talking about my friend Tandy's mom.

"Yeah, Tandy's mother is single." I was sure he already knew this since the newspaper chronicled how I'd loused up Mrs. Westlake's wedding by uncovering her fiancé's criminal past. That story made me look like a heroine, too, not that anybody ever talked about that part.

"She wears pearls the size of golf balls. I have a sack of golf balls I fished out of the water hazard at the country club. Her necklace looks like she went in my golf bag and stole my balls," Daddy said. He wiped his mouth, refolded his napkin, and placed it next to an empty plate. "She's an idiot."

Couldn't argue with him there. My friend Tandy Westlake has the brains of a physicist, the lean, toned body of a swimmer, curly strawberry blonde hair that hangs in ringlets, and compelling brown eyes the shade of milk chocolate. Her mother looks just like her, minus the smarts. But she's wealthy, and in Fort Worth, rich people tend to marry their own kind.

I tried again. "Well, what about someone else, then? I mean, you're a good-looking guy. And there are a lot more women out there than men who are your age."

"I did meet a lady at Tranquility Villas who took a shine to me. Nice gal."

Window shopping for women at Tranquility Villas wasn't exactly what I had in mind, so I remained cautiously optimistic when I asked him her name.

"Her name's Jillian Wicklow."

Orange juice spewed through my nose. My grandmother gave me a dirty look. Teensy snickered. Jillian Wicklow suffers from a closed-head injury. She can carry on a conversation with you and then not remember it five minutes later. Call it "eraser brain." How do I know this? Because she's Aspen Wicklow's mother. Once, when I went into the break room at WBFD, I overheard her talking about it with the station's helicopter pilot, Chopper Deke.

My daddy doesn't need a woman who's not operating with

all of her faculties.

I turned to Gran. "Do you know any single ladies at the country club Daddy could ask out on a date?"

"It wouldn't be proper, Dainty. Your father's divorce won't be final for at least six more weeks."

"Longer, if the tramp contests it," Daddy snarled.

Gran did a heavy eye roll. "You picked her, not me."

Daddy got up from the table and patted a full belly to show Gran his appreciation for the home-cooked meal. "You know, sometimes I really enjoy getting together with you people. But not today. Somebody get me the remote. We're watching football."

He stranded us at the table and headed off into the living room in search of a comfy chair to beach in. Which made me rue the day when our family reunions would be held in a mental hospital.

CHAPTER FIVE

Around five o'clock that afternoon, in preparation for the evening meal, Gran announced that we were having Thanksgiving dinner in the formal dining room, and pressed Amanda and me into service. I halved the cloth napkins and the sterling silver with Amanda, and instructed her how to set the table, while Gran watched with a critical gaze, eyeing each piece of crystal and china like she was seeing an old boyfriend's ugly wife.

I educated Amanda on the provenance of Gran's china. It was already an antique when the Rothschilds gave it to my grandparents as a wedding gift. "This is called a place setting. These are bread-and-butter plates, and these are cream soups, and these are their underplates." I demonstrated. "They go here, here, and here."

Gran sniffed in contempt. Other than the help, she'd probably never had anyone inside her home who didn't already know the etiquette of table setting.

It surprised me how Amanda took it all in—the napkin on the left with the forks on top in descending order: dinner fork, salad fork, and up at the top of the plate, the dessert fork; and on the right, the knife and spoons, large to small. When we finished, Gran left the room, secure in the knowledge that we hadn't damaged her hundred-year-old Limoges.

"I could probably feed my family for a month for what it costs for one of these place settings," Amanda mused.

"You could, except Gran always counts the silver after guests leave." This just popped out; I didn't mean anything by it.

Amanda said, "I don't steal."

"Don't take it the wrong way." The reality was that I'd spent the sum total of about one whole week with Amanda, give or take a few hours, and I really didn't know her. I didn't have any reason not to trust her, and she'd saved my bacon down in Mexico more than once. Teensy's, too. But Bruckman didn't like her; he pegged her for a con artist. "Arrange the crystal glasses this way." I showed her where to put the water and wine glasses, assuming we were having wine, which didn't seem to be such a good idea since I suspected Daddy'd turned into something of a boozer while married to Nerissa.

Periodically, Gran moved in and out of the room to inspect the layout. Finally, she pronounced it "perfect" and moved on to the kitchen. By six o'clock, Amanda and I were ferrying hot platters and casserole dishes into the dining room, and by six-fifteen, Gran rang the little silver dinner bell for us all to gather at the table.

Daddy took his place at the head of the table next to the meat platters. "I want turkey and dressing, and ham and tamales. And I want gravy. I hope you made extra because this boat's mine."

"There's plenty." Gran unfurled her napkin and smoothed it across her lap while the rest of us followed her lead. She made eye contact with Daddy. "Beau, say the blessing."

Daddy instructed everyone to join hands.

This meant Gran had to hold hands with Amanda. She promptly put the kibosh on this by saying, "Not necessary, son, it's flu season," but we all knew influenza had nothing to do with it.

He said, "Let's bow our heads."

I glanced around, wondering what to make of my own family.

Mine was the last chin to drop in prayer.

Dear Lord—Help me tolerate these people so I don't end up in jail—

I blew out a sigh, realizing the actual prayer didn't matter now that I'd already started my own.

The doorbell rang.

Gran looked up in astonishment. We all exchanged awkward expressions. The only way anyone could even come onto the Prescott estate to ring the doorbell is if somebody left the gate open. Or pole-vaulted over the brick and iron fence surrounding the property. I glanced around for someone to blame, and noticed all eyes move to me in a collective shift.

Daddy and I were the last to arrive.

Gran voiced what the rest of us were thinking. "Who in the world is that?" Lively blue eyes thinned into slits. "And, who left the gate open?" She directed this accusation to me.

Certain that I'd shut the gate, I shot Teensy a withering look. She glanced everywhere except into my eyes. Guilty.

Gran said, "Don't answer it. It's rude to drop in on people uninvited."

"Yeah, let's eat." Daddy'd put in a hard day in front of the TV, yelling at the referees and scolding his favorite football players for their mistakes, which burns up a lot of calories and makes a man hungry.

The doorbell sounded again.

Gran said, "Beau, say grace."

As we ignored the front door and bowed our heads in prayer, two air horns went off outside.

I experienced one of those jarring, *What the hell?* moments. I looked at Gran, who tried to incinerate me with a glare. Holidays cause me to momentarily forget that there's no due process at the Prescott compound. You can be tried, convicted, and receive the figurative death penalty on circumstantial evidence—or in this case, no evidence.

"Why are you looking at me? I didn't do anything."

"This is your fault, Dainty."

"Why pick on me? It could be Teensy's fault." I pointed the finger at my guilty sister.

"Don't blame Teensy because you neglected to close the gate."

Then a voice broke into a song, belted out by my ex-boyfriend, Strayer Drexel Truett, III. I fleetingly wondered if Teensy set this up, but she acted just as shocked as the rest of us.

The last time I saw Drex, he was trying to get into The Rubanbleu ball as my date, and was being told by Rubanbleu doyennes that I'd already arrived with my escort and—guess what?—it wasn't him. Right after The Rubanbleu ball, the night I went home with Bruckman and the same night I got the frantic phone call from Teensy saying she'd been bludgeoned half to death and left on a dirty back street in Mexico, I texted Drex—twice—in immediate succession. The first text read: "I love and miss you, darlin'," followed by: "Damn it. Wrong person," just so he'd think I had a life.

I finally recognized the first strains of Drex's pathetic rendition of "Help Me, Rhonda." That's not even my name. I didn't know whether to call him a therapist or a vocal coach . . . or an ambulance—that's just how infuriated I was.

Gran's whole body seemed to sigh. "I swan, Dainty. You're sucking the life out of me. Get rid of that racket."

Amanda sniggered. Her eyes disappeared behind lids squeezed tight. Fine laugh lines crinkled at the corners.

I froze with embarrassment.

Teensy sat there, wide-eyed, inert as a gas while Daddy eyeballed the food.

I amended the prayer I'd started in my head earlier.

Dear Lord—

Help me adapt to jail.

"I didn't invite him." Mortified that Drex would have the gall to show up here, I didn't budge, either.

The air horns went off again.

The next thing I knew, Teensy rocketed out of her seat and made a beeline for the front door.

Gran shoved her napkin at Amanda. "Here—don't just sit there—take this and drape it over your arm. Go stand by the kitchen door and act like you work here. And, no back-talk. Be quick about it."

Amanda stiffened. "You expect me to do *what*?"

I hallucinated: Gran expected Amanda to pretend to be the help.

I hallucinated again: Amanda did as she was told. That triggered a heavy eye roll on my part.

Just kill me now.

Drex stood in the doorway looking GQ gorgeous in his blue jeans, boots, and Polo shirt, gripping the air horns in one hand, and a dozen yellow roses in the other.

Dude—you really think you can buy me off with flowers?

He said, "Hi, Dainty. I brought these for you." He meant the air horns. "And these are for you, Miss Eugenia." Gran got up and relieved him of the flowers and toddled off to find a vase.

Way to schmooze.

"Have a seat, young man." Gran motioned Drex to take Amanda's empty seat, which meant he'd be sitting next to me. "We were just about to say grace."

When I was six, my parents sent me to the "Little Miss Debutante" class The Rubanbleu puts on each year to instill proper manners in grade-school girls who will become future debs. I received a certificate of excellence at the time; now, I had trouble recalling what they taught me, but I was pretty sure there wasn't anything in the curriculum about how to demurely knee a grown man in the stones.

Being trapped at the family table was bad enough. Being trapped at the family table with Drex by my side was like making a cameo appearance in somebody else's bad dream; or having Hollywood show up to film *National Lampoon's "A Prescott Family Thanksgiving";* or having your face appear on the Jumbotron during the "Kiss Cam" segment while you're sitting next to a nose-picking moron you're pretty sure you saw on a Wanted poster down at the post office. I didn't think it could get any worse, even with Amanda fuming at the kitchen door, gritting her teeth and giving me slitty-eyed looks.

I cleared my throat. "Since this is Thanksgiving, shouldn't we invite Amanda to join us?"

"Oh. Well." Gran looked uneasily at Amanda. "We'll understand if you're more comfortable dining in the kitchen, Amanda—" she shooed her toward the breakfast nook "—where the rest of the help eats." This was less of an invitation and more of a suggestion.

"Delighted to join you." Amanda flashed a gap-tooth smile I knew to be fake. "Let me pull up a chair."

Gran set her jaw, but she stepped over to the chinoiserie china cabinet to get another setting of china, and a sterling place setting.

"I want to eat," Daddy announced.

"After we give thanks." Gran shot my father a reproachful look and returned to her seat after setting Amanda's place.

The doorbell rang again. Amanda's cocked eyebrow said, *Now what?*

My blue-haired grandmother appeared thunderstruck. "Would someone please fill me in? What in the world's going on here?"

"It's my counselor. He's a psychologist." Teensy pushed back from the table and tossed the cloth napkin next to her plate.

"We're dating."

Daddy piped up. "That's unethical. I plan to report him. Why would anybody in their right mind do that?"

"Don't be silly, Daddy." Teensy scampered toward the front door. "People do it all the time."

"Well, I don't care if everybody's doing it," he cupped his hands to his mouth and called out after her. "A prison tattoo's always a better idea when you're locked up." His eyes slewed over to me. "Has she lost her mind? Did you know about this?"

I bobbed my head *yes* for the first question, and shook my head *no* for the second one.

Gran's lips pinched at the corners. "Let's table this discussion and eat. Beau, call your daughter to the table."

Daddy yelled, "Teensy—get in here. You're holding up dinner."

Drex inclined his head my way. "We need to talk."

"And the horse you rode in on. Get away from me." No need to mention who said that.

Teensy appeared in the dining room with an odd-looking man who looked to be twenty years her senior, which would put him in his early forties. His eyeglasses looked a bit large for his face, and his brown hair had been cropped unusually short, as if he'd recently had his head shaved, and it had grown out over the course of several months. Still, the glasses couldn't obscure the small patches of gray that had formed at the temples. When he first said *Hello* to our group, I thought he had a youthful voice more befitting a teacher, or a store clerk, and I wondered what my sister saw in someone who didn't have a more commanding tone. Then I reminded myself that Teensy's underpinnings are fragile, and that she could probably use someone nonthreatening in her life. I mean, just this morning, at breakfast, my sister learned how hard it is to remove chunky peanut butter from one's eye.

Teensy introduced him around the table as Dr. Wright. As she ticked off our names, each of us gave a perfunctory nod by way of hello. Then she arrived at Daddy.

"And this is my father, Beau Prescott. Daddy, this is Mr. Right."

Talk about a Freudian slip. The looks Amanda and I exchanged across the table caused such an electrical force field I thought our hair would crackle and stand straight up.

"Dr. Wright." He stuck out his hand for a shake. Then his eyes cut to me. "You're even prettier than you are on TV."

So sue me. I could see that his compliment just blistered Teensy's haunches. My face cracked into a smile.

"Doctor?" Daddy gave the man's sweater vest, khakis, plaid shirt, and tassel loafers the once-over. "No. You're not a real doctor."

"With all due respect, sir, I have a Ph.D." He stood, marooned, as if he'd stumbled into a shooting gallery sporting a duck mask.

"Yeah? So if you had a heart attack on a cruise ship, who'd you want the steward to call . . . a Ph.D., or a medical doctor?"

Dr. Wright indulged Daddy with a smile. We'd just met the man, and he had no reason to suspect he'd be dining with a family of lunatics, even though he'd probably already started performing our individual mental evaluations—Lord only knew what Teensy'd told him about us. After all, the acorn doesn't fall far from the tree: My sister's hair is pink; my grandmother's hair is blue; my father's trying to pickle his liver; and—*hold onto your hats*—there's a pygmy seated at our dining table. I didn't even want to factor Drex into the equation.

"Where do you live?" Daddy asked. "Where's your practice?"

"I live and work in Dallas." He said this with pride, as if living in Dallas were a good thing—which, let's be brutally honest, it isn't.

I swallowed hard. For the record, none of us care for Dallas. Not even Gran, who lives in the gilded cage my deceased grandfather inherited from his parents. To us, Dallas is merely the conduit by which one passes through en route to God's country, what some people know as "Cowtown," and others call Fort Worth.

"It's the ninth biggest city in the United States, pal. Big-D. It's a Category Five on the Saffir-Simpson scale of hurricanes. Dallas would screw you twice it if had an extra dick."

My eyes bulged. I thought I'd misheard. My blue-haired grandmother swooned.

Blood rushed to my head. I didn't grow up with this language—my mother wouldn't have put up with it, and it certainly wasn't Rubanbleu appropriate. My father had a reputation for toughness, but he mostly conducted himself as a gentleman, even in business deals. This demonstration of bad manners convinced me he'd gone off the deep end.

Not to mention the food was getting cold.

I studied these loons with cold scrutiny. So far, Amanda was the only one enjoying the Prescott family Thanksgiving.

"If you want to grow a decent practice," Daddy said, "move to Fort Worth."

"I like it where I am."

"Yeah? Well just make sure business isn't so bad that parents are teaching their kids to drive in your empty parking lot, pal."

I looked at Amanda, and immediately realized that—*hold onto your socks*—between Teensy's new man, and my father having a psychotic break, the weirdest person sitting at the dinner table had suddenly become a challenger in the "Most normal person in the room" contest.

My father flexed his one-upmanship muscles. "What kind of car do you drive?"

"I don't understand. What does this have to do with me taking your daughter out?"

"I want to know what you're squiring her around town in. A Lexus? Jaguar? A beat-up Chevy? Because my girls deserve the best, pal."

Ah . . . so now we deserve the best?

Drex inclined his head in my direction and muttered, "Good thing I drive a BMW," and yukked it up like a high-fiving high schooler in the boys' locker room.

I whispered, "Get away from me."

Dr. Wright said, "I drive an extended-cab diesel pickup. The luxury version."

"Well, congrats on your behemoth, gas-guzzling truck. How smart do you think that decision was when gas is sky-high?"

"I make a decent living. I can afford it."

"The bigger the truck, the smaller the penis."

We all took bracing breaths.

"Beg your pardon?" Dr. Wright. Stricken.

Amanda said, "Man, I'm happy eating Thanksgiving with the white people."

"I'm just saying a big-ass, extended-cab, diesel pickup might suggest you had to compensate for having a little needle dick." Daddy.

Gran swooned. "Beau—the blessing. Now," she said with a certain urgency. Then she asked Dr. Wright if he'd be joining us for dinner.

"That'd be great. Thanks."

I decided he was an idiot.

We played musical chairs again. The doc slid into what had formerly been Teensy's seat and watched as Gran set another place at the table for my sister.

"What?" Teensy looked at Dr. Wright, miffed and sarcastic. "I suppose you want to sit next to my sister, the TV personality, huh?"

"My seat's fine." Dr. Wright said pleasantly. "This way, I can look at her."

Teensy set her jaw.

The discussion on whose was bigger continued. The doc may have thought this was how polite society made idle conversation, when he asked Daddy what kind of vehicle he drove, but it only came out as a challenge when Daddy answered, "A big-ass extended-cab, diesel pickup, but I'm not covering up for having an inadequate penis."

"Well, with all due respect, sir, it appears you drive a gas guzzler, too."

"Hey, pal, I can drive a damned bus if I want—unlike you, I own an oil company. You, on the other hand, screw with people's heads. Don't call me when you run out of gas."

This offensive behavior toward our guest actually convinced me Daddy's health had improved. He'd turned back into a real bastard so I suspected the rehab center would soon be actively working on his discharge.

Gran returned to her chair. "I think we should eat before the food gets cold. Remember what they say: Hot food is the best food."

Amanda looked up expectantly. "Thought you wanted to say grace."

"Of course." The pained smile on Gran's face resembled a snarl. "Perhaps we should let one of our guests give the blessing." She shifted her gaze to Drex.

"Sure thing, Miss Eugenia."

Not so sure.

My whole body wilted. Having Drex in the house was like having a piano in the kitchen. It's pretty, but it's in the way.

"Join hands," Daddy said, and everyone clasped the hand of the person next to them until we'd formed a circle. Everyone but me, that is.

When Drex reached for my hand, I backed him off with a sterling silver knife. "I wouldn't if I were you," I said through gritted teeth.

"Isn't it wonderful having Drex here?" Gran asked, clearly snowed by a bouquet of flowers.

Incredulous, my mind cast back to the previous month, to when Gordon Pfeiffer hired me to figure out who his wife was having an affair with. I did a slow burn. The pictures I took of a naked Drex and the boss's equally naked wife, Paislee, locked in a doggie hookup in front of the upstairs bedroom window, photographs I took from a treehouse in my boss's backyard, sealed their fate.

I could've answered my grandmother. Could've told her why Drex and I weren't together anymore. In fact, I wanted to, but then, why would I? After all, nobody wanted to ride in the back of an ambulance crying, "Hang on, Gran, hang on . . ."

CHAPTER SIX

My out-of-body experience worsened in inverse proportion to the cooling food, as my ex-boyfriend led us in prayer.

"Dear Father . . . Mother . . . Spirit—whatever You are—as I sit here today I'm thankful for the changes in my life . . . for getting my law license—even though I really hated all those people at the law firm where I interned, and I hated the clients they brought in even more. And for being able to go places like the national forests in Paislee's Winnebago . . ."

My eyes popped open. Well, not just open. They damned near shot out of their sockets like champagne corks.

". . . and I'm thankful for friends like Dainty, who's still speaking to me even though I was a rotten boyfriend and chased women behind her back—"

I sat ramrod straight, and slid Daddy a sideways look. His eyes were practically bungee jumping out of his head. Plus, he crushed my hand. I may be the stupid one in the Prescott family, according to him, but I'm still a Prescott, and that trumps a cheating ex-boyfriend.

"—and for all this food, and the caterer who made the food—"

Gran took this as an insult. "There's no caterer. What kind of person do you think I am? I wouldn't trust a caterer to prepare food for my family on Thanksgiving."

Amanda's shoulders bobbed with stifled laughter.

"—and for the employees who work at the store where Miss

Eugenia bought the food; and for the pig and the turkey that gave their lives so that we could eat them; and for Mr. Prescott, who's sitting at the end of the table smiling at me—"

That's not a smile, you idiot.

"—he's my brother. Well, not really my brother. My brother is Van, but he's not speaking to me because of what happened with Dainty . . . or maybe it's the other way around. Anyway, Mr. Prescott's my blood brother, and I'm glad I ran into him at an AA meeting, even though I chose a group over on the east side of town so I wouldn't run into anybody I knew . . ."

Lo and behold, there's my daddy, the lush, skulking around town doing the same thing.

". . . and I'm thankful we hooked up and he agreed to be my sponsor, and that I'm not drinking, and he keeps me sober—"

"Not anymore." Daddy's cheeks had turned beet red. To Drex, he said, "Do you even know what the word 'anonymous' means?"

I kept waiting for Gran's reaction. But her head stayed bowed, further convincing me she couldn't take any more drama and had turned off her hearing aids.

Amanda's shoulders heaved with silent laughter.

Drex continued. "I'm thankful Teensy came home from Mexico, but she owes me money, and it's starting to affect our friendship—" he slid Teensy a sideways glance "—so I'm not going to loan her any more. And Lord, the other night I saw a shooting star and didn't even know what to wish for because I'm already truly blessed—"

"For the love of God, can't we just eat already?" Teensy. "And, just so you know, the only reason I asked for a loan was because my drunken father cut me off financially, and I didn't have any cash to take on my trip to Mexico."

"Although I'm running low on money," Drex went on, "I really, really, *really* don't want to have to go back and practice law. I think that would make me drink."

Cue Daddy and his throat-clearing rumblings of disapproval.

"Get a grip." *Moi,* under my breath.

"So before I conclude, I think we should go around the table, starting with the Prescott's help, and each say something you're all thankful for. What's your name?"

"Amanda. And I'm not the help."

"You're supposed to say what you're thankful for," Drex prompted her.

"I'm thankful my family's starting to look pretty normal." Amanda turned to Gran. "Your turn." Since Gran looked like she'd nodded off, Amanda poked her. "It's your turn to say what you're thankful for."

"I heard you the first time. I'm thankful to be surrounded by family. And I'm thankful I have a thirty-year-old boyfriend who keeps me young."

"What?" I yelled this.

Daddy shot me a look. Hand to face, he shielded his mouth to keep Gran from lip-reading. "Imaginary boyfriend."

"Gran has an imaginary thirty-year-old boyfriend?" I cackled in disbelief.

"She's doing better than you," he grumbled. "You don't even have an imaginary boyfriend, let alone a real one."

Gran prompted Teensy. "Go ahead, dear."

My sister took a deep breath. "I'm thankful I'm in therapy. And that Texas has the death penalty so we can watch Nerissa fry."

"We don't fry people, Teensy, we stick needles in them," I said.

"Right. Lethal injection. Whatever. I'm thankful I found Mr. Right."

"When did that happen?" *Moi.*

"Shut up, Dainty, it's not your turn . . . oh, yeah, I'm thankful I finally got my shit together—"

Gran groaned. Then she and Daddy admonished Teensy in stereo.

"—and that I have a new job, and a new car—"

"You got a new job and a new car? When did you get a new car?"

"While you were gone."

This unwelcome disclosure turned into a real whiskey-tango-foxtrot moment. My head swiveled to Daddy. He refused to make eye contact.

"Would you let me finish, please?" Teensy, acting put out.

I should've been the one who was put out. These people didn't get me a new car. *Au contraire.*

"Wait—when did you get a new job?" I felt like somebody'd whacked me upside the head with a pistol butt. "For that matter, *where* did you get a new job?"

Gran intervened. "She got a job while you were gone. Actually, she's had a handful."

I learned Teensy'd gotten—and lost—four jobs in the two weeks I'd been gone. She got laid off from the first one due to "cutbacks." A few days later, she drove past her old workplace and saw a "Now hiring" sign in the window. Next, she took a job as a support worker at a daycare. After forty-five minutes of trying to calm a violent, autistic kid, he beat her with a *Happy Ways to Behave When I'm Upset* book that she'd given him the day before.

Then she lost her job at a retirement community when she ran over an old lady's foot with her work golf cart.

She didn't actually *lose* the fourth job so much as *quit.* The way Teensy told it, the babysitting job she auditioned for went awry after the mother left her alone with her kid on a trial run while she ran errands for a couple of hours. The five-year-old pulled a knife out of the cutlery drawer and told her he'd cut off her tits if she didn't get him an ice cream sandwich out of the freezer, and, apparently, she believed him.

She lost out on the fifth job when she couldn't find her lip gloss and told a woman at the cosmetic counter at Harkman Beemis, "I need a lipstick. Something like yours. Something that says, 'I'm a bitch.' " This woman turned out to be the person conducting her interview. According to Teensy, the meeting lasted long enough for her to say they were no longer hiring but would keep her application on file. The lady promptly dropped the paperwork in "File 13" before Teensy skulked off. Imagine that.

Teensy continued to regale us with her reasons to be grateful. It reminded me of one of those Academy Award acceptance speeches where everybody got thanked—right down to the gofers who made coffee—while the real contributor to the actor's success got left out.

"And I'm thankful the university granted me an extension to finish this semester since the closed-head injury set me back . . ."

The more Teensy talked, the more my cheeks blistered with heat. What started out as a slow burn spontaneously combusted. "And you're thankful for me—that I rescued your ass from a Third World country. Say it."

Gran swooned.

Sparks shot from Teensy's blue eyes. "You're so selfish, Dainty. This is my turn. You'll get your turn."

"Say it." I produced a balled-up fist and shook it, just like when we were kids, before our mom would intervene and diffuse the situation by using reverse psychology on us. That unexpected disconnect made me think of the time our mother broke up a brawl that erupted between my sister and me in the kitchen. At the root of this fight was the last brownie in the pan that we were told to share. Teensy picked up a knife and prepared to slice it in half, until our mother announced that whoever did the cutting got last pick. A fight broke out when Teensy cut an unequal portion, and then grabbed the biggest piece. At her wits' end, Mom yelled that she'd had her fill of us. She went to the cutlery drawer, handed each of us a steak knife, and sent us to opposite corners of the room. On the count of three, we were instructed to run at each other. Teensy realized we loved each other and burst into tears. Our mom was a sharp cookie.

God, I miss her.

I realized I still had my fist locked and loaded when my eyes flickered to Amanda, mocking me across the table by doing little bobs and weaves.

Teensy concluded her filibuster by grudgingly thanking me for rescuing her, and passed the torch to Dr. Wright. I wanted to smack her.

Daddy said, "Make it quick. You're not even supposed to be here."

Dr. Wright said, "I'm delighted to be spending this evening in your lovely home, and at your lovely table. With your lovely daughter. *Daughters.*"

"Yeah?" Daddy said, "We'll just see about that." Then he took the mantle. "I'm thankful for the food. The food we can't seem to be able to eat." He paused to consider his empty plate. Then he turned to me. "Hurry up."

"I'm thankful that I have a new job, and a new life . . . and screw you, Drex, for ever letting me go in the first place."

"Dainty." Daddy and Gran scolded me in stereo.

Amanda hooted.

Suddenly enthused, Drex alerted. "So you're saying we should see other people?"

"Save it. I'm way ahead of you," I snarled.

"Let's just eat." Gran calmly picked up the closest dish, and started the rotation by passing it to Amanda, who helped herself to the mashed potatoes before passing the bowl to Drex.

"No. I don't want to eat." And when I announced I didn't want their food, what I meant was, "Holy cow, these people are freaking insane." Feeling horribly defiled and offended on so many levels, I slapped my napkin onto the empty plate. It was pretty freaking impressive.

"Is this about the Columbia thing? It's a done deal, Dainty. Let it go." Daddy picked up a casserole dish. "Here—try your grandmother's sweet potatoes."

I love Gran's sweet potato casserole covered in pecans with marshmallow topping heated to a crusty golden brown. To drive home my point, I turned up my nose at it.

My blood boiled. "Is that all you have to say for yourself?"

Drex put his two cents' worth in. "Listen to your father, Dainty. He's right."

I whirled around to face him. "Shut up, suck-up. I don't even know why you're here. Shouldn't you be with Paislee Pfeiffer?"

His jaw dropped open. "You know about that?"

"The whole town knows about it."

He shrank in his seat and inclined himself in the opposite direction.

Gran turned into Chatty Cathy and changed the subject. "Isn't your high school reunion happening over Christmas break? Do you have a date?" She conspicuously eyed up Drex.

"It's not my high school reunion. It's a midyear get-together for all the people who weren't able to come to the official reunion."

"Well, maybe Drex would be willing to take you."

" 'Willing to take me'? *Willing to take me?*"

"Dainty, if you can't keep your voice down, you'll be asked to leave the table."

"I don't need help getting dates." I kept my voice even and

metered. And lethal.

"I'd be okay with taking you," Drex said.

"I wouldn't go to a dogfight with you." I shot him a look meant to cut him dead.

Amanda laughed. "This is fun. Dinner with the white people. Who'd have thought?" She did a little chair dance until I opened fire on her with a death-ray glare.

Daddy piped up between bites. "I went to my high school reunion. Huge letdown. Everybody had turned into their parents. The guy voted 'Most Likely to Succeed' couldn't be there. The governor denied his pardon. And the biggest oddball in the class showed up in a Rolls Royce with a racehorse blonde on both arms. How's that for irony?"

I'd had enough. In the court of Beau Prescott, Teensy's new man had been found guilty of being Mr. Wrong, my sunny disposition had turned thunderous, and I couldn't get out of the room fast enough. I decided to do the sporting thing and save Amanda, too.

"Amanda, would you like to go upstairs and get settled in?"

"No, thanks." A grin split across her face. "I'm enjoying this lovely dinner."

"Yes, well, wouldn't you rather come upstairs for a few minutes so I can show you where things are?"

"No, thanks."

I wanted to body-slam her against the floor.

I thought about my family, and how they all have permits to carry firearms. You're not supposed to be able to get one if you're a mental case, but apparently Gran got hers before she went nuts, and Daddy got his before he went bonkers, so I guess they can thank their lucky stars they were grandfathered in. For a few seconds I took comfort in the fact that, now that my sister's gone off the deep end, she probably can't get one.

I suffered through the meal in relative silence. When I'd had all I could take, I asked to be excused from the table.

Gran balked. "Where are you going on Thanksgiving? Everything's closed."

"I'm going to the TV station. I have work to do."

"What kind of work?" Gran looked at me, slitty-eyed.

"I've been working on a project for Mr. Pfeiffer. I need to finish it." On the brink of tears, I pushed back from the table. I didn't plan to stick around to see if things could get any worse, but occasionally I forget—I'm Dainty Prescott, and when Mercury's in retrograde, my life augers in. My sister, the debutante, had just crammed a Parker House roll into her mouth like a field hand and was chewing furiously, giving me a flapping hand gesture to wait while she washed bread down her throat.

In a slightly more refined move, she delicately dabbed the corners of her mouth with a napkin. "Oh, you don't have to worry, Dainty. The project's finished. You can relax and spend the evening with us."

I narrowed my eyes in suspicion. "What do you mean 'finished'?"

"I finished it for you. I turned it in to Mr. Pfeiffer on Monday."

The room suddenly blurred. Then it came back into sharp focus. "You what?" The tinny, high-pitched ring in my ear turned into a fifth generation echo of myself. "How could you finish my project?"

She put on a hang-dog expression—like the ones on sad bassets in those adopt-a-pet commercials—the same way she used to do when we were kids, and she pulled out all the stops to sway the argument in her favor. Too bad for her that I was wise to this little pantomime of sadness.

"No need to thank me. It was the least I could do to help you out while you took off in search of Nerissa. So I went to

69

your boss and asked him if I could help. He told me about your project, and I finished it for you, and turned it in."

I started a new prayer in my head.

Lord—help me to be able to convince a jury not to give me the death penalty.

My fury had narrowed the entire world to the space between my sister and me. Now, it abruptly widened, making me vaguely aware of the dumbstruck stares of the rest of the people at the table. Reality set in, and everyone was treated to the latest episode of the "Dainty and Teensy" show. As I railed away at my sister, I hardly noticed Daddy get up from the table and head toward the kitchen.

I ended my rant with a denouncement. "Suck-up."

"Oh, please, you practically invented suck-up. You hold the patent on it. People should have to pay royalties on your suck-up rights to be able to use it."

Daddy returned from the kitchen carrying two large butcher knives. One was an inch or so shorter than the other. He held them aloft and gave Teensy and me a choice. "Whoever picks the smaller one gets a two-second head start."

He remembered.

I could almost picture tomorrow's headline. The front-page story would start with, "All stunningly beautiful and extraordinarily talented Dainty Prescott ever wanted was to share a happy Thanksgiving with family and friends," and end with, "She then turned the knife on herself."

"Nobody puts Baby in the corner," I slapped my napkin down next to my plate.

I missed my boyfriend . . . well, ex-boyfriend. If I'd played my cards right, I would've been spending the holidays with Bruckman. With the grace and elegance of a forties starlet, I glided into the kitchen, snagged my black cashmere coat off the hook on the hall tree, and stepped into the pantry where Gran kept a spare set of keys for the Caddy.

Chapter Seven

WBFD-TV operates out of a stand-alone concrete and glass building that takes up approximately one city block and backs up to a residential neighborhood. It has a cinder block wall in the shape of a horseshoe that buffers three sides of the building and parking lot, and a gated area in front that Gordon recommends the staff keep locked from nine o'clock in the evening until seven o'clock in the morning. I'm sure that has nothing to do with the people living in the residences on the other side of the wall, especially the psychotic naked guy who occasionally dashes out his back door hollering, "I don't want to clip my toenails, you crazy bitch." He lives alone. Every time he does this, I run, not walk, through the parking lot.

This area of town just isn't safe after sunset. The houses behind the station have a creepy feel, with many of the homes having bars on the windows, and dancing pit bulls chained in a handful of yards. I hosted a "Fight Crime" fundraiser in the parking lot outside of the TV station the last semester of my senior year at Texas Christian University during my internship at WBFD-TV. Only three people showed up, and two of them robbed our booth. I'm pretty sure they were miscreants who lived in the houses on the other side of that wall. And once, I made eye contact with a man standing on the balcony of an apartment building across the wall, on the other side of the train tracks. He ran his finger across his neck and stared at me. Then he broke into a smile, and motioned me over. Made me afraid to leave the station.

Back to the building itself.

The front doors to the lobby remain open during normal business hours between eight and five o'clock, but the metal door at the back of the building wasn't monitored with a vengeance until maybe a month ago after an incident occurred that freaked out Gordon and the rest of the employees.

The event that led to our increased attention to safety and security began when a bullet Rochelle fired from a .38 caliber Smith & Wesson grazed a man who'd been stalking Aspen Wicklow. Rochelle had taken to frequenting a particular bar looking for the man who beat and raped her best friend's daughter and left her for dead in a ditch. This Bronson-esque vigilantism set in motion a string of events that had lasting consequences for the rest of the people in the WBFD workplace; among them, Aspen's boyfriend, Spike Granger, the sheriff of Johnson County, who shot the rapist as he tried to bludgeon Rochelle into a pink stain. One would think that'd be enough to swear off bars for good, but, no, not Rochelle. She exchanged phone numbers with Ulysses S. Bumgardner, a dwarf she met one night while plastered, but once she sobered up and spurned the man's advances, he subsequently followed her to the TV station early one morning.

Prior to the appearance of Mr. Bumgardner, employees used the back door to dash in and out on food runs, and to let guests inside who were invited to appear on the early show. On the morning Mrs. Schmidt's first grade class arrived to join WBFD's meteorologist, Misty Knight, for the weather report, they entered through the back entrance, which allowed Rochelle's dwarf to file in with the rest of the children. The shootout that occurred when Rochelle's spurned suitor took Aspen and Steve Lennox, one of the news anchors, hostage caused Gordon to make a few safety changes regarding people gaining access to the studio during off hours. As far as I knew, the big rock next to the back door hadn't been used to prop it open since that unfortunate incident.

Now, I wondered if it was still there, available for one of the neighborhood thugs to bash a naïve intern's head in.

Not to mention that a homicidal maniac, still at large, had been stalking Aspen ever since she did a story on missing young women who'd been found murdered.

I hadn't been issued a key card that would allow me access to the front door, and I'd only recently become a paid extern, so I called ahead and asked one of the photographers to let me in. To my surprise, Chopper Deke met me at the gate.

His mouth curled into a polite smirk. "Couldn't stay away from me, could you, toots?" He said this in a two-pack-a-day voice.

"Get over yourself and open the gate."

He flashed his key card and the gate groaned open. Chopper Deke said, "You look hot. Actually, you look like shit. But the car looks hot." He ran his hand along the hood of the Caddy as I rolled through the gate at a snail's pace. "Where'd you get it?"

I gave him an uninvitingly blank look, explained that it belonged to my grandmother, and asked him not to slobber on it. To keep from getting his foot run over, he moved beneath the mercury vapor street lamp. The glow cast off by the light blued his face and his cotton-white hair.

"Tell the truth—do you ever think about that kiss?" He said this with a leer. His eyes gleamed stubbornly.

I wanted to jam my fingers into my ears and make babbling noises until I drowned out the voice screaming inside my head, but I let the silence speak for me. I could only express a strained hope that, one of these days, Chopper Deke would quit hitting on me.

He stood guard until I cleared the gate, and when I headed toward the back of the lot to dock the *U.S.S. Eugenia,* he hollered at me to pull it into one of the spaces reserved for the on-air talent. I parked next to Aspen Wicklow's old Honda.

"It's safer. If anybody says anything, tell them to take it up with me." His face cracked into a grin. I was familiar with the tone, and the sentiment behind the voice. The guy had helped me before. Maybe he could help me again.

Chopper Deke escorted me into the building. He actually looked less creepy now that the street lamps no longer made his face appear cyanotic. When we got inside, he shrugged out of his leather pilot jacket and hooked it on the coat tree near the door. For convenience, I layered my cashmere coat over his.

Then I noticed the smell. Masked by the strong scent from the pine tree Gordon had brought in for the staff to decorate for Christmas, I couldn't place the strange odor other than to know that I'd never whiffed anything like it before. I felt my face contort into a gruesome shape.

"What the heck is that smell?" I turned to Chopper Deke, thinking it might be him.

"Don't know. My allergies flared up when the cold front blew in, and I can't smell a thing." His eyes locked on my cleavage despite the fact that the outfit I had on wasn't exactly seductive. "Didn't affect my vision, though. What brings you up here this time of night?"

I'd been dreading this and had put it off for as long as possible. "Believe it or not, I'm here to see you."

"Daydreaming about me, huh? Bet you wake up in the night and do nasty things to yourself while you fantasize about me, don't you?"

"Do you always have to act like a pervert? I came up here because you're probably the only person I know, who's still

75

speaking to me, who can answer my questions."

"Pop the top two buttons on your shirt."

"Again, I ask—hoping I won't be called to testify—do you always think about sex? Or do you have moments when you act normally?"

"Hey, toots, 'normal' is what's normal for you. For me, talking about sex is normal." He teased me with his eyes. His smile widened enough to see a missing molar. "Want to talk in my office?"

Chopper Deke had an office? News to me. I'd only worked here a few hours each week during the previous semester, and still had a lot to learn about the layout of the place.

He led me to the second floor, past the mezzanine and off a side corridor. Normally, I would've felt uneasy following him down a long, deserted hallway, but Chopper Deke had played an integral part in Teensy's return from Mexico. I trailed him to the end of the hall, past Production, where he opened a door for me. As I entered the room, a sensor engaged and the light automatically came on. Chopper Deke skulked in behind me like a criminal behind his bail bondsman, looking both dangerous and borderline sinister. The window shades had been left open, which permitted a western view of downtown Fort Worth.

The skyline flickered like Christmas tree lights.

Had I not been in the company of Chopper Deke, this would've been romantic.

He motioned me toward a leather sofa, and he headed for a recliner that didn't fit with the rest of the tasteful, western-themed décor. This looked like the same white trash, motorized easy chair we'd witnessed movers haul out to the dumpster when Gordon had his office redecorated after sweeps month propelled the station from last place to third place in the ratings.

He flopped back into the seat, grabbed the lever on the side of the chair, yanked up the footrest, and viewed me with the intensity of a poker player.

I got right to the point. "I'm having trouble understanding my sister . . . what she's going through."

"What do I look like, a counselor?"

"I just meant that she seems to be having some sort of post-traumatic stress, and she's not acting right."

"What do you expect me to do about it?"

"Mr. Quintanilla told me you were in Vietnam. And that it made you . . ." How could I delicately put this without offending him? ". . . well, crazy."

He forced the back of his spiked blonde head into the chair's covered-foam cushion and guffawed.

"My sister's gone off the deep end."

"She's been through a lot. What'd you think would happen when she got back home?"

I didn't answer. I thought she'd be the same as always. He implied Teensy needed TLC. I implied she should be spanked with a three-hole board.

He continued to stare. I could feel familial obligation sucking at me, and figured I'd made a mistake coming here. My father may have gone middle-aged crazy, and, for sure, my grandmother was a rigid aristocratic wingnut, but I always thought I'd have my sister. These days, I couldn't tell who she was, or what she stood for. My eyes misted. I blinked back tears.

Chopper Deke's face got all funny looking. Lines in his forehead relaxed. Right before my very eyes, the station's helicopter pilot, who I'd previously thought to be vile and crass and amoral, turned into a good guy.

Startled into honesty, he said nice things. "Look, kid. When I was in the military, a lot of bad things happened. More than half of the men I served with were killed in action. The chopper I flew took a direct hit and went down in a three-canopy jungle.

Know what that is?"

I shook my head.

"Three layers of trees. You get to the bottom and can't see the sun. It's like midnight. So there we were—the ones who survived the crash—and you know what we were staring at?"

I didn't realize I'd been holding my breath. It seeped out in increments.

"Gooks." His eyes thinned into slits. "Angry little slope-heads who wanted to kill us. I was scrappy and no stranger to brawls. I wanted to live. Had a girl back home—Nancy Lynn. Knocked her up. I carried her picture everywhere until it was so dog-eared and tattered I stopped passing it around. Didn't matter in the end. They took that snapshot, and everything else of value from us, and prodded us back to camp at gunpoint. Ever hear of the Hanoi Hilton?" He paused.

I'd heard of it. This was where U.S. POWs endured miserable conditions, including torture and interrogation.

"Shall I go on?"

The air between us had become energized. Chopper Deke no longer seemed perverted and sinister to me. Spellbound, I nodded.

He recounted a new part of the Hanoi Hilton they nicknamed "Little Vegas" because a lot of the downed pilots had trained at Nellis Air Force Base.

"Living with a bunch of guys, you long for things like privacy, and having your own room. We each got our own room, all right," he said with a hint of sarcasm. "Here in America, they're known as cages. So for three hundred and sixty-two days, I lived in a little cage, stark naked, about five or six inches from the water. Rats need water. They'd bite us through the wires of our cages to see if we were dead."

I winced.

"They fed us rotten rice full of maggots. Or, we did without food. Forget everything you ever heard or read about the Geneva Convention. Humane treatment didn't exist. Those were the nights we were glad the rats came up to the cages."

I felt a tug of affection for this coarse man as he told more stories, each more ghastly than the one before. It was all I could do to keep from hurling. I looked at Chopper Deke—really looked at him—and saw a brave and determined man I was honored to know. For no good reason, I felt the urge to kiss him. Not in the way that I kissed Bruckman, but in the most grateful and patriotic of ways, like when a firefighter pulls you out of a burning building. It just seemed right. I fought the urge.

"Prior to my unfortunate stay at 'Little Vegas,' I weighed in at a hundred and seventy-two pounds. By the time we were liberated, I weighed a hundred and seventeen pounds, and had all kinds of parasites and nutritional deficiencies. But I won't bore you with the gory details."

"I'm so sorry. So very sorry." I whispered this with the utmost reverence, and he fanned away my attention with a flick of the wrist.

"I learned a few things as a POW. One, everybody has a breaking point. Two, you do whatever you can do or say to survive. Maybe it wouldn't be such a bad thing to cut your sister a little slack."

I felt physically ill. He must've sensed a change in my demeanor because he invited me downstairs to the break room for a soda. I accepted.

But when he opened the door and swept me inside the lounge area with a flourish, a terrible odor struck like a punch in the nose.

"Oh, gag. What's that smell?" He stood in front of the vending machine, plunking quarters down the chute, while I buried my nose in my sleeve, Dracula-style.

Instead of answering, he asked what kind of carbonated drink I wanted. He selected one of the colas, and I asked him, again, about the horrible odor as the can rolled down the channel and clunked against the stop.

Chopper Deke touched his nose. "Like I said, my sniffer's on the fritz." Then he motioned me over to one of the bistro tables, but I thought better of it. Between this gagging smell and Deke's imprisonment story, I declined.

"Thanks for the drink . . . and you're right. I'll try to lighten up on my sister."

Then Chopper Deke walked me out to Gran's car.

"So whatever happened to Nancy Lynn? Did you get married?"

He shook his head. "Wouldn't have worked. War changes a person."

"What about your kid?"

"Never met her."

"You have a daughter?" It was hard to imagine Deke as a father. "What's her name?"

"Don't know. Don't care."

But the pain in his eyes told a different story. Suddenly, I knew what I could do to repay him.

The night air sent a chill through me. I shuddered realizing I'd left my cashmere coat behind and didn't like to think about returning for it.

"Quick question—have you caught wind of any stories as to whether those extradition officers who transported my step-mother made it back safely?" I OCD-checked the parking lot at least ten times waiting for an answer.

"Quit worrying. They're big boys. Let 'em do their jobs." Deke said this in the same impassive way someone comments on a luggage tag, but I caught him doing a quick eye scan of our surroundings and knew he must've been worried, too.

As I fished the keys out of my purse and unlocked the door, he ran his hand lovingly over the hood.

"Looks like we'll have two beauties at WBFD now," he said.

Not hardly. Since beauty was in the eye of the beholder, I set the record straight. "My dad sold my car while I was gone. As soon as I get new wheels, you won't see Gran's Cadillac around here again."

He did a little face scrunch. "Not talking about the Caddy, toots. I meant you and your sister."

Teensy wouldn't dare show her face at the TV station now that she'd taken over my project once I'd left the country. And once I'd disabused Chopper Deke of the notion, I left him to fondle the car while I hurried inside to collect my overcoat from the hall tree.

It was gone.

I'd seen these rude people in action; it wasn't unusual for someone dashing out to their car and back to grab the top coat on the hall tree, if theirs was buried underneath. Instead of hunting it down, I left the building and headed back to the car without it.

CHAPTER EIGHT

Once I'd left the station, I headed off down the highway.

But not back to Big-D.

I felt the electric force field of Jim Bruckman's house calling, and pointed the snout of the Cadillac toward Airport Freeway. The closer I got, the more the low-grade sexual current in my body increased.

In my head, I rehearsed what I'd say when he came to the door. Just for the record, I don't do "sorry," so thinking up ways to make amends without actually using the word had me stymied. By the time I turned onto his street, I'd nearly perfected my canned speech. Bruckman lives in a ranch-style home that sprawls across a one-acre lot. All of the houses on this street were built in the fifties and sixties when land in Tarrant County, just east of downtown Fort Worth, was more plentiful, so surrounding homes had been built in similar styles on similar-sized lots. But Bruckman owned the most desirable piece of real estate in the neighborhood—his house topped the hill, which gave him a bird's-eye, almost panoramic, view of downtown Fort Worth through the plate glass window in his living room.

There was one other interesting fact about his street. It only had one security light at each end, which made traversing the middle stretch of roadway a bit scary with the headlights off. If not for the fact that most of the homes already featured Christmas lights, Bruckman's house would've been next to

82

impossible to see in the dark. Only the light overhanging the front door burned with a soft, incandescent glow.

Was he even home?

I rolled up in front of the house and didn't see his pickup in the driveway. Maybe he'd gone to his parents' house for Thanksgiving, but maybe not. Maybe he'd garaged his truck. I swallowed what felt like a golf ball in my throat and whispered, "Please don't let this be happening," to no one in particular.

I knew what I had to do. It was either that, or stay ostrich-headed.

I walked up the driveway and rang the doorbell several times. When he didn't answer, I retraced my steps. Halfway back to the car, I heard a noise like an acorn hitting the ground . . . or a serial killer trying to get the jump on me. I glanced over my shoulder in time to see a dark figure approaching me from the side of the garage. I screamed and threw my purse. It also threw its purse due to the fact it was my shadow on the wall.

This almost made me require the defibrillation paddles. While not yet ready to admit the desperate need for anti-anxiety medication, I had to admit this skittish behavior could be an indictment on me as the owner-proprietor of a private investigations firm.

The need to know Bruckman's whereabouts worked on my last raw nerve. I turned on the headlights and headed to the end of the street and took a left to get back onto the freeway. I'd made this drive before, back when Bruckman and I first started dating a few months ago. To prove that I could pull surveillance without the target's knowledge, and to stop him from making fun of me by calling my fledgling business the Debutante Detective Agency, I followed him from work one afternoon. The destination brought tears to my eyes when I discovered he'd gone to see the widow of his best friend—a lady a few years older than me who'd once been his girlfriend or fiancée . . . whichever.

Gran's car seemed to instinctively know where to go. It didn't shore up my confidence knowing the ex lived ten minutes away. I kept my eyes on the road, passing smears of neon signs that advertised restaurants, bars, and other businesses. I knew I shouldn't be doing this—Bruckman had made it clear: If I returned to Mexico looking for Nerissa, we were history. He said no girlfriend was better than a dead girlfriend; that he'd witnessed enough death on the job to last a lifetime; and, if I couldn't mind him—*mind him!*—then I could go my own way . . . all of this to the sounds of Fleetwood Mac singing "You Can Go Your Own Way," in the background while Bruckman played air-guitar, and hopped around on an invisible stage.

I'm a seventh-generation Texan. And while I'm respectful (read: most of the time) to my elders, professors, bosses, service people, businessmen, and the like, I don't "mind" anyone. It's not like I wanted to schlep around the desert looking for my wicked stepmother—I had to. She needed to be held accountable for what she did to my family, and, come hell or high water, I couldn't let it slide.

There was ample time to abandon this crazy idea as I made the last turn to the ex's home, an eighties tract house with a zero-lot line. It'd been one thing to go by Bruckman's place looking for a shoulder to cry on. It was quite another to go house-to-house, hunting him down. That's what stalkers do.

Again, I tried to talk myself out of this. What could I do if I saw his pickup parked in her driveway at one o'clock in the morning, and all the lights out? Stir up a racket in the front yard by declaring my love for him via the medium of interpretive dance? Park the car down the block, disguise myself as the Virgin Mary in the nativity scene on the neighbor's front lawn, and watch the house all night? I certainly couldn't pass myself off as one of the wise men—this was crazy.

Yet, I had to know. I'd been idling at the corner, afraid to turn down her street. While working up my courage, my cell phone chimed with a text message from Teensy. It was a romantic text, clearly meant for Dr. Wright. Not only can't she spell, the clichés she uses are horrifyingly embarrassing. The fact that she sent it to me instead of him made me want to slam her head against the bathtub. And yet . . .

Thanks to Teensy's misrouted text message, I completely took leave of my senses. Under the soft, creamy glow of the dome light, I decided to type a romantic text message of my own to Bruckman on my cell phone, telling him how important he was to me, and how much I loved him. After debating whether to go on pouring my heart out, I pressed the send button. In Rubanbleu terms, less is more.

Finally, I shifted the Cadillac into gear and rolled around the corner. Sure enough, there was Bruckman's pickup. I didn't think things could get any worse. Then the front door opened.

Bruckman stepped out onto the porch. He probably wouldn't have paid any attention to Gran's car if I hadn't made a hard right and whipped onto the intersecting street. Surprisingly, my heart didn't stall. It didn't stall because I'm pretty sure you can't have a heart attack and a stroke at the same time. In my hasty getaway, I felt a thud against the back of my seat. My eyes flickered to the rearview mirror. Toxic green eyes peered back at me. Through high-pitched screams and an advancing blur, I lost control and careened into the curb and then over it, thanks to the feral station kitty that apparently crawled into the car, fell asleep, and then woke up when I swerved to go around the corner.

At the second house from the corner, I plowed under the jaunty nativity scene in the homeowner's front yard. While the big ugly cat hissed in the floorboard, I also took out their mailbox as I careened back onto the street.

But, hey—good news. This shameless debacle was enough to

tear Bruckman's eyes away from his ex's slinky robe. If there's one thing he loves more than a good-looking girlfriend, it's a good car chase. As he receded in my rearview mirror, I watched him fling open the driver's door on his truck and jump in. I didn't have to hear the peel-out to know he'd come after me. Headlights the size of chigger-eye diamonds grew larger as he gained on me. If I could make it to the freeway, I could shake him. Better yet, if I could make it to the freeway, I could sucker-punch him by going straight under the overpass, and avoid Airport Freeway altogether. After braking to a screaming halt at the stop sign, I floored the accelerator and shot through the intersection like the Stars's winning hockey puck.

I checked my rearview mirror. Bruckman's headlights went from chigger-eye diamonds to the size of the Hope Diamond as he gained on me. I bounced under the overpass and made a sharp left onto the frontage road, briefly losing sight of him. But instead of taking the on-ramp to the freeway, I drove into the stall of one of those convenience store car washes, cut my lights, leaned across the passenger seat and flung open the door. The cat took off and I closed myself back inside. Then I plunked a bunch of quarters down the chute, and drove onto the conveyor belt. Sayonara, baby. Who's the ace investigator now?

Splashes of water froze in midair. The wind from the blow dryer turned them into little shards of ice as they hit my cheeks like a pin cushion. I realized one of the back windows had been left slightly rolled down, and that spray from the car wash had dampened the brocade upholstery in the back seat. When the car wash spit out Gran's Cadillac, I glanced around. No Bruckman.

At least I had that going for me.

For now, I needed to dry out the seat as much as possible, and rolled the back windows all of the way down. Air circulating through the vehicle might actually take care of the matter; if so, Gran would never have to know.

I realized by crossing the freeway, I'd entered a ratty part of town. One more block over, and I'd need a gun. If I could snag a handful of paper towels from the dispenser and hop back into the car without anyone getting the jump on me, I'd be long gone, and I'd be fine. The towel dispenser happened to be bolted to the outside wall of the car wash. Because of the direction my car was pointed, I cleared the bricks enough to open the door, take a step out, and grab a handful.

With shop towels in hand, I whipped around to jump back into the safety of Gran's car, and screamed bloody murder.

Bruckman stood next to the hood with his arms braced and a scowl on his face, looking as hacked off as the first time we met, back when he arrested me for refusing to sign a ticket for the red light he claimed I ran.

It took a few seconds for my heart to jump-start itself.

"Holy cow, Jim. You scared the living daylights out of me."

"What're you doing, Dainty?"

"Doing?"

"Right. What're you doing?" He opened his arms up to our surroundings.

"Well . . . I . . . thought I'd take Gran's car to the car wash." I couldn't help stammering. The orange glow cast by the sodium vapor street lamp turned his blonde hair the color of a ripe apricot, and darkened his cornflower blue eyes. It was like staring at one quarter of a Warhol painting—like the four-section canvas he painted of Marilyn Monroe, only it was Bruckman as an orange Adonis—and once again, he took my breath away.

He gave a slow headshake. "You always go through the car wash with the windows down?"

"Window. Just. One. Window." I held up a finger.

"Are you stalking me?"

My answer came in the form of a vehement headshake.

"You have a beef with the Baby Jesus? Or maybe room service at the inn wasn't up to your caliber?"

I wondered if pulling a hit-and-run on the Baby Jesus would cause the trap door to Hell to spring open. But then I decided I was already there since Bruckman would probably arrest me for criminal mischief, or reckless driving—or both. The arrest, alone, would get me kicked out of The Rubanbleu, which would be the social death knell for me—and let's face it—these days, membership in The Rubanbleu is all I have. Of course, me being broke, there'd also be the pesky problem of not being able to post my own bail.

"So how'd you find me?"

"If you're going to hide in a car wash, you probably ought to take your foot off the brake."

My whole body wilted. I admit it; I'm just not that smart. Or devious.

I said, "Tonight, I experienced the most horrible Thanksgiving, ever." The quiver that started in my chin made its way down my body. Next thing I knew, I'd become a blubbery, shivering, crying sensation. "I came to see you but you weren't home. And then I wondered if you were with . . . *her.*" I delivered my confession through shoulder-wracked sobs.

"Dainty, Dainty, Dainty." The slow headshake continued.

"Do you . . ." Again. Had to know. ". . . love her?"

"No." His whole body seemed to sigh. "What am I going to do with you?"

"Are you going to arrest me?"

"Arrest you?" He glanced up at the sky, as if the decision could be found in the stars. "No. But I *am* taking you into custody."

Then the unexpected happened. Bruckman pulled me close and wrapped me in his embrace. Just as quickly, he shoved me away, as if I'd become part of his new catch-and-release program, and said three powerful words that I never expected to hear . . .

"Damn, you stink." His face hardened into a ghastly contortion. "You reek like fertilizer."

To make matters worse, the inside of Gran's car smelled like urine. While fleeing Bruckman with the back window down, I felt what I thought was rain coming past the glass. Turned out to be urine mist from the cattle trailer in the next lane. Not to mention the feral cat that unwittingly became part of my animal relocation program.

I sniffed my hands, my clothes, my armpits. The odor of ammonia blistered my eyes. "I can't go home like this. Gran will kill me."

Bruckman eyed me with cold scrutiny. Against his better judgment, I'm sure, he made me an offer. "Come on back to the house. I'll vacuum the water out of Mrs. Prescott's car with my shop-vac, while you throw your clothes in the washing machine and take a shower. Not sure I can get the smell out of the car, but I probably have something in the garage I can spray on it that'll mask the smell for a couple of days."

Wait . . . what? Me, at Bruckman's house, naked in the shower? I entertained all sorts of ways to parlay what now seemed like a stroke of genius on my part into a romantic evening that would get us back together. Then my cell phone chimed to let me know about the text message that had just come in. Thinking it was Teensy again, writing more smut to Dr. Wright, I almost didn't check.

Thirty minutes ago, I didn't think things could get any worse for me. In fact, despite my part in what could be categorized as a "criminal episode," they'd actually gotten better. Then I looked at the text message and the whole shebang tanked.

It read: "I think we need to discuss this."

It seems, in my psychotic haste to declare my love for

Bruckman, I inadvertently sent the text message to my boss by mistake. According to the rest of the message, I'm to be in his office at five o'clock in the morning. Since it's almost two o'clock, that only leaves three hours to clean up, tidy the car, get home to change clothes, and head off to WBFD-TV. I might as well look super-gorgeous if I'm going to be fired.

CHAPTER NINE

After showering at Bruckman's and laundering my clothes—he didn't lay a hand on me, sadly, and largely ignored me while tending to Gran's car—I returned to Gran's house fit to be tied. I heard chattering coming from Teensy's room and realized she was still awake.

"Teensy Prescott," I yelled up to the second floor, "you come down here this second. I want to talk to you." She needed a Caterpillar and a dragline to clean up her room, which she'd filled with colorful bags from Dallas's most upscale shops, and I wasn't going to compete with a gift for a place to sit.

"Come on up." She said this in a chipper lilt, which infuriated me all the more.

"Not without a global navigation system."

"You make it sound like there's kudzu twining through the furniture." She appeared, half-naked, at the top of the banister overlooking the rotunda. When I eyed her up on the immodesty issue, she pulled a role reversal, snapping at me like she was the grown-up, and I was the big baby. "What? Amanda and I were trying on clothes."

Amanda squealed, "Master has provided Dobby with clothes. Dobby is free."

I glanced past Teensy's shoulder, at Amanda and the guilty expression riding on her chisel-featured, milk-chocolate-colored pygmy face. I decided not to reveal Amanda's big secret, a shocker I learned quite by accident down in beautiful Meh-hee-co when we shared a room at Hotel Malamuerte.

"I just came from the TV station."

"So?"

"Is there anything you'd like to tell me?"

Her eyes made a furtive dart up to the ceiling, down to the floor, across the landing, and back down to me. "No."

"I talked to Chopper Deke. You'd better tell me he was pulling my leg."

"About what?"

"How long were you hanging out at the station?"

She did a one-shoulder shrug. "A week maybe. Long enough to finish your project."

Realization fully dawned. Dread filled my body. "This job you mentioned earlier," I said in a half-crazed voice, "where is it?"

"Oh . . . that." Her big blue doe eyes narrowed into slits. "What difference does it make?"

I bristled. "You'd better tell me right this second before I come up there and bitch-slap you so many times you'll look like you have a bad case of rosacea."

"Ha. You, and what army?"

I gauged how fast she could make it to her room if I took the stairs in twos, and decided she had ample time to slam the door in my face and lock it. When she gave me an uninvitingly blank look, my voice crescendoed to a piping shrill. "How could you?"

She looked at me, peeved. Then her peevishness turned haughty. "I'm sure I don't know what you mean."

But I suspected she knew exactly what I meant.

"I did a good deed by finishing your project so your boss wouldn't be left in a lurch." She flip-flopped her hand through the air as if this were insignificant in the grand scheme of things. "You should feel honored that he thought enough of you to let me complete it."

"Honored? *Honored?*" The pressure in my head built like a tire inflated with too many PSIs.

"Yes. You should thank me instead of twisting off. As in, 'Thank you, Teensy. Thank you for thinking of me.' "

"Thank you? I should *thank you*?" I sounded like the skip in one of our mother's scratchy old vinyl record albums.

"Well, Dainty, once again, we didn't know whether you'd return from Mexico, or not. Same reason Daddy sold your car."

She made it all sound perfectly reasonable the way she stood at the railing, calm as a Hindu cow, while I—normally the picture of poise and serenity—frothed at the mouth.

"Come on up if you compose yourself and want to talk. We need to discuss Gran. She's gone off the deep end." She turned her back on me and headed for her room.

I took the stairs in twos. Without so much as a backward glance, she picked up her pace. By the time I reached the top of the landing, I glimpsed the back of her leg disappearing through the door. Then the lock snicked shut and I was treated to a close-up view of the smooth satin paint job on a solid core door.

"Open up." No need to explain who said that.

"Not until you're over being mad."

Which would be . . . never. We exchanged insults through the door.

"Traitor." Me.

"Ungrateful." Teensy.

"You're such a cow."

"I'm not the cow. You're the cow."

"You're the cow," I insisted.

"You're both cows." Amanda. Insufficiently muffled, I might add.

I had to convince Teensy to let me inside, and she wasn't going to do that if she thought I'd resort to violence. Which is simply un-Rubanbleu, and something I'd never do. Unless she had it coming, which she did, and unless I thought the ladies of The Rubanbleu would never find out, which I didn't think they would.

"I intend to get to the bottom of this. And I have to catch some sleep. The TV station's having an open house in a few hours, and I have to be there to help set things up."

Teensy's muffled voice came from the other side of the door. "Oh—didn't I tell you?"

"Tell me what?"

"We have to hang around tomorrow for Child Protective Services. They're coming by at ten."

This made no sense. "You mean Adult Protective Services," I corrected her, "not Child Protective Services."

The lock clicked, and the door cracked open a sliver. In that little sliver of space, I saw Teensy's left eyeball and part of a nude breast. "I'm letting you in. But only as long as you behave."

"Fine." Which meant not so fine. The door swung open. She stood, half-naked, in sheer bikinis. I figured Amanda must be having the time of her life getting a peep show from my sister, but at this point, I hardly cared. "Why's APS coming to the house?"

"Not APS. I told you it's CPS."

"Why? There aren't any kids who live here. Why would Child Protective Services want to talk to Gran—unless—" hand to mouth, I gasped "—did Gran witness someone abusing their children?" She stared at me, blank-faced. "Oh, no." I drew back a little. "Did you abuse somebody's children?"

"I didn't tell you?" Her brow furrowed. She touched a finger to her lip. "That's funny, I thought I did."

"Spill it."

I waited to hear my sister spin a tale about how she'd lost someone's kid on one of her babysitting expeditions, and instead got to listen to something much worse. Apparently, while Amanda and I were boarding a plane to the Metroplex, Teensy was developing into a reluctant witness for the State of Texas. According to her, Gran had just stepped out of the shower, and was in a great debate with herself agonizing over what to wear to her weekly bridge game at the country club, when the doorbell rang. It seems Teensy accidentally forgot to close the driveway gate when she drove in, which allowed a wolf pack of elementary school kids selling candy for their school to stray onto the property.

Buck naked, Gran grabbed the closest thing to a cover-up—a green flannel one-piece garment that looked more like a bed roll that Teensy bought her for Christmas five years ago that she never wore. That would be because Teensy, the consummate impulse buyer, didn't possess my fashion taste as a teenager, and hadn't put any thought or imagination into Gran's gift until she saw it advertised on late night TV.

According to Teensy, Gran hurried to the door while my sister ate cold cereal in the breakfast room. She went on to say that, while Gran isn't prone to buying anything sold door-to-door, she'd apparently made an exception because she recognized one of the neighbor kids as Old Man Spencer's grandkid. Without thinking, she turned around to grab her purse, exposing her naked backside to a bunch of children.

"And now CPS is dropping by to investigate."

Amanda hooted.

"Well, you'll have to handle it yourself. I have an appointment for laser hair removal, and then I have to be at the TV station."

Amanda hooted again, and then made "pew pew" noises and pretended to shoot my underarms.

I gave our houseguest a pointed look. "Do you mind?"

Later, in the privacy of my own bedroom, a thought made

me misty-eyed: Not only had Teensy horned in on my job, she'd stolen my friend. Well, not exactly my friend. I want to go on record that Amanda and I are not friends. Oh, sure, I'd come to appreciate her slightly more than when we first met. Okay, fine— I liked her a lot more than when we first met. But I chalked that up to what we'd gone through together—like men in the armed forces who came to rely on the man in the trench next to them during times of battle. Irrefutably, we'd formed such a bond. But Amanda didn't fit within in my social circle, and she'd never be Rubanbleu-approved.

And yet—okay, fine, I stand corrected—the undeniable reality was that Teensy stole my friend.

I decided to check out the back of my eyelids. There, I crawled into bed and pulled the covers over me without even shrugging out of my clothes.

My eyes burned. A tear leaked out.

Now it felt like Thanksgiving.

Chapter Ten

I arrived at WBFD-TV at five in the morning, anxious to clear up my wayward text message with Gordon before the morning drive-time show began. Apparently the dead rodent problem at the station had been taken care of. I assumed this was the case as I watched one of the feral kitties that lived along the tree line outside of the station projectile-vomit a soggy, death-scented wad of matted fur, along with tiny masticated organs, onto the pavement next to the space where I parked Gran's car.

In an effort to look more important than I am around here, I grabbed a handful of papers off Rochelle's desk and headed for my boss's office, only to be intercepted by one of the new interns, a coed from Southern Methodist University She handed off a note to me. It read, "If you can, please take a shower once in a while." The office I've been using is next to the break room where the dead rat smell's coming from. I crumpled it up and shoved it into my jacket pocket.

Gordon didn't holler at me to come in when I did a little knuckle-rap on his door, so I gently opened the handle and peeked inside. I found him seated behind the desk, with his chair swiveled away from me, ranting about his "useless employees." I slipped in and waited for him to put down the phone. Turns out he was talking to himself.

When he saw me, he swiveled around. "Top o' the morning, Prescott. We need to talk."

My mind cast back to the last time he said this—while I

stood drip-drying on old newspapers after the blood-thirsty dog he forgot to warn me about drove me into his swimming pool.

With a sweeping hand gesture, he directed me to the couch. "Sit."

"Mr. Pfeiffer—" I dropped onto the cowhide sofa like a warm bag of rocks.

"Gordon," he corrected me. Like we were friends. Which we were not.

"Gordon—I can explain—"

"I'm doing the talking. And you know why?" He didn't give me a chance to guess, just fixated on my blank stare, and continued. "Because I'm the boss."

My mouth formed words, but the pointed look he shot me from across the desk drove them back down my throat.

"I can see why you might have a crush on me—"

Oh, good Lord. He thinks I'm into him.

"—after all, I used to be a pretty good-looking man."

How long ago was that?

"And you've, no doubt, heard stories about my sexual prowess, back in the days when I used to go carousing with Chopper Deke—"

Heavy eye roll on my part.

"—but I'm middle-aged, now, and I can't even remember half of those moves—"

My eyelids fell to half-mast.

Please don't make me have to hear this.

"—except for that finger action—" He crooked his index finger a couple of times. "But half the time my arthritis keeps me from pulling it off."

Finger action?

I bit my lip to keep from barking out a laugh, but it only created a blood blister on the inside of my mouth. To squelch the hysterical cackle building up from my gut, I buried my face in my hands.

"Come on, Prescott, you know it's for the best," he said, in one of those *There, there . . . "Father Knows Best"* kind of voices.

My shoulders heaved with silent laughter.

"It's bad enough my soon-to-be ex-wife is young. I can't have people running around saying I robbed the cradle."

With my palms still shielding my eyes, I nodded.

"Aw, come on, Prescott, it'll be okay. You'll get over me. Try somebody closer to your own age. Don't give up."

I shook my head, prepared to add another name to the fast-growing list of people in my life who'd gone off the deep end.

"I mean . . . I know I'm a good catch."

I sneaked a peek when he said this, and caught him slicking back his receding gray-brown hair with the flat of his hand. Then he adjusted his wire-rims, seating them back into dented impressions in his flesh to keep the weight of the Coke-bottle lenses from pulling them down the bridge of his bulbous red nose.

Yeah. Right. Good catch. Got it.

Again, I head-bobbed into my hands.

"Stop crying, you hear? It's not the end of the world. Here. Take this."

By this time, tears of mirth poured from the corners of my eyes. I sneaked another peek. Gordon keeps a box of tissues at the ready for the talent he frequently screams at, or for when he fires them. Or for Misty Knight, our weather girl, because she's hormonal. And for the SMU interns Rochelle makes cry. He leaned across the desk and waved one in my direction like a surrender flag.

When I get flustered, my cheeks turn a pleasing shade of pink. When I'm embarrassed, they flush beet red. Fearing my emotions would betray me, I snatched the tissue from his grasp, and crushed it to my nose. From the hang-dog expression on his bulldog face, he clearly thought he'd broken my heart.

"Look, I feel bad about this, Prescott. Let me make it up to you. You want to do the news this morning?"

"What?" I gasped, but inside my head, my voice screamed, *"What?"* Nothing had prepared me for going on-air this morning. I blinked in incredulity. "Where's Aspen?"

"Wish I knew. Hasn't shown up, hasn't called in. I was about to see if your sister wanted—"

"I'll do it." No way was I going to let Teensy squeeze me out of the job that was rightfully mine. "I want to be your go-to girl. Not just today. I want to fill in whenever you need me."

"Fine. I'm counting on you, Prescott. Don't let me down. Getcha something pretty from wardrobe."

I almost cackled. The last time I pulled something from wardrobe, the only decent article of clothing turned out to be a pashmina, owned by the makeup girl, that I turned into a colorful, wraparound top. Secured by an extension cord plucked from a wall socket on my way into the studio. Women wanting to duplicate my original look actually called in to find out where they could buy my outfit. My sense of style, fashion, and resourcefulness certainly worked in my favor that day. Gordon's preoccupied with the on-air talent's appeal. He knows if people get bored with us they'll change channels. I rose, only to be waved back onto the cowhide sofa by my boss's meaty hand.

"One more thing."

I didn't like the warning in his tone.

He stretched against the seat back of his chair. Flexed his fingers. Hemmed and hawed a few seconds, and then came out with it.

"We get letters from viewers every day. People write in about all sorts of things: They don't like the anchors; they don't like the anchors' clothes; they want to know if the investigative reporter's eyes are bloodshot because he's tanked up. Conversely, they write in to inform us about things they like: They like that Aspen Wicklow cries when she tells them about some poor kid gunned down in a drive-by; they like her red hair and want to know if she colors it—she doesn't. They want to know if she's married . . . or how to meet her . . . or where to send flowers. We call those letters 'fan mail.' "

Fan mail.

My heart quickened. He wanted to tell me I had fan mail. I could hardly contain myself.

Fan mail!

Fan mail is what keeps a broadcast journalist employed. Well, that, and being pretty.

Gordon made serious eye contact with me. Intense, direct, laser-beam eye contact. "All mail goes through me before it's distributed. I decide what the talent should know about."

Chills crawled across my skin. My mind conjured up self-serving scenarios. Did another station from a major market see me do the news? Did one of the affiliates want to hire me away? Was Gordon feeling threatened that he might lose me to a bigger market? My heart raced with possibilities. Maybe that was just what I needed to get over Bruckman. My mind spun with opportunities: I could move to New York and live in a Manhattan high rise with the ton of money I'd be paid. I could buy a new wardrobe. Catch Broadway shows. People who recognized me on the street would snap my picture. Those who hadn't caught my show would take my picture anyway, due to the commotion whipping up around me.

I'd need a bodyguard. He'd be gorgeous, of course—like Bruckman—only he'd be smarter than Bruckman because he'd never issue me an ultimatum like Bruckman did when he blew me off for going back into Mexico. And one day, when I was powerful, he'd escort me down the red carpet, to the premier of

The Dainty Prescott Story, in my thirty-five-pound, bugle bead designer gown. Whereupon Bruckman would call my name from his place behind the roped-off area, and I'd recognize his voice. And the rest of the Dainty Prescott story would play out like this:

"I made a huge mistake letting you go. Please take me back."

That'd be Bruckman's opening line.

Then, I'd shield my eyes from the camera flashes exploding all around me, and narrow my eyes to feign confusion, like: *Who is this? Do I know him?* Because I wouldn't want Bruckman to get the big head and think I'd been pining away for him all those years. And finally I'd launch into fake surprise at seeing him after so many years.

"Well, I do declare. If it isn't—" And here's where I'd pretend to forget his name. But only for a second *"—Jim. Jim Bruckman."*

And then he'd drop to his knee and pull out a diamond ring the size of a headlight on Gran's Cadillac, and—

I hauled up short. Gordon had been talking. He'd said something while I was daydreaming, and now he expected me to answer him.

"I'm sorry, what?"

"I read everything. Understand?"

Of course I understood. He was about to tell me something wonderful and I'd missed it. Something that would turn Teensy's treacherous act of stealing my job into an unintended favor. I wanted to yell, "Spill it, already," but I kept my composure and let this moment unfold—like an Oscar nominee for best supporting actress, waiting, with dignity and grace, for her name to be announced. *Moi.* Dainty Prescott. Anchor extraordinaire.

"The good stuff, I distribute."

I caught myself nodding. "Get to the point," I wanted to say, "and let's hear the good stuff."

"The bad stuff, I withhold. It's rare that I mention bad stuff to the talent because . . . well, you know, I don't want negative critique to affect future performance."

Bad stuff? Negative critique? I began to come down from my selfish high. The intensity of my boss's stare was starting to creep me out.

"I say 'rarely,' " he went on, "because there are times when telling the person who's the subject of these poison pen letters seems the prudent thing to do." He paused. "You follow me?"

I didn't have a clue where this was headed. I'd only done the news broadcast a couple of times; first, as an unpaid intern, when I had to do the news on the spur of the moment as part of my Radio-Television-Film grade at TCU; and again, while sitting in for Aspen Wicklow when she went to her interview at CNN.

And now.

Gordon abruptly ended the conversation. We exchanged awkward looks. Then he opened his right-hand drawer. Everyone at the station knew Gordon kept booze in his desk. For a fleeting moment, I thought he was going to toast me with liquor for being so popular with the viewers. Instead, his meaty hand came out with a fistful of letters, rubber-banded, to keep them together. As he thrust them across his blotter, I distinctly heard a high-pitched noise come from deep within the building. It sounded like a scream.

My head snapped back.

Gordon inclined his head toward the door for a few seconds but returned his attention to me, as if this happened all the time and he found it more annoying than problematic. "The only reason I'm telling you now is because this has escalated into a safety issue."

Safety issue?

Turning my attention to the letters, I stared, slack-jawed. My mind reversed to an email message I ran across on my personal computer when I got home from Mexico the first time. It popped up in my email after WBFD ran all that footage on me about rescuing my ungrateful sister—the kind of message that announces someone wants to meet you—like those posted by dating sites. Only I'd never subscribed to a dating site. That's simply not the way debutantes of The Rubanbleu meet eligible, wealthy men. When I opened up the link with the sender's picture, I jumped back. It was like opening one of those serene email attachments where you're going along enjoying the video, all hunched in concentration, studying the photos of the world's most beautiful sights, when—no joke—a scary face pops up and screams at you. I deleted it.

I took the stack of mail from my boss, and re-opened the first envelope, pulled out the letter, and did a quick eye scan.

Just as I'd imagined.

My face cracked into a smile. Gordon had been messing with me.

This letter had nothing but praise for *moi*, Dainty Prescott. The viewer liked me and considered me to be an asset to WBFD. He didn't watch our station, and only saw me doing the news while channel surfing. But he said he'd be glad to tune in if I had more air time. It was signed "Best of luck in the future, Tim."

My cell phone *pinged*, notifying me that a text message had come in. I ignored it.

"This is good." I rattled the paper at my boss.

"Keep reading," Gordon said, flat-voiced.

The next note had been written on *Hello, Kitty* stationery by a girl wanting to know where I'd purchased my gorgeous red dress. She meant the pashmina I'd converted into an impromptu top about three seconds before I went on-air. She signed it, "Marie," and penned a little heart over the "i" in lieu of a dot.

"Also, good," I announced knowingly. If this kept up, Gordon would have to return me to the paid externship he'd created specifically for me. My boss sat as inert as a gas.

I opened the third letter in the stack—*whaddaya know?*—another communication from Tim saying he'd tuned in to watch me, only to see Steve Lennox broadcasting, instead. He asked for my work schedule so he could be sure and catch me on TV.

I glanced up at Gordon. I'm pretty sure he hadn't blinked since he'd passed my fan mail across the blotter. I opened the next one in the pile. Tim again, short and to the point. It read: "Did you fall off the planet?" He'd drawn a happy face beside his name. I checked the postmark. The letter came in while I was down in Mexico looking for my treacherous sister.

The next missive from Tim took a downward turn. "You can run, but you can't hide." He'd penned a frowny face after his name. I looked at Gordon looking right back at me. When I hesitated, he said, "Keep reading."

I probably held two weeks' worth of correspondence in my hand; each letter got progressively worse than the one before it. Halfway through the pile, I stopped. Gordon still sat across from me, silent and unmoving, studying my reactions with the intensity of a forensic scientist as I pored through my mail.

The intercom buzzed. While he reached over and depressed the button with one of his sausage fingers, I seized the opportunity to check my incoming text message.

It was another romantic text from Teensy, meant, once again, for Dr. Wright, and once again filled with misspellings and clichés that made her appear to be a world-class twit for writing and sending it to the wrong damned person for a second time. This "sexting" habit of Teensy's was getting pretty disgusting. I deleted it.

"Whatever it is can wait," Gordon barked into the telephone speaker.

"Gordon, I think you need to come out here." Rochelle's voice came across the speakerphone, all calm and efficient.

"Just handle it—whatever it is. And don't bother us again, y' hear?"

"But, Gordon, you have to—"

His face turned fire-engine red. "I don't have to do a *cotton-pickin'* thing."

"Gordon, listen to me—"

"Not. One. Cotton. Pickin'. Thing. Understand?"

"Don't say I didn't warn you," she said, with an inflection of sinister undertones.

He severed their connection and cut his eyes back to me.

Midway into the next letter, I glanced up from the page. "Am I supposed to answer these?"

"Yeah, Prescott. We need to keep our viewers happy."

His answer was so full of bluster I couldn't tell if he was serious. "What am I supposed to say?"

His gaze broke from mine; his attention flitted up to the ceiling before resettling on me. "Well, let's see," he deadpanned, "here's an idea—start with: *'Dear Valued Viewer: We appreciate your comments and have passed on your request to our Snowball Department in Hell. Sincerely, Us.'* "

Okay, messing with me seemed to be par for the course. This was the first reaction I'd gotten out of Gordon about the mail.

"Of course you don't answer them," he growled, "keep reading."

At least we were on the same page. Literally.

When I reached the next-to-the-last letter, I shuddered. The abominations Tim wanted to perpetrate on me were not only graphic, but sadistic. My stomach roiled.

Teary-eyed, I looked up without finishing. "I think I'm going to be sick."

Gordon grabbed the nearest trash can, and practically flung

it at me. I shoved my face into it and whiffed whiskey fumes from an open bottle. I backed my nose out past the outer rim, but hovered my face in the general direction, and willed myself to calm down. In moments, the nausea passed. I positioned the trash can on the floor in front of me, within easy reach.

"You okay, Prescott?" After I gave a queasy head bob, he said, "Would it have been better not to know?"

I shook my head. "No need to be ostrich-headed."

"That's a good girl. Oh, one more thing." Gordon's expression suggested this *thing* wouldn't be a *good thing*. I arched an eyebrow. "This came for you yesterday." He reached into the same drawer and pulled out a shoebox, along with brown-paper-sack wrapping that bore no return address.

"Did you look inside?" I asked, already easing away, with my back forcing a deeper impression into the cowhide sofa. "Is there something dead in there? Because if there is, I don't need to see it."

"You need to see this."

I sucked it up and lifted the lid. The box was filled with dolls' heads—just the heads—dismembered from the little limbs and torsos. I shuddered. "So this is like *build-a-bear*, only without the bear?"

"That's what I love about you, Prescott. Wait—did I say *love*? I meant that figuratively. Not literally. I meant *like*. Not *love*. That's why you're here—to clear up that whole love-smitten teenager issue you've got going on with me."

"I'm twenty-three."

"To be clear, I don't love you and I never will."

"I get that." Said nastily. "It won't be a problem." But what I really wanted to say was that the receipt of this box made me scared to walk to my car without an escort.

A commotion ensued just outside Gordon's office. Beyond

the door, I heard Rochelle's strident voice call out, "He isn't in."

"As I was saying," Gordon went on, "that's what I *like* about you. You get bad news and you deal with it. Not like these other mamby-pamby, titty-babies that work here. Which is why I feel bad about giving your sister your job."

"Wait—*what?* You already gave Teensy my paid externship?"

"Yeah. But nobody expected you to come back. We all pretty much figured you'd get yourself killed down there, you being a debutante and all." He must've noticed my gaping jaw because he went on the defensive. "What was I supposed to do, hold the job open for seven years until you were declared legally dead?"

Hello—still alive. Sitting right here.

My voice shrilled. "But you created that job for me."

"Ironic, isn't it? Come to think about it, you're not really qualified for it."

Not qualified for it?

"You took the qualifications directly from my application. I stood right here and watched you write it. You asked if I had any skills the SMU interns didn't have, and I said, 'Yeah, I made the Dean's List one semester; and I made everything in wardrobe look better than it did on anybody else.' "

"Yeah. Tough break, Prescott."

My head spun with ideas, none of them good. So—just to recap—my boss called me in and sat me down on his cowhide sofa in order to tell me I didn't meet the qualifications of the paid externship position that he created specifically for me? Oh, yeah, and as a bonus, he passed out hate mail. Right. *Way to be appreciated.*

Energy depleted, I wilted. "What am I supposed to do, now?"

It was hard to concentrate on my own problems with Rochelle escalating the drama beyond Gordon's door.

She hollered, "You can't go in there," and we were treated to sounds of a scuffle.

The pressure inside my skull had developed into a pounding headache.

Gordon pulled his wallet out of his back pocket, parted the flap, and pulled out two one-hundred-dollar bills. "Don't worry, I'll think of something. Take this."

A female silhouette, plastered against Gordon's glass door, jarred us.

Gordon said, "What the hell?"

"I don't want your money," I said, with a modicum of drama. I needed to steer my boss back onto the subject of *moi*, Dainty Prescott. Future anchor. "I need a job."

The door to Gordon's office opened and a big bruiser wearing a navy blue blazer sauntered in fisting what looked like a legal document. I barely took note of the shadowy figure who trailed him in and blocked the door, but I recognized the point man as one of the detectives who worked with Bruckman. He'd given me a piece of lifesaving advice at our first meeting when I rode in with Bruckman under the FWPD's police buddy plan. I'm not talking about the *Don't fall for Bruckman* part, but, rather, the other advice: *Never let yourself be tied up. Fight for your life right there.*

"Fort Worth Police," the detective announced with authority, without giving me a second glance. For all he cared, I could've been part of the décor. "Gordon Pfeiffer?"

Then, I noticed the guy behind the lead detective. Piercing, cornflower blue eyes took my breath away. Spectacular eyes narrowed into the squint of an assassin.

Bruckman.

I sucked air.

"I'm Pfeiffer," my boss said. "Who the hell are you? And what makes you think you can just auger in here without a damned appointment?"

"Search warrant." The detective slapped the paper into Gordon's hand. Stunned, I watched as Gordon's eyes drifted over the page.

"For what?" Gordon said, all blustery and beet-faced. "I demand to know what this is all about. Is this about that *Asleep at the Wheel* piece we did last month? Because if it is, you'll be hearing from my legal department."

"We have reason to believe you murdered your wife."

CHAPTER ELEVEN

Instead of putting his hands behind his back, Gordon tossed me his wallet.

"Take the money out," he barked, "I'm hiring you. Do the news and then call my attorney. Not the station's attorney—not my divorce attorney—my personal attorney." The detectives were walking him out as he told me this. My balding, portly boss raised his voice as they exited through the station's main entrance. "Start unraveling this bullshit. And get rid of that jewelry." His voice trailed as the door closed him off from view.

I stood slack-jawed.

When finally I slunk out of Gordon's office, I became aware of the rumbling din filling the rotunda. The front lobby had started to fill with dignitaries and luminaries who'd received invitations to our open house. It also bloated up with the unwashed public. Still reeling, I watched Rochelle and the new male intern from SMU backing people away from Gordon's office, and herding them upstairs to Production. With about a half hour to primp, get into the studio, and onto the set, I headed to my little office by the break room, pulling off my pearl earrings one by one, and loosening the catch on my eighteen-carat gold bracelet.

When I rounded the corner, I hauled up short at the sight of yellow, Day-Glo crime scene tape. Fort Worth police had cordoned off the break room. The horrible smell from the night before had been made worse by opening the closet door, which explained the massive line to the bathrooms, like in Soviet Russia. No wonder the SMU interns thought I needed to bathe. Someone—probably one of the paramedics standing around like a clove on a ham—had thrown a Mylar blanket over something, or someone, on the closet floor. Clear, brownish liquid had oozed out past the door.

And, trembling in the corner, with a tall uniformed police officer towering over her, was Kim Lee, the station's Korean clean-up lady. "I no clean. No damned way."

While my mind tried to process this scene, I felt Chopper Deke's breath on my neck.

"What died? Or maybe I should say, *Who died?* Took an antihistamine this morning; cleared up my sinuses just fine— maybe a little too fine."

Uniformed officers moved us along.

"Holy cow," I said in a breathy voice, "I think I'm going to be sick."

"Suck it up, blondie." Deke grabbed me by the back of my neck and steered me into my office.

I was treated to a view of Teensy sitting at my desk, yukking it up with Stinger Baldwin.

Hand on hip, I sashayed up to the desk and parked myself in front of her. "What're you doing?" It was a stupid question since we both knew the answer. She'd horned in on my job.

"I'm talking to Stinger."

I looked at Stinger, WBFD's investigative reporter. "Would you excuse us for a moment?" I said with fake sweetness. Then I turned to Deke. "Same for you."

I unlatched my bracelet. Along with the earrings, I tucked it into my bag.

Teensy, looking perky and purple in her cashmere sweater and suede skirt, grabbed Stinger's wrist and clamped down hard. "You don't have to go." For me, she laid down the gauntlet with equally put-on sweetness, "He's staying."

Deke said, "If he gets to stay, I get to stay."

Public displays of emotion are very un-Rubanbleu, and simply not done. I decided to break with tradition.

I narrowed my eyes. "You're not getting my job, Teensy."

"Already did."

"We'll see about that." I stormed off with purpose in my step. While strutting past the break room, I took in a deep breath and held it as long as I could until I reached wardrobe.

I poked my head inside, but didn't see anyone around. Which meant I could pick out my own clothing, but it also meant I'd have to do my own hair. Since the Texas humidity had wilted my hair during my short walk from the parking lot into the building, I needed someone to fluff up my thin, fine hair and spray it until it could withstand a category four hurricane on the Saffir-Simpson scale. Teensy could help, but I'd rather eat glass than ask for her assistance. I took a comb, ratted the fire out of it, smoothed it down, and lacquered my big Texas hair to a fare-thee-well.

Gordon insists that the female anchors wear bright colors in gem tones. According to him, they photograph better. So I culled through the blazers, blouses, and salesman samples and found a fuchsia shirt that looked small enough to fit me. Since I would only be seen from the waist up, I paired it with a small rosette that I found in the hair-clip drawer. This, I secured at my collar. Just call me Dainty Prescott—trendsetter.

I repaired my lip gloss and headed for the studio, excited to be delivering the news.

The open-house invitees were being ushered into different rooms, upstairs and down, where they could watch the broadcast on monitors. While Misty Knight, WBFD-TV's meteorologist, did the weather forecast, a couple of the SMU interns explained to the guests how the chroma key wall worked.

Here at the studio, we call it the "green screen." It's a blank screen that video can be shown on, and gets its name "green" because it appears chartreuse when there's no film footage being played on it. When Misty stands in front of it doing the weather report, meteorological images of air currents, precipitation, cloud cover, temperature, or Doppler radar pop up on the green screen.

Before the stations in this market switched from video to HD, or high definition, the photographers used to torment Misty by putting up the wrong video; while Misty—who, by the way, is a degreed meteorologist—gave the weather update, it wasn't unusual to witness a car chase going on the green screen behind her. Or cheetahs chasing a gazelle across the Serengeti. You'll never convince me this happened by accident.

Inside the studio, I scanned my copy of the news for any names that I might have difficulty pronouncing—like the time I delivered the broadcast about the Thai dignitary with a foot-long surname who came to Fort Worth to be honored at a banquet for making a huge donation for the building of a new, all-purpose psychiatric facility. Hey, I did the best I could. It didn't help that the photographers showed film footage of swine, memorializing a local farmer's attempt to get his albino pig into the *Guinness Book of World Records*. I can't help it if the lady thought they were making fun of her weight.

Speaking of ham, I'm a bit of a showboat when it comes to being on TV. I photograph well, and I really want my own talk show someday. But I admit it—with a dead body down the hall and a handful of local luminaries watching me on monitors in different parts of the building, the butterflies in my stomach were making me nauseous. I felt even more nervous than the time I did the *Live at Five* broadcast and my clothes came unraveled on the set.

I fidgeted in my chair as a member of the crew clipped a

mike to my blouse and fed the excess wire beneath my collar. Normally, the floor crew makes sure all the lights are working; the audio department makes sure the mikes are working. If an anchor has a smudge or sweat, a floor director will point that out, but we're all grown-ups and take care of our own personal needs—like makeup and hair, and putting on our own mikes. But this morning, they decided to help me because I'm new at this, and green as a gourd. And because we have so many visitors.

I glanced down at my hands and realized how badly I needed a manicure. I could also use a pedicure. The problem with choosing between the two is like playing dodge ball with a mortal enemy: it's hard to choose between targeting the feet or the face.

The heat from the overhead can-lights was already starting to affect me; the crew girl patted a dry cloth to my forehead before dusting on some last-minute powder above my brows and onto my nose and chin. Still, I'd never felt such exhilaration as when I faced the camera. Well, that's not entirely true. Jim Bruckman could make me feel this way—call it a gift.

The music lead-in crescendoed. My pulse quickened. The producer gave me a finger countdown, *Three-two-one.*

And, I'm on the air.

"Good morning, I'm Dainty Prescott, filling in for Aspen Wicklow. In today's news the 'Cat Burglar of Monticello' struck again last night in the wealthy Fort Worth neighborhood, making off with over a hundred thousand dollars in jewels . . ."

I didn't look at my copy, not once. It's important for ladies of The Rubanbleu to be immaculately groomed, and my hands simply weren't. Instead, I read off the teleprompter while delivering a polished report.

"And, that's the morning news. I'm Dainty Prescott. We hope you'll join us for the remainder of our program, and again for the noon update." For no good reason, I added, "Top o' the mornin' to ya," as if I'd turned into a leprechaun and popped in from Ireland.

I admit it. I'm a bit of a ham.

The drive-time show's closing music grew louder; I sat perfectly still, with a frozen smile beaming across my face, until the producer gave the *That's a wrap* motion—a twirling finger gesture—and the broadcast cut away to a commercial.

I ripped off my mike and rocketed from my seat. I needed to do whatever I had to do to figure out why my boss was in such a jam, and yet my grandmother, the blue-hair, had created her own jam. As much as I felt the sucking sound of familial obligation, my grandmother wasn't bankrolling me. It seemed more prudent, at the moment, to follow the money.

On my way to find Teensy, as I plotted out the day in my head, guests at the open house complimented me on what a great job I did on-air. The stack of hate mail had almost faded into a distant memory until a man stepped into my path and scared the living daylights out of me. I recognized him immediately as a resident of one of the neighboring houses beyond the wall behind the studio. It was the crazy guy who yells stuff at *unseen others,* and by that, I mean people nobody else can see. He's also the same psycho who talks smack to people in the neighborhood who the rest of us can actually see. We met for the first time when he chased me through the parking lot with a stapler nipping at my derrière.

In a flat, fathomless voice, he said, "I know you."

Reflexively, I covered my face with my hands and let out an unearthly scream of the damned that shut down the rumbling din of guests. When the blow I'd expected to feel didn't come, I peered out from between my fingers. He'd merely raised his meaty hand to give me a fist bump.

How was I supposed to know he wasn't trying to kill me?

Horrified, I stammered, "Have a nice day," and ran for my office.

A couple of representatives from the Medical Examiner's office had arrived, and the cops turned the break room over to them. I glimpsed a body bag being hoisted onto the gurney, and overheard another verbal exchange from the Korean clean-up lady, over the clacking wheels.

"I no clean. No damned way."

I had no idea who she was talking to until I heard Rochelle chime, "Damned right you'll clean that up. That's what you're paid to do."

I skirted the cordoned off area and hurried to my office. Like Elvis, Stinger Baldwin had left the building, but Chopper Deke was flopped in a chair, entertaining Teensy while she performed a hostile takeover of my office. She lowered the newspaper she'd been reading and peered over the top enough to see me from her place behind my desk.

"Find anything interesting in the paper?" I sliced my sister an eyebrow-encrypted message. Because of the timing, it had been too late for any eleventh-hour carjackings or shootings to make the deadline for coverage in *The Dallas Morning News* on Thanksgiving Day. Still, I feared there might be an article or obituary in today's paper about the man Gran shot.

Teensy said, "Like what?"

Since my sister didn't pick up on my hint, I fed her a little more information. "Oh, say, like there might be any newspaper reports on knifings . . . beatings . . . *shootings*?"

She shrugged.

"Nothing along Harry Hines Boulevard?" I prompted.

Teensy experienced a light-bulb moment. "Oh. No. Nothing like that." She cast Chopper Deke a furtive glance to make sure he hadn't cracked our code. Then she refolded the newspaper. "Just so you know," she gamely informed me, "from here on out, Amanda will be sleeping in your room."

For a second, I worried Teensy'd discovered Amanda's big secret. But then I found out that sleep deprivation kept them from being big buddies. Apparently, Amanda's banishment to the attic came about because she had flashbacks about cartel violence from our Mexico trip, and lamped Teensy three times.

I tuned up in protest. "Your room has two beds."

"Not my problem. Get a rollaway out of the attic."

There's no rollaway. My room *is* the attic.

Great. I get a cot, and the opportunity to listen to Amanda snore like a wild boar.

Teensy flashed a smile more saccharin than sweet. "Ready to go take care of this mess with Gran?"

Still reeling from my sister's treachery, I couldn't deal with Gran today. Since Amanda and I arrived night before last, I realize that my grandmother has become so obsessive-compulsive—if not, out-and-out, *rat-in-a-drain-pipe* crazy—that the best way to piss her off and cause her to direct a hissy fit at me is to drape my overcoat over one of the hangers in the entryway closet.

I flattened my palms against the desktop, leaned into her face, and took a stand. "You're doing it. Not me. You. I have bigger problems to deal with today, and that doesn't include bailing your grandmother out of a jam. So . . . *ha*."

"She's your grandmother, too. So . . . *ha-ha*."

"I'm starting to wonder. I'm willing to be tested."

Teensy jutted her chin in defiance. "She was your grandmother first. So . . . *ha-ha-ha*."

My blood boiled. "I ought to slap you 'til your nose bleeds."

"Easy does it, bitches." Deke sat bolt-upright in the chair.

I whirled on him. "Don't call me a bitch. She's the bitch." By way of illustration, I pointed to my sister.

"I'm not the bitch. She's the bitch," Teensy mocked me.

"You're both bitches. Knock it off."

"She's wrong," I said.

"You're wrong." Teensy smirked.

"If you get into a catfight, I want to see torn clothes and lots of skin." Deke, again, apparently realizing that we made a scarier pair, together, than he did by himself.

"You're so bad." Teensy egged him on with a sly smile. "How'd you get so bad?"

"You're both bad," I snapped. I heard the muffled *ping* of my cell phone through my purse, notifying me of an incoming text. I willed it to be Bruckman. I needed to be with that man, and if I couldn't be with him, then I at least needed to put things right with him.

I dug for my phone. Once again, my bad luck held. Teensy sent me another romantic text that was meant for Dr. Wright. The fact that this kept happening made me want to slam her head against the floor.

I eyed her with contempt. "I'm leaving. And you'd better take care of this mess with Gran." Then I showed her a quick fist as I flounced toward the door.

My office phone bleated and Teensy snatched up the receiver.

"Teensy Prescott's office."

My jaw dropped. I saw red. "This is not your office. Give me that phone."

"Why yes," she purred into the mouthpiece, "she's right here. I'll get her for you . . . why no, thank *you.*"

She held out the receiver and I yanked it away. "Dainty Prescott," I announced, like the calm, capable newscaster I am. I backed my haunches into the edge of the desk and settled in for what I hoped was an important call.

The man on the other end of the line told me, blow by blow, what I'd been doing for the last half hour. As he recited my movements, my heart thudded like hoofs on a dirt racetrack.

Then he mentioned what I was doing every second I was on the phone with him. I immediately stopped fondling my hair, and did a quick lean-in to view the digital display screen on the base. I wanted his number, but the call had been placed from a non-published account, so it didn't appear on the digital readout. Now I was scared to leave.

"Tim?" I spat the name.

Dead silence.

"Is this Tim?" Nothing but raspy breaths came from the other end of the line. "Why are you doing this?"

At the exact same time this crippling fear kept me from leaving, I had one of those sickening, *The call is coming from inside the house,* moments. That realization heightened my anxiety, making me want to hightail it out of there. Chopper Deke, who'd been studying my face with cold scrutiny, must've thought I'd gotten bad news because he jumped out of the chair and guided me to sit in it.

"Don't call me again."

I let go of the receiver. It clattered to the desk about the same time Teensy's new boyfriend sauntered in through the doorway.

"Hey, princess," he said, as she rose from the chair behind my desk and ran to him. They engaged in a passionate, tonsil-extracting kiss before he turned his attention to me. "Hey, princess."

Sulky, pouty Teensy chucked his arm. "She's not the princess. I'm the princess."

"Of course you are." Dr. Wright introduced himself to Chopper Deke, who unexpectedly postured, and got all scary looking until the whites of his eyes ringed his pale blue irises like the planet Saturn. He clasped the doctor's outstretched palm, which nearly degenerated into an arm-wrestling match as Deke's handshake turned crippling. I'd seen something like this before out at our ranch, when two bulls locked horns while a pasture full of cows looked on.

I retrieved the dangling telephone receiver and dialed out. My recovering sorority sisters might be out-of-pocket, but there was still one person I could brag to about my success. The line purred at the other end; then Gran answered.

"I did the news this morning." I glanced over my shoulder to make sure Teensy got the message, but she and Dr. Wright were still making us sick with their neck nuzzling. "Did you watch me?"

"You did great—especially since the camera added twenty pounds to you."

While keeping a close eye on Teensy, I cupped my hand to the mouthpiece and whispered. "The expression is that the camera adds ten pounds, Gran, not twenty."

"Well then you probably ought to weigh yourself before going on-air next time because you look like you've been taking steroids."

"Gotta run." My rock-solid feelings of self-esteem for pulling off a particularly difficult newscast lasted all of one minute before my grandmother dashed them.

I gathered my composure and addressed Teensy's boyfriend. "Would you mind escorting me to my car?"

"I'll do it." Chopper Deke.

"I don't mind." Dr. Wright extricated himself from Teensy's grip and offered me his arm. My sister backed me off with a lethal glare.

"I'm good," I said, grabbing my purse and giving his crooked elbow a wide berth. "Let's just go."

CHAPTER TWELVE

I wasn't conscious of leaving the building, but when my face hit the crisp outside air, I realized the noise level had greatly diminished and the station lay behind me. As Dr. Wright escorted me through the parking lot, I noticed something on the hood of Gran's car at the same time I heard my name called out behind me.

When I turned to look, Rochelle had framed herself in the doorway. Gordon's assistant, looking beautiful in her red Escada suit, is exactly what I'd always imagined Snow White would look like when she turned fifty and went through menopause after a life of bitterness at the hands of the evil queen. Or maybe Rochelle was the Evil Queen. She motioned me back with a frantic hand wave, so I left Dr. Wright with a *Be right back,* and a *Please don't leave.*

When I reached the steps, Rochelle's nose inclined at a disdainful tilt. "You have to come back inside and apologize to that man you frightened."

"I—*what?*"

"You scared him. He only came here looking to meet celebrities—in your case, a celebutante. And now you have to apologize to him."

"Are you kidding? What about me?"

"I'll never understand your generation. It's always about you-you-you when it should be about me-me-me. Now get back in here and let's get this over with."

"I'm not apologizing. That man scared the wits out of me." I whipped around, and walked away.

"Gordon doesn't want the on-air talent making enemies."

Instead of retorting that Gordon wasn't in much of a position to do anything about it, I inwardly smiled. Uppity Rochelle actually regarded me as a member of the on-air talent.

She cupped her hands to her mouth and spoke magic words with the magnetic pull capable of yanking me back to the front portico—*I can help you get your job back* . . .

As I allowed myself to be drawn into her web, a looming presence appeared over her shoulder.

Rochelle must've sensed the immense form slipping up behind her because she grabbed him by the arm as soon as he came even with her. She pressed him through the doorway while making glowing introductions.

"Dainty, this is our neighbor, Mr. Bilburn." She made a sideways thumb gesture to indicate the man lived in the neighborhood on the other side of the privacy wall.

I'd already met a representative sample of those neighbors from afar, and didn't like to think about what could happen if we didn't have such a wall in place to separate us.

"He watches us all the time." When I corkscrewed an eyebrow, Rochelle clarified this. "On the news. Mr. Bilburn, this is Dainty Prescott. Dainty has something to tell you—" gray eyes that looked as cold and translucent as ice cubes locked on mine; Rochelle's voice went suddenly gelid *"—don't you, Dainty?"*

I knuckled under. Not because this Bilburn guy had the capacity to squash me like a bug, but because the Evil Queen possessed greater powers.

"I didn't mean to startle you back there," I said, turning my toe out, *à la seconde,* like I'd learned in ballet. This wasn't an attempt to show off my formal dance training, I just reflexively enhanced my chances of escape by positioning myself to bolt if he tried to grab me. "I thought I was about to get hit."

Off to one side, Rochelle mouthed without sound, "Say you're sorry."

I wasn't about to. "So . . . are we good?"

Mr. Bilburn had a large, chocolate pie face. And when his face split into a big grin, his dark almond-eyes nearly disappeared into the folds of skin plumping his cheeks.

"We good." He stuck out a catcher's mitt hand for a quick shake, and I realized it wouldn't take many foot pounds per square inch for him to dislocate my shoulder, if he'd had a mind to.

I rejoined Dr. Wright and we fell into step, angling across the parking lot toward Gran's bloated car.

"You don't look so hot," said Teensy's psychologist-slash-boyfriend.

"I just said 'See you later,' to a viewer who stared at my chest for the past two minutes. He said, 'You sure will,' and then winked at me. How do you think I should feel?"

Dr. Wright did a one-shoulder shrug. "I'd say you handled it pretty well."

I gave him a brusque headshake. "Sorry. It's nothing. I always get keyed up when I do the news."

"I thought you were pretty good."

"You saw it?" I slid him a sidelong glance.

Bright eyes turned sheepish. "Well, no. Not really. But I know you did a great job. Actually, while you were doing the drive-time show, I was battling traffic and trying not to become part of your story. I thought it'd be nice to pick up your sister and take her to breakfast. Next time, I'll forget about breakfast and head over for lunch."

"Lucky you," I said in a congratulatory tone I didn't feel. "So . . . how long have you been treating my sister?"

"I really can't discuss her therapy. Doctor-patient, and all that. But I can tell you we met about a month ago, not long after y'all returned from Mexico."

I didn't ask how they met; I didn't really care. I merely wondered how Teensy was paying for her therapy sessions now that Daddy had applied a financial tourniquet to what he'd starting referring to us as a couple of hemorrhaging spendthrifts. I fleetingly wondered if Gran might be bankrolling her. Neither of us had two nickels to rub together, so somebody else had to be footing the bill.

"Who pays you for her treatment?"

"Can't tell you that, either," he said with a smile. "But if you'd like to come in and see me some afternoon after regular business hours are over, I'd be happy to do a separate consultation with you—*gratis,* of course. It actually might help with her recovery."

"Yeah, sure," I replied absently. Now that we'd almost walked the entire distance, I could see what had been left on Gran's hood.

My breath caught in my throat. The item turned out to be a Barbie doll that had been broken into pieces. The hair had been cut and styled like mine; its head had been removed, and impaled on the tip of the windshield wiper. Hand to mouth, I sucked air.

"What's wrong, princess?" Dr. Wright hooked me around the shoulder in a one-armed, protective embrace.

I stood, speechless, as my fear of someone calling himself Tim reignited.

He gave me an avuncular squeeze. "What is it?"

"Nothing." I took a picture with my camera phone and then gathered up the dismembered Barbie parts and put them in Gran's car.

I wanted to talk to Bruckman.

I *needed* to talk to Bruckman.

Bruckman, in all his wisdom, could tell me how to handle this.

But I figured he'd be assisting with the interview of my boss, and let's face it—this was no interview—this seemed like more of an interrogation. Until I had Bruckman's full attention, I'd just have to manage on my own.

That's when I decided to stop at the spy store and pick up supplies. And, at the top of my mental list, I checked pepper spray.

I hadn't been on the Interstate more than a few minutes, when it dawned on me that driving Gran's bloated Cadillac for two days on three-fourths of a tank of fuel didn't mean the car was getting good mileage. It meant the gas gauge was broken.

I limped the car over to the shoulder and shut off the engine. Then I put on the emergency flashers and hoped they had a longer shelf life than the empty gas tank. As I rummaged through my purse for the cell phone, I debated whether to call roadside service for the fourth time in two months. The last time I called, the guy who showed up turned out to be the same guy who helped me the first two times. When he got out of the truck the third time, he snorted, and then doubled over, snuffling with laughter.

About the time I'd decided to forget roadside service and call my friend Salem's brother, my eyes flickered to the rearview mirror. A big, white pickup, with flashers engaged, pulled in behind me. For a second, I got all crazy thinking *This could be Tim,* and poised my thumb above the 9 button in case I had to dial 911 for help.

But when the driver's door on the truck opened into traffic, and the driver stepped out, I breathed a sigh of relief.

Dr. Wright. With perfect timing. No wonder my wretched sister nicknamed him Mr. Right.

I lowered my window halfway down and gave him a sheepish, "Hi."

"Car trouble?"

"I think it's out of gas."

He chuckled at my predicament, angling his body where he could keep an eye on the traffic while conversing with me.

"Damsel in distress," he said knowingly. "Lucky for you, I carry a spare gas can in the back of the truck. Why don't you hop in the pickup, and we'll drive across the highway and fill it up?"

As soon as he offered, I thought, *Would you mind doing it yourself, pretty please with sugar on it?*

But my real thoughts had less to do with indolence on my part, and more to do with caution, as in, *Hey, buddy, I don't know you.* About the time I was fixing to explain to Teensy's boyfriend that I'd become jaded and suspicious after surviving my first trip to Mexico, Dr. Wright gave a frantic arm-wave to oncoming traffic. I hunched involuntarily at the squeal of brakes. As he tried to become part of the Cadillac's door, tires screamed against the asphalt in rapid succession. I sealed my eyes tight, waiting for the impact, I felt the wind-rush from the speeding driver as he swerved away and blew on past us.

He said, "C'mon, princess. It's not safe out here. These people are crazy."

And just like that, I climbed into his truck. As soon as I buckled myself in, my mind had a flight of ideas—all of them bad. Like: Did he carry duct tape? Rope? Knives? Other weapons designed to kill or maim? But as soon as he pulled onto the highway, put his blinker on, and took the first off-ramp, I realized how crazy I'd started to act since I'd become aware of the hate mail from Tim.

I reviewed the threat letters in my head. Went over the things he said he wanted to do to me—nasty, filthy, vile, and degrading acts he wanted to perpetrate on me. Then I relived the moment I freaked out when poor Mr. Bilburn just wanted to shake my hand. And next, when the scary phone call came in, I began to wonder: *Is Tim someone on the other side of the world, or in the next cubicle?* By the time Teensy's boyfriend pulled into the gas station, and nosed his pickup in next to one of the fuel pumps, I realized just how paranoid I'd started to get.

While Dr. Wright pumped gas into the plastic can, I noticed the store logo of a chain of sweets boutiques Gran liked, and excused myself with a "Be right back."

The last time I drove past one of these shops, Gran chided me because I didn't stop and pick up a box of those Black Forest truffles that she likes. Cue screaming, where she called me "self-centered and unappreciative." This time, I wouldn't make the same mistake.

From my place at the cash register, I watched Dr. Wright tighten the lid on the gas can, and checked my wallet to see what size box I could afford. If I had to reimburse him for the gas, that would only leave me with five dollars of disposable income. After all, I still had to return to the filling station in order to fill Gran's guzzling behemoth with enough gasoline to get back home. Plus, I'd have to use the pumps at the self-serve island—an indignity I had to get used to, now that I'd recently become "Dainty Prescott, former heiress."

I selected the small box of Black Forest truffles, and returned to the truck as Teensy's boyfriend loaded the gas can into the pickup bed. We made small talk on the way back to Gran's car, with him saying things like, *Gee, your sister's really something;* and me agreeing with him even though I was actually thinking, *"Something" doesn't begin to cover it—she's a nut job;* and hearing him ask what might make a nice gift for their three-week anniversary, and me agreeing that, *Yes, dinner at an expensive Italian restaurant, along with a dozen blue roses*—blue is Teensy's signature color—*a box of double chocolate chip cookies, and a book of poetry he'd been working on since he met her that he'd had bound into a memory book with photographs of them, would make a nifty gift,* even though I was thinking, *Straitjacket—size small.*

"I wish I'd known your sister when she was little," he said, waxing nostalgic. "She's such a strong-willed young lady. And intrepid. Tell me something about her: like what her deepest fear is."

I snorted. This was the same girl who used to be afraid of monsters in her closet. Once, when we spent the summer out at our ranch, I tried to prove there weren't any monsters by sticking my hand under the hanging garments and waving it around near her shoes. A scorpion stung me with its barbed tail, and I shot out of the closet screaming bloody murder. Then I got a spanking for making Teensy's irrational fear worse, since she immediately regressed, and my mother had to dress her for the next six months because she refused to go anywhere near her closet.

"I can't think of a thing," I said.

"So what's your deepest, darkest fear?"

Until this morning, my biggest worry was ending up without a job, without any money, and finding out that Gran took a reverse mortgage out on her mansion. But with the onslaught of hate mail, my greatest fear was to end up like one of those dolls in the shoebox. Before I could answer, I realized Dr. Wright had missed the off-ramp for us to circle back to Gran's car. My heart quickened.

"So what is it? Your fear, I mean. What're you afraid of?"

My voice caught in my throat. "You missed the turn."

"So I did." While his eyes flickered to the rearview mirror, mine darted furtively around the interior of the truck, looking for things he could kill me with.

He moved into the middle lane and accelerated. My stomach roiled.

"What's your name?" I swear I saw shock register in his eyes. "I mean, I can't keep calling you Dr. Wright, right?" My heart pounded with the same cadence as the message swirling inside my brain: *Don't be Tim, don't be Tim, don't be Tim.*

He passed the official pace car and whipped into the slow lane. "Mitchell."

"What?" I had a white-knuckled grip on the door handle.

"My given name is Mitchell." He flipped on his blinker and the truck drifted into the upcoming turn lane. "Sorry about that. It's just that you're so easy to talk to, I wasn't paying attention to the exit."

"No problem." I let go of the door handle. Fingertip indentations, left in the padding from the ferocity of my grasp, disappeared, and I found myself wondering whether I should take him up on his offer for a free consultation. Maybe he'd give Gran and Daddy one, too. That way, if he was really thinking about keeping Teensy around for the long haul, he could figure out exactly what the family pathologies were, and save himself.

When the red light cycled to green, he made the final turn at the overpass. I spotted Gran's car a half mile up, gloating.

I said, "Chocolate allergies."

He took his eyes off the road long enough to slide me a sideways glance. "Beg your pardon?"

"You asked me what my deepest, darkest fear is. I just told you: I'm afraid of developing an allergy to chocolate." He laughed, but I had a question for him. "Why's it so important to know about these deep, dark fears, as you say?"

He looked at me like I had a screw loose. "I want to help your sister. And, I think I can. But, so far, she's not been very forthcoming with information. Still, I think I'm in love, and I want what's best for her."

"You don't see a conflict of interest between your personal and professional relationships with her?" As soon as I asked, I realized how much I sounded like Daddy, and wished I could take the words back.

Apparently, Dr. Wright caught a glimpse of Beau Prescott, too. "You sound like your father. Last night, after dinner, he called me into the living room. I thought when he poured me a drink we were going to kick back and watch A&M play. You can imagine my surprise when he called me a 'sex-crazed dipstick' and told me to keep my mitts off his daughter."

I barked out a laugh. Really, I couldn't help it. That wasn't what Daddy said and we both knew it.

"I know y'all have problems with him. Your sister told me about it. But he's just acting that way because he loves you. And this upcoming trial with his child bride has to be keeping him on edge."

I gave an almost imperceptible head bob.

"Do you have anyone you can talk to—I mean *really* talk to? Like a boyfriend or a fiancé?"

I shook my head no.

"That might be a good thing." He put on his flashers and rolled up behind Gran's car. "No point worrying people over piddly stuff. Things have a way of working out." Then he hopped out of the truck, grabbed the gasoline from the pickup bed, and walked over to the Cadillac with me in tow. When he unscrewed the gas cap, he jutted his chin in the direction of traffic. "I need you to watch the cars for me. If you see anyone weaving, or not paying attention, yell out."

CHAPTER THIRTEEN

I returned to the filling station to refuel Gran's car. Dr. Wright followed me until he was sure I'd safely pulled in on the self-service side. Then he gave me a quick wave like the Lone Ranger, *Hi-ho, Silver, away!* and left me to fend for myself. I pumped my own gas until I overfilled the seemingly bottomless tank, and it belched out fuel. After I paid, got back into the vehicle, and hit the road, I noticed the gas gauge on "E." Stupid car. Then I thought about Teensy's new powder-blue roadster with the metallic paint job, and me, being without my Porsche, and I wanted to spit galvanized nails.

My first stop took me to the spy shop, where I replenished my pepper spray. Then I wondered why I didn't own a gun when every other red-blooded Texan owned one, so I drove to the indoor firing range and had a look around. I'd been there once before, when Daddy took me with him. After finding a large enough caliber revolver that still fit comfortably in my hand, I bought a taser.

I hated driving Gran's car.

I hated wimping out on the gun purchase.

And, I hated to admit it, but, just when I thought I had life by the tail, I'd picked up a stalker.

But what I really hated to admit was that Teensy had a boyfriend who loved her . . . while I didn't.

Later that afternoon, as soon as I let myself in through Gran's front door, Teensy burst through her bedroom door looking like

she'd survived execution. Then she ran to the landing screaming like a pregnant lady having a home birth. Since I didn't see
anyone chasing her with an upraised hatchet, I assumed this
was just another component in the continuing, escalating
psychodrama that was rapidly becoming *de rigueur* in this house.
I stood near the front door, ready to dash, in case she came
down the stairs to hit me for failing to screw the mouthwash
cap on just so.

She took a step toward me; I took a backward step toward
the threshold.

She took the first couple of stair steps, and I retreated across
the threshold. Seeing how this would play out, she hauled up
short and addressed me like the total whack-job she's turned
into.

"I need your help, Dainty."

"For what?" I had to make sure this wasn't a trick.

"Doc texted me—"

"Doc?"

"Dr. Wright. My boyfriend. Everybody calls him that."

"Ah-ha."

"Doc just texted to tell me he was breaking up with me. He
said he can't deal with my instability—if you can believe that—"

"Imagine." I still hadn't fully reentered the house. "Unstable.
What's he thinking?"

"Exactly." Teensy gave me one of her exaggerated head bobs
as if to say we were on the same page. Which everyone in this
house knew we were not. "Well, I was so upset I texted him a
list of grievances and other things I don't like about him, but
before my text went through, he texted me again, saying, *Just
kidding, princess, you know I love you.* You've got to help me,
Dainty."

"Why should I help you? Besides, I don't know how to
retrieve a *sent* text."

She tuned up the whining. "But you're my sister." Then she gave me a hang-dog expression and her bottom lip started to quiver. "You always know what to do."

This was the first glimpse I'd had of my "real" sister since the hair-raising rescue in beautiful, enchanted Meh-hee-co—and I say that with the utmost sarcasm. When I returned to that swill pit of a country to bring back my stepmother, I had no idea Teensy would become diabolically possessed during my two-week absence.

I grudgingly stepped back into the house and shut the door as she scampered down the rest of the stairs. When she reached the bottom, she handed me her phone.

To be sure Teensy gave me the correct details, I intended to double-check who said what, but scrolled up the digital display too far and caught the tail end of an X-rated comment detailing moves Teensy's boyfriend wanted to show her to improve her sexual dexterity. For a moment, I considered the only way to take my mind off what I'd just read would be to gouge out my eyes.

I finally found the breakup messages, put a couple of seconds' worth of thought into it, and sent another text. I pretended to be the cashier from Poca Jamoca, a coffee house in the strip center about two miles from Gran's, and told Dr. Wright that the girl who owned the phone had left it in the store, and some Mexican dude picked it up and wrote something before they could retrieve it.

Then I handed it back. "You owe me."

She checked out what I'd written. Then she looked up from the screen. "You're not getting your job back."

"Let me ask you something," I said. "Do you even know what Dr. Wright's real name is?"

"Uh, yeah." She said this as if it perturbed her. "It's Doc."

"You think his Christian name is Doc," I said dully.

"Well, I don't know if he's a Christian." Her eyes rolled up toward the ceiling and back. "I mean, we haven't really talked about religion yet. I guess you do that the same time you have the conversation about kids, right? Do you think that's important, given that it's still early in the relationship?"

My eyes fell to half-mast. My sister was not only treacherous, she'd probably lost seventy-five IQ points since she got back from Mexico, making her officially dumber than dirt.

With her fingertips barely grazing the mahogany banister, my self-centered sister prissed halfway up the stairs with great elegance, had a light-bulb moment, and turned. "Don't you want to know about the CPS deal with Gran?"

I did. And I didn't.

Haltingly, I asked what happened.

"Not sure. They did their little home visit—" she flip-flopped her hand through the air "—and then they left. It lasted all of thirty minutes. I think they felt sorry for her. I really don't know. You should ask Amanda."

"Why would I ask Amanda?"

"Because she's the one who talked to them."

"Wait—you let Amanda handle the interview? Are you crazy?" But then I thought, *Oh, wait, that's stupid, of course she's crazy,* and wanted to smack my forehead with the heel of my hand.

"I thought it best."

"What?"

It wasn't that I didn't hear her; it was merely my way of giving her a chance to change what she'd just told me. If I'd said, "Say what?" instead, she would've known it was time to run.

"You thought it best?" I parroted, projecting my voice in an upward spiral. "What's more important than tending to the woman who's allowing us to stay, rent free, in her house?"

"As soon as the CPS lady got here, Gran told me to get a shovel and go out to the sunroom and re-pot two of her plumeria plants. When I asked why, she said, straight-faced, that it'd be good practice for when I inevitably went to jail for doing something stupid; that I might be qualified to do my community service at a nursery instead of wearing a reflective vest and spearing trash by the side of the highway with all the other low-lifes."

"Have you lost your mind? You don't turn over a serious interview for your grandmother to a non-family member. What were you thinking?" I checked myself. "You were busy texting that psychologist guy, weren't you? Texting, instead of thinking."

"Fine, what*ever.*"

As she pranced back to her room, I decided that *Fine, whatever* is Teensy-speak for, *Why yes, I do need a slap upside my head for insolence.*

I went looking for Amanda, and when I didn't find her, I quickly changed into a pair of black yoga pants and a black "T." Since I wasn't sure how late I'd be, I wanted to be able to pull reconnaissance if necessary. But first, I'd need to return to the spy shop to buy more surveillance equipment with money I'd pulled out of the hidden stash in my drawer if I had a chance at helping Gordon.

Then it struck me. If Paislee Pfeiffer was dead, then Drex must be suffering something awful. Or maybe he was about to become a suspect.

Then I realized I hadn't seen Tig Welder, WBFD's star investigative reporter, since I'd returned. He had a motive—he was having an affair with Gordon's wife, too. I put him on my mental list of suspects. Who knew how many flings Gordon's wife was having at the same time? But, still, at the top of the list, I had to start with the man who had the most to lose—and that was my boss.

I practically skipped down the stairs. I'm not sure why, but I actually liked the fledgling business that Bruckman called the Debutante Detective Agency. Not as much as being an anchor for a third-rate TV station in the Metroplex, but I still liked it.

Okay, I confess. I loved it. Especially when I'm scared out of my wits and adrenaline courses through my veins. It's like the best and worst feelings, all rolled up into one.

I stopped in the kitchen and looked through the pantry. If I got stuck somewhere, I wanted to make sure I had a couple of nutrition bars to keep up my energy. I also had a hiding place so that other people in the house couldn't find the cookies I like. Teensy has a hiding place, too, but I know where hers is; she doesn't know where mine is. Then I got angry inside all over again, thinking about how Teensy stole my job.

So, *ha.* Teensy's cookies? Don't mind if I do.

When I turned around with an armful of junk food, my startle reflex kicked in as I came face-to-face with Gran.

I jumped at seeing her.

"You remind me of me when I was your age. And yet you look so much like your mother," she said almost semi-loving and wistful, "only chunkier." She wore an expensive five-carat emerald surrounded by a ring of quarter-carat diamonds in a platinum setting around her neck, and her latest acquisition from Harkman-Beemis, another designer suit in a subdued-but-elegant shade of gray. I gathered after her morning with the CPS people that she'd joined her friends at the country club for their weekly game of bridge. Her gaze went steely. "What are you up to?"

"Snacks. I may have to pull surveillance tonight," I said as if I held the fate of the planet in my hands.

Bright blue eyes turned into sparking, glittery beads. "What was the name of that anchor in the national market?" She poked her finger into the air a couple of times as if to jog her memory.

"You know . . . the one they fired? You know . . . the one who got *fat*."

I returned half of the junk food to the pantry. Kept the cookies, though. All of them.

"Just so you know, Gran, I lost six pounds the last time I was in Mexico. So, actually, counting the ten I lost when I went down there for Teensy, I'm down sixteen."

"Well, then we know where to send you when you get chubby, don't we?" She gave me a grandmotherly smile that was anything but.

For the record, I was never chubby. I was perfect. Now I look borderline anorexic. I re-hid my cookies, but hung on to my sister's.

"Do you intend to go out in public dressed like that?"

For reasons I don't completely understand, Gran has issues with yoga pants. So I justified my clothing by saying I didn't want to wear my good clothes. Then I tried to make myself out to be really important—Dainty Prescott, super-hero. "You never know when you'll have to subdue somebody."

Her jaw tightened.

"Come on, Gran. Don't be mad. I won't run into anyone we know." I wanted to say, *Believe me,* and decided I'd better not.

She gave me an aristocratic sniff.

I pulled out the sack from the candy boutique with the box of Black Forest truffles in it, and handed it to her. "Brought you something."

"What is it?" She recoiled as if I'd scooped up Old Man Spencer's basset hound's poop.

"Your fave. Go on, open it."

Gran took the bag. Cue screaming, where the Village Scold chastised me for "blowing money."

"Your gas gauge is broken."

"No, it isn't."

"It is, Gran. I ran out of gas. On the highway. It was scary."

She wanted to know if I'd had "enough sense to call for roadside service." I told her about Dr. Wright giving me a lift.

"I don't like him. Every psychiatrist I ever met was half nuts." Then she went off on a wild tear. "Like that gypsy you dragged home with you—"

"Amanda's a pygmy, not a gypsy."

"Fine. Pygmy. That pygmy you dragged home needs to get a job."

"She's a visitor. Just visiting. Already has a job." Of course I didn't want to have to explain the nature of Amanda's job. I didn't want to explain this, oh, say, let's use the term "quirky" aspect to Amanda's personality to Gran, because I didn't want to have to call 911 and get the fire department to speed over and revive her. Nor did I want to say that if Amanda needed pocket money, she could turn tricks down on Maple Avenue, in Big-D, and earn enough cash in one night for a down payment on a decent car. I didn't want to tell her this because it only reminded me that they'd gotten rid of my Porsche, and talking about it would just depress me.

"I have an idea. Why don't we sit and talk about your day?" I moved to the breakfast nook, put my food stash on the table, and took a seat in an effort to encourage her to do the same.

The breakfast room overlooks an outdoor terrace on one side, giving a bird's-eye view of the swimming pool. The room is done in muted blues that are restful to the eye. There's a white wool Oriental rug on the floor beneath an American walnut gate-leg table from the late 1700s, plain walnut chairs with seats upholstered in blue plaid silk, and a Baccarat chandelier hanging from the ceiling. I like the feel of being outdoors without having to put up with bad weather, insects, and, on occasion, the piping screams of the nearest neighbor's grandchildren.

Oddly, Gran joined me in the nook. I started the conversation with chit-chat, remarking, first, about the beautiful orchid in the middle of the table, and asking where it came from.

"It's your sister's. She got it from her new beau. At least that's her version. Personally, I don't think he's really her boyfriend; I think she sent them to herself."

"C'mon, Gran. She introduced him to us last night. The doctor. Dr. Wright." Gran kept shaking her head, no, so I continued to ferret out answers to more serious topics. "So, how was your day?"

"Remember those *Charles Dickens: A Christmas Carol* tickets I gave you for your birthday? Well, I need them back. I know how you love the ballet, Dainty, but Mr. Spencer decided he wants to go see it."

Should've known.

In my effort to have a meaningful conversation with my grandmother, I forgot to mention she's an Indian giver. The last time she did this to me, she didn't even bother to give me a replacement gift. I probably haven't received a gift from her that actually remained in my possession since I was seven, and that was only because Gran had no use for my "My Pretty Pony" stable.

"Remind me tomorrow and I'll get them for you."

"I'd like them now."

While Gran admonished me for running through the house, I dashed up two floors, to the attic, and retrieved the tickets from my jewelry box. When I returned, she was standing at the sink, making herself a cup of white tea.

"Here you go." I handed them over. When I re-seated myself at the breakfast table, I saw that she'd placed a speckled muffin on a bread-and-butter plate from her "everyday" set of 150-year-old Limoges for me. I did a quick lean in for a whiff, and immediately identified the speckles as fresh blueberries. She only bakes them on special occasions, so I figured this was left over from the morning's CPS debacle.

I tried again. "So, Gran, how was your day? Anything interesting happen?"

Anybody get criminal charges filed for lewd conduct? Indecent exposure with a child?

My grandmother poured hot water over her tea bag. She returned to the table with the china cup chattering against the saucer from the shakiness of an unsteady, elderly hand. Next she squeezed a lemon wedge into the brew, covering her hand as she did so to prevent any rogue splatters from shooting across the table at me.

"Well, let's see . . . your gypsy friend—"

"Amanda's a pygmy. Not a gypsy. We covered this already."

"—your pygmy friend—"

"Amanda," I said with emphasis. "And just so you know, Amanda isn't my friend, she's the person who helped me get Teensy back from Mexico. And now she's our houseguest."

What a Judas—I denied Amanda again, and felt terrible about it.

"—your pygmy acquaintance, Amanda, introduced me to a very nice lady from the government . . ." She pronounced it "Guv-mit" like a true Southerner. ". . . and then the new Mexican housekeeper served us tea. I never really did understand why the government lady wanted to see me, but she seemed nice, and the visit was pleasant enough. And I made a new friend." Her voice trailed. "And afterward, Mr. Spencer drove me to the country club, and we had lunch together, and then I played bridge with my friends while he played poker in the men's tavern, and then he drove me home."

I stiffened. That CPS investigator was no friend.

I tried to keep the alarm out of my tone. "Do you remember what you and the lady from the Guv-mit talked about?"

Oh good Lord. I pronounced government *the same as Gran did.*

I'm turning into Gran.

I bit the top off the muffin, savoring the crispy, sugary cap overhanging the fluted wrapper.

She cast her gaze to the ceiling, thoughtfully, before answering in the most genteel of voices. "Why yes, I do. We made small talk, such as how she should probably get her priorities straight. Like, go get me a chocolate meringue pie from the Jewish deli. And that's how we might've left it had it not been for her saying she was starving to death. I told her from the looks of things, she ought to be able to hibernate 'til sometime after the big thaw next spring. The whole reason for the meeting seemed bewilderingly silly. You know, if I'd killed Mr. Spencer when I first met him, I'd be out by now and there wouldn't have been a grandkid panhandling at my front door in the first place."

I passed a blueberry through my nose. Believe me, the force of having a double-aught buckshot, pellet-sized blueberry shoot out your nostril is much more painful than it sounds. I never thought of my grandmother as having a sense of humor, but I think she might've been messing with me.

After I recovered from my un-Rubanbleu table manners, I excused myself from the table and ferried my plate to the sink. Once I rinsed it off and left it for Gran to dry—she doesn't like for us to handle her dishes—I turned around in time to see her appraising my yoga pants.

Glittery blue eyes thinned into slits. "If you wear those things out in public, I'm going to send your father after you, dressed in a Speedo."

"I'm not changing," I said emphatically, then went back into the pantry and foraged for my cookies and two bags of chips to haul out to Gran's car.

CHAPTER FOURTEEN

After I changed out of the yoga pants, and slipped into a nice
pair of tropical wool slacks in a Rubanbleu-approved shade of
charcoal, I headed back over to the spy shop and bought additional surveillance equipment with Gordon's money. He
promised me I could keep all of the spy gear after I found
out who his wife, Paislee Pfeiffer—correction, the late Paislee
Pfeiffer—was having an affair with. And while my boss can be a
benevolent dictator at times, I felt sorry that he was probably
sitting in some Spartan interrogation room down at the Fort
Worth Police Department with beads of sweat popping up on
his forehead.

I paid for what I thought I'd need—and just to be clear—a
few extra things that'd be nice to have around for future cases.
Thanks, Gordon. Thanks for getting yourself thrown in the clink.

I tried to get Gordon to answer his cell phone but each time
I called, it cycled into voicemail. As a last resort, I drove by his
house.

I'd been to his place a grand total of three times: First, when
I took Drex as my date to the Labor Day office picnic, a month
or so after Gordon and Paislee bought the new place; second,
when I knew Drex and Paislee were having an affair, and I went
back to take evidentiary photos, and discovered the Pfeiffers
were dog-sitting a big, black Beauceron for Paislee's twin
sister—the swimsuit model—and my camera and I ended up in
the deep end of Gordon's swimming pool after the dog tried to

eat me; and third, when I returned with a new camera, and ended up flat on my back when the tree limb that concealed me snapped.

On this particular night, I didn't see any house lights burning except for the two gas lamps mounted on either side of the massive double doors of this two-story, sandstone French château. I tried Gordon's cell phone again, but no luck. Then everything changed.

Taillights blazed in Gordon's driveway. I flashed my brights and the vehicle slowed. I jumped out of Gran's Cadillac and waited for the car to come to a stop at the mouth of the drive. Sure enough Gordon rolled the window halfway down. His eyes appeared bloodshot in the ambient light of the street lamp.

"Prescott. I've been trying to get you all day." Then he explained that he'd been to the M.E.'s Office and identified his wife from the morgue's video monitor.

My eyes bulged at this disclosure.

"Go home and get some shut-eye—I need you to do the drive-time news tomorrow. Nobody's heard from Aspen Wicklow. As soon as you're done, come back over here and go through my wife's stuff. See if you can find anything out of the ordinary."

"Why don't you do it? You knew her better."

My boss sighed. "Apparently, I didn't know her at all. Besides, you're females. Right-brain thinkers. Just give me a list when you're done." He shifted the car into park and fiddled with the keys. Then he handed over the house key and recited the alarm code. "Easy to remember. It's my birthday—oh-three-one-one. Come back tomorrow, after the news. Then let me know what you found."

"Will you be at the station tomorrow?"

"Don't know, Prescott. Depends on whether or not the police believe I didn't kill my wife."

"About that, Mr. Pfeiffer . . ."

"Gordon."

"Right. Gordon. I'm really sorry about Mrs. Pfeiffer."

"Yeah." He looked away, but I noticed a tear beading along the rim of his eye. "Me, too, Prescott . . . me, too."

I returned to my grandmother's estate a few minutes before the news at ten began, only to find Gran sitting in one of the leather wingbacks in front of the big-screen TV in the casual living room. A roll of wrapping paper with a Christmas theme lay on a nearby coffee table, along with scissors and tape. Several boxes had been wrapped, minus bows, and I assumed that Gran had done this.

We exchanged hellos, and I asked Teensy's location.

Gran volumed down the television. "Were you aware that today's cars have seat warmers?" I had no idea what this had to do with my sister's whereabouts. "Teensy took me for a spin in her new little hotrod. She didn't tell me it had seat warmers."

"Did Amanda go, too?"

Gran scoffed at the notion. "It's a two-seater, Dainty. Really. Where's she going to sit?"

I felt the rise of a slow burn that came from missing my Porsche. "Where'd y'all go?"

"Your sister needed a driver's license, so we drove out to the Department of Public Safety. Those people were no help at all."

"How so?"

"They wouldn't give it to her without a copy of her birth certificate. In order to get a copy of her birth certificate, she either needed a driver's license or a passport. In order to get a passport, she needs a copy of her birth certificate or a driver's license. She doesn't have any of those things because they were stolen in Mexico." Gran sighed. "Identity thieves have simply ruined it for the rest of us."

"So what happened?"

Her tone developed an edge. "What do you think happened? We left. And as soon as your sister drove out of the parking lot, a state trooper pulled her over and wrote her a ticket for not having a driver's license."

"Good thing you tagged along." Merely visualizing Gran behind the wheel of a finely tuned convertible caused my eyes to throb. "So . . . I take it you had to drive Teensy's car back since she didn't have a valid driver's license?"

"More or less."

Uh-oh. Didn't like the sound of that. "What exactly does that mean?"

"What it means, Dainty, is that Amanda came and got us."

I hallucinated. Amanda?

According to Gran, Amanda went out earlier in the day and got herself a job. After that, she went over to one of those tote-the-note places and took out a payday loan for a car. Which turned out to be a good thing since, in Gran's effort to leave the DPS parking lot, driving Teensy's new sports car, she wrapped it around a light pole.

"You what?"

"I'm going to bed," she announced, unapologetic and terminating the discussion. Then she shut the television off with the remote and glided out of the room with her silk kimono billowing at the hem. As she headed for the stairs, she said, "Put up the wrapping paper and clean up the rest of that stuff, would you?"

I did as I was told, but I also read the name on the gift cards for the boxes Gran already wrapped. They were all for my sister; none for me. I decided to snoop. When I opened each one and peeked inside, I realized what happened to a couple of my favorite outfits. Gran went into my closet, gift-wrapped them, and gave them to Teensy for Christmas.

I went to the refrigerator to pour myself a glass of orange

juice, only to find that Teensy had stuck a pre-glued note on the side of the box that read: *I licked the carton.* It only had a little bit left when I swished the container, but I went ahead and penned *So did I* underneath her note.

Next, I decided to scramble a few eggs before going to bed. I did scramble them, but not the way you might think. I dropped the carton on Gran's freshly waxed floor, and spent the next ten minutes sopping up the mess. Like every day since my birth, my name is Dainty. And unless your parents named you Grace, you'd probably have trouble keeping a straight face introducing yourself, too.

Even though I was still hungry, I decided to cut my losses and head upstairs for bed.

For no good reason, as soon as I flipped off the light switch and stood in the dark, empty kitchen, I felt a gut-wrenching void. I missed Daddy. The telephone in Gran's kitchen is one of those old-fashioned, rotary model Princess phones that came into vogue in the late fifties. The original, delicate shade of blue had darkened with age, but the phone still worked and I used it to call Tranquility Villas. When one of the night-shift staff members answered, I asked to speak to my father. I didn't want anything from him—not like money, or the keys to the River-crest estate Teensy and I grew up in—I just wanted to see if he was still acting crazy. I heard a sound like the rustle of fabric, and my father's voice came over the line.

I launched into a heartfelt message, pouring out my feelings over the past year since he'd neglected me. I tried to tell him how badly I missed Mom, so he'd understand why he shouldn't have expected us girls to take to Nerissa, just because we had "a lot in common with her." Of course we had a lot in com-mon—we were all in high school at the same time. I confessed that, down deep in my heart, I really did want to see him happy; and that I'd put a lot of thought into it, and figured maybe it really would be a good idea if he asked Aspen Wicklow's mother out on a date. And then I told him to ask Mrs. Wicklow if she knew where Aspen was, because as far as I knew, nobody else had the answer.

Then I asked what kind of day he'd had.

He told me he'd been at the urologist's earlier. "And right before they stuck a tube up my goober, the angry, skinny Mexican technician answered, 'Like a *sumbitch*,' when I asked her if the procedure would hurt. Then I asked her if it would help if I made it bigger. She said, '*Ju* wish.' "

The more details I got about the procedure, the more I wanted to muzzle him. I didn't mean to make light of his predicament, so I crushed a paper towel to my mouth to keep from snuffling with laughter.

Then he resorted to colorful language, adding, "That pretty much sums it up. So don't ask me what kind of day I had."

I told him I was sorry we'd been estranged for so long, and that I'd try to make more of an effort to see him, now that Nerissa was locked up in jail, awaiting trial for murdering my mother, and trying to murder Daddy.

When I was done, he said, "I don't have a problem with it. Stop contacting me, and get a real job."

I trudged upstairs to my bedroom in the attic and found Amanda already tucked into my bed. She'd pulled the covers up tight beneath her chin, and looked like a pen jutting out from a pocket protector. Then I heard the musical intro to *The Rockford Files* and saw that she'd hauled up a small TV from one of the guest bedrooms, and wired it up to cable.

I gasped with pleasure.

Shifty black eyes cut in my direction. "How's it going?"

"You got us TV?"

"It was the least I could do for making you sleep on the rollaway. But I *am* your guest, so I ought to be able to sleep where I want."

I was so excited I didn't even care what she'd said or done to make the CPS people go away.

"Gran said you got a job." I clasped my hands together, prayer-like. "Please tell me you didn't resort to your usual occupation. You can't do that here. My grandmother won't let you stay if she finds out you do that."

"Don't worry, diva. I haven't been able to find the good places in Dallas to pimp myself out, so I got a job at a pizza parlor, delivering pizza. I have court-ordered restitution coming up soon, remember?"

Until Amanda mentioned restitution, I'd completely blocked out that unfortunate incident back in El Paso. Although Amanda claimed she'd rescued a Bichon from fiendish people who were guilty of cruelty to animals, the court apparently didn't see it that way since the judge gave her thirty days to make restitution. Later, Amanda also claimed the dog had run away, but I suspected she'd found it a safe home with an elderly lady who treated it like a sultan so she wouldn't have to return it to its former owners.

As for court-ordered restitution—if Amanda didn't make timely payments to reimburse the family for the cost of the dog before the deadline expired, the court could issue a warrant for her arrest.

"What's the job like?"

Eyes shrewdly narrowed. She gave me a slow stare and enunciated every word. "It's a pizza delivery job."

"At least it's honest work." I tried to put the best possible spin on a lousy job. "You never know, it might be exciting."

"Diva, the only way it'll be exciting is if I get robbed."

She shifted her attention to the television and upped the sound by remote. I went over to the delicate French vanity and opened my laptop computer. As it booted up, I turned on the portable printer. While Amanda watched another back-to-back rerun of *The Rockford Files,* I typed out a list of things I'd done and the time I'd spent doing them to make it easier to invoice Gordon. Then I typed out a to-do list for the next few days. When I finished, I saved the document as "Shit I have to do to get my job back," printed both pages out, and shut down the computer.

Amanda's show went into commercial, and she muted the volume.

She took a deep breath and slowly blew it out. "Your family's crazy."

"Ya think?" I oozed sarcasm.

"Did Gran tell you she called me to pick her and your sister up at the DPS?"

I told her Gran might've mentioned it, but that I'd like to hear her version on how that came about. Then I cracked a smile. The very idea that Amanda felt comfortable enough to refer to my blue-haired grandmother as Gran—and the scenario working itself out in my head as to what Gran would do if Amanda actually called her that to her face—caused me to snuffle with laughter.

"Bitches were out screwing around at the DPS, and, *ai diva*—" Amanda launched into a barrage of Spanish curse words "—if your grandmother had been taking a driving test, she would've flunked before she drove out of the parking lot."

"She wouldn't tell me how Teensy's car got wrecked. I don't suppose you'd know, now, would you?" My excitement built.

"Only because I had to listen to your sister bitch to high heaven all the way home." Amanda gave a derisive grunt. "After the trooper ticketed Teensy for failing to display the driver's license she no longer has, she and Gran switched places so Gran could drive them home. Or, rather, that was the plan. But about ten seconds after your loony grandmother gave it the gas, she started screaming about her ass being on fire, and swerved into a pole.

"By the way, your sister's a raving psycho. She called me crazy and hit me with a shoe, and said I needed to be locked up in a mental hospital because I didn't screw the cap back on the toothpaste tube right. Then, she traipsed all the way up here to talk about raccoons, all nice as you please. I spent ten minutes explaining why getting a pet raccoon isn't such a hot idea. This marks the third time we've had this conversation since I first got here."

"Exactly. They're nocturnal. We'd never get any sleep."

"That's the part that bothers you?" Amanda sat up in bed. "What about rabies? And the fact that they tear up everything they come in contact with?" She turned and plumped her pillows. "Well, feel free to thank me; I talked her out of it." She gave me a pointed look. "Exactly. You're welcome."

"Yeah, I heard her talking to somebody on the phone about where to get a wallaby. That's the thing about the 'new and improved Teensy.' It's like she developed Attention-Deficit Disorder from that unfortunate blow to the head."

"Ya think?" Amanda mocked me. "Stop laughing. She found out you stole her cookies and went on a rampage. She paced back and forth, yelling about how you're going to end up being a common criminal, living on the street, on drugs, all because you ate her Snickerdoodles."

"Listen, Amanda, I'm sorry you have to bunk in here. Teensy's room is a lot nicer, and I know the beds are more comfortable."

She fanned the air with one of those *Don't give it another thought* hand waves. "It's a relief. After we went to sleep, your grandmother came in and turned on the TV. She set it on one of those evangelical shows. I startled her when I asked if I could assist her, and she confessed she's been setting it on the religious channel so your sister's subconscious will absorb it and turn her into a God-fearing human being, all because while we were in Mexico tracking your stepmother, Teensy was hanging out with the riffraff in Deep Ellum."

I let out a nervous chuckle. "Teensy's boyfriend asked me if I wanted to come in for a free consult. Should I?"

Amanda did a one-shoulder shrug. "I'm not much into shrinks. After we got across the border, I was diagnosed with antisocial behavior disorder, so I joined a support group. So far it's worked out pretty good. We never meet."

I barked out a laugh. Amanda's funny in a dry humor sort of way.

"Maybe I ought to take Dr. Wright up on his offer. He said I might be able to provide information that would help Teensy. And I liked the *free* part. It's not like I have money, you know?" At the moment, I was so broke I didn't have two quarters to do a load of towels.

"Tell me about it." Amanda did a little eye roll. "After Border Patrol released me, I was so broke that I had to dry myself off with a chamois sample that came in the mail, every time I got out of the shower."

"What happened to all that money I paid you?"

"Meh—" she distributed invisible cash to the air between us "—a little here, a little there . . ."

For the longest time, I tossed and turned, thinking about Tim—was he someone I knew, or had inadvertently offended? Not to mention, I couldn't believe I let Amanda sleep in my room. Even though she snored like an overweight sixty-year-old man with sleep apnea, I eventually fell into a fitful sleep.

CHAPTER FIFTEEN

While deep in the throes of a Technicolor dream, I felt the slap of a hand against my forehead and came half-awake. Then fingers poked my eyes, my nose, and then my mouth, before I came fully awake to Amanda's hysterical laughter. She'd confused me with the clock radio.

After Amanda rolled over, pulled the covers over her head, and went back to sleep, I showered and got ready to go into the station. Halfway down the stairs, the smoke alarm attached to the kitchen ceiling went off. To be sure, Teensy's no cook. She either incinerates the food, or poisons us. Part of the problem with her inedible cuisine is that she tends to substitute ingredients when she discovers Gran's out of something—like the time she baked biscuits, but replaced the baking powder the recipe called for with baking soda. And because Gran didn't permit the wasting of food, she made us eat them. All of them. Every. Last. One.

On this particular morning, my sister dressed like a carnival exploded. I watched, slack-jawed, as she dragged a chair across the floor and climbed up on the seat to reset the smoke alarm.

You kidding me?

I mean, honestly, are you kidding me?

You couldn't find a hat and gloves within the entire color spectrum to go with your multicolored, slung-together, fashion disaster outfit?

Huh. The lack of effort is duly noted.

I whiffed the malodorous air. If Teensy planned to turn this

153

into a routine we needed to invest in a canary on a perch, and keep it at the foot of the stairs to warn us. There had to be more sulphur in Gran's kitchen than Hell's waiting room. After the smoke cleared and the warning bells were silenced, Teensy went back over to the stove.

"What'd you burn this time?" Like I needed to ask. Opting for cereal, I headed to the pantry.

"What'd you burn this time?" she asked. Then, she narrated my actions. "Dainty Prescott has disappeared into the pantry. As we wait, breathless with excitement, she's coming out with a box of cereal she selected."

I arched one brow. "What?"

"What?" she said. "She's moving to the refrigerator . . . she's opening the door . . . and, yes, she's pulled out a carton of milk."

"Are you mocking me?"

"Are you mocking me?"

I felt like I'd boarded a plane, been hijacked to a foreign country, and didn't speak the language.

Although my sister hasn't had one iota of formal training to be a broadcast journalist, in order to buttress her abilities to do a job that it took me four years to prepare for, in order to prove to Mr. Pfeiffer that she has what it takes to deliver the news, Teensy alternated between repeating everything I said, and narrating everything I did at the precise moment I said and did these things, until the only way I could escape the insanity was to leave early for work.

When I drove through the gate at WBFD, Chopper Deke was waiting for me, and motioned me to park in the reserved space with his name painted on it. According to Chopper Deke, Gordon instructed him to escort me across the parking lot and into the building, but left out the reason.

Ever since the night Rochelle got drunk and gave her phone

number to that dwarf who came to the TV station and held everyone hostage until he could speak to her, Gordon hired a security guard to work the graveyard shift. We actually met for the first time when Mr. Bilburn, the crazy guy who lives on the street behind the station, chased me with that stapler.

As Chopper Deke and I walked across the parking lot, he filled me in: Gordon was worried about my safety. That made me think of the incident with Mr. Bilburn at the open house. Life had to be hard for someone who was almost like a separate species, but I still wasn't convinced the guy might not be trying to use up one of my nine lives.

Chopper Deke sheared my thoughts. "So what's going on between you and Pfeiffer? Y'all got a little thing going between you? Hmmm?"

Offended, I still decided to set him straight because I owe Chopper Deke big time. "It's not like that. I work for him. I'm on special assignment. And : . ." *Go ahead, admit it,* I told myself, ". . . I'm being stalked."

Now it was Chopper Deke's turn to be offended. His eyes looked like they might slingshot out of their sockets, and I was instantly treated to the deranged face of a man whose irises were ringed in white. "Who is it? I'll kill him for you. Say the word."

"Thanks, that won't be necessary."

When we'd traveled halfway across the parking lot, Gordon burst out the front door wearing a "Freddie" mask—presumably left over from Halloween—and angled over to where Tig Welder had parked his Hummer.

I asked Chopper Deke if he knew what was going on.

"Gordon went through the building looking for Tig. One of the photographers ratted Tig out. So Gordon found out his star investigative reporter went on a bender, got too drunk to drive home, and probably went outside to sleep it off in his dickmobile."

As Gordon went around to the driver's door, Chopper Deke continued to grip my elbow with enough force to convey a certain urgency as he steered me toward the building entrance. I couldn't see into Tig's vehicle—it was still dark outside and the SUV had heavy, if not outright illegal, tinting—but I watched as Gordon pounded on the window and put his face up to the glass. A dark shape rose up in the seat like a pop-up target.

Tig woke up and pepper-sprayed him. Too bad his window was rolled up. While Gordon headed back inside, Tig bailed out of the Hummer, watery-eyed and foaming at the mouth from the effects of chemical mace. After Chopper Deke swiped his magnetic card across the door opener and the two of us stepped inside, Gordon left Tig sitting on the front steps, gasping for air, and came back in to brag about it. Apparently that's the most fun my boss has had around here since he found out about Paislee cheating on him—not only with my then-boyfriend, Drex, but with—*hold onto your skivvies*— Tig.

Then Gordon summoned me into his office, left Chopper Deke standing in the foyer, and shut the door behind us.

He motioned me toward the cowhide couch and said, "Sit."

Déjà vu all over again.

I told him about the additional equipment I'd bought and asked if he could reimburse me right away. At the moment, I don't even have gas money. He pulled out his wallet and shelled out a couple of hundreds while informing me that he's staying at his friend Byron's house. I've never met Byron, unless he was the jolly guy in the Hawaiian shirt at the Labor Day party, and I didn't press the matter.

Gordon sat in his swivel chair and spun around to face me. I knew he had something on his mind, and just wanted him to spill it and get it over with.

"The security guard took off early," he said. "His wife went into labor."

There was a pregnant pause. I wasn't sure where this was leading.

"Want me to buy a card, and get everyone to sign it?" I asked helpfully.

"That's Rochelle's area of expertise. I don't know where she finds those hateful cards—you know the ones with the double entendre?"

I knew exactly what he meant. She'd picked one out for my birthday the previous month. I didn't know whether to kiss her for remembering I even had a birthday, or slap her for the rude message it contained.

Gordon was still talking and I'd missed what he said. I tried to look alert . . . and interested.

"—but Rochelle can handle it. I wanted you to know the reason Richter walked you in this morning."

"Richter?"

"Chopper Deke."

Right. Deke Richter. I'd only recently learned his last name because it wasn't stenciled on his reserved parking space, and up until recently, I'd spent the majority of my time at this station ducking him.

"So when you came in, did you notice anybody watching you?"

I stiffened. I'd spent so much energy making sure Chopper Deke didn't put his mitts on me that I'd never even glanced at my surroundings. I answered Gordon by way of a head shake.

He opened his right-hand drawer and pulled out an envelope. From my place on the sofa, I could only read my name. No postmark. No return address. No postage stamp.

Even as he passed it across the desk, I saw that it'd been

opened. And it had my name written on the front in block print. I couldn't help it; I stared as a serpent of nausea coiled in my gut.

"Someone left this on Rochelle's desk yesterday. Probably one of the people who came to the open house."

I gradually became aware that my intake of air had increased. Halfway to hyperventilating, I actually watched the fabric of my silk blouse pulsing from my rapid heartbeat. I gutted it out and slid the letter from its envelope.

Before I read a word on the plain white paper, I looked for a signature. Sure enough, it was signed "Tim." I swallowed hard. Instead of smiley-versus-frowny faces, he'd drawn a crude stick figure wearing a triangle-shaped dress, like the ones commonly found on bathroom doors, only this one had a little hangman's noose around its neck.

Tears blistered behind my eyeballs. But instead of breaking down in front of my boss, I set my jaw and read. The letter came off like hostage negotiations: This Tim dirtbag wanted me to stick a fresh flower in my hair the next time I did the news, and to give a little laugh if I delivered a sad story. He expected me to wear chandelier earrings—which are *so* déclassé if worn out in public before the cocktail hour—and to show my cleavage. If I didn't do all these things, there would be consequences.

Not that Gordon would approve these demands in order to preserve my safety, but I considered what the consequences from my blue-haired grandmother would be if I carried out these requests—especially the baring of cleavage. None of these requests are things a debutante of The Rubanbleu would do. Unless you're attending the annual debutante ball, you're expected to dress in muted colors and classic styles, avoid trendy fashions, and wear only pearls or jewelry set in fourteen-karat gold or higher. In other words, understated elegance.

"I don't know what to say. Do the sponsors even provide

chandelier earrings?"

"You're not doing it—any of it." Gordon leaned back in his swivel chair and eyed me up. "I don't negotiate with terrorists, and neither do you."

"Of course not," I said, but my brain was screaming, *For the love of God, stick a freakin' flower in your hair and unbutton your blouse down to the third button.* "But what do I do?"

"You want to be a newscaster, do the news. This station's not a joke anymore, Prescott; we're third in the ratings thanks to Aspen Wicklow." The worry lines in his face deepened. "Speaking of Aspen, have you seen or heard from her?"

I shook my head. Aspen and I aren't friends. There'd be no reason for her to call me. We're openly cordial to each other, and the Debutante Detective Agency recently did a job on her behalf—paid for, believe it or not, by Rochelle—but that's about it.

"Have you talked to the sheriff of Johnson County? Spike Granger?" It was common knowledge around the station that Aspen dated the man. Sheriff Granger reminded Rochelle of "Dirty Harry" but Gordon considered him something of a loose cannon for the unorthodox way he dealt with criminals and bureaucracies. I'd only met the guy once from afar, when Rochelle hired the Debutante Detective Agency to do some reconnaissance on his personal life. Okay, I spied on him. But Aspen thought he'd reconciled with his ex-wife, a leggy, racehorse blonde who ran off with one of Granger's friends. Turned out he hadn't. "Maybe the sheriff knows where she is."

"Good idea, Prescott. Makes me tickled pink that I thought of it—*yesterday*. Now . . . you want to do the news this morning or not? No chandelier earrings. Use the earrings our sponsors sent over. No flowers. No flashing of boobs. No inappropriate laughter."

"But he said if I didn't do it, he'd—" my words nearly choked me "—he'd strangle me with my pantyhose."

Gordon locked me in his gaze. "In or out, Prescott? Because I can get somebody else to do it if you're not interested."

I knew good and well who he had in mind. I was trying to get my job back, not hand it to Teensy on a silver platter.

I sealed my fate. "I'm in."

"Good. Then when you're done, get over to my house and start doing whatever it is that your little detective enterprise does. And don't go handing out keys. Or throwing any rave parties while I'm at Byron's." Horrified, I told him I'd never do such a thing, and then he said, "I have an idea that if the cops think I harmed my wife, it's only a matter of time before they'll be getting a search warrant."

I pulled a dark blue blazer from wardrobe, and checked my hair and makeup one last time. Then I took my seat behind the anchor desk a full half hour before the broadcast started. The closer it got to air time, the more my irrational fear built.

Was the person sending me these threats living on the other side of the wall, or the other side of the globe? Were they sitting in front of their TV, or in the next room?

The floor crew came out to make sure all the lights were working. I put my own microphone on and finished preening while the audio department made sure all of the mikes were working. The floor director gave me the "thumbs up" so I knew I looked good. I saw, by the clock, that I had less than three minutes, so I waited until the red indicator light came on the studio camera. I felt zombified, as if I were moving in slow motion, but when the producer gave me the count, I gave a smile bright enough to temporarily blind the entire viewing audience, and did what I do best.

I'm Dainty Prescott, broadcast journalist.
This is my job.
This is me.

Then I delivered the news report.

After I finished, I pulled off the mike and shot out of my seat like a calf out of a chute. I needed to do two things today, and I wasn't sure how long each would take. First, I needed to swing by Gordon's house and take a look around. I didn't really expect to come across anything out of the ordinary, because I didn't really know his wife, so how would I know if anything was out of place or missing? But Gordon was paying me, and I wasn't in a position to argue, and if that's what he wanted from me, I planned to do it. How else would I ever get my job back?

Second, I needed to see Bruckman. I wanted to show him the letters I'd received from Tim. And, let's face it, I needed help.

I decided to go see Bruckman after I snooped around in Gordon's house. If I got lucky, my professional encounter with him about the letters might actually turn into a personal encounter later that evening.

CHAPTER SIXTEEN

The last time I saw the inside of Paislee Pfeiffer's bedroom, I'd worn camouflage cargo pants and concealed myself outside her bedroom window, inside a child's treehouse that the previous homeowners left behind when the Pfeiffers bought the house. I watched through a pair of binoculars as my then-boyfriend, Drex, boffed my boss's wife.

This time, before I ever walked through the front door, I wanted to make sure the big, black Beauceron belonging to Paislee's twin sister was either outside or completely gone. I'd met this dog before, and didn't like what I saw.

I walked around to the side of the house and punched in the key code to the gate. The gate was constructed of wood slats that integrated with the privacy fence, and had an inward opening. As soon as I heard the audible click from the release of the magnetic lock, I gently pushed the gate open a sliver, enough to poke my head through and have a look around.

I never even saw him coming.

The dog body-slammed the wood, and in a prolonged moment of terror, I knew he wasn't there for a slobbery meet-and-greet. The gate face-planted me, and banged shut.

By the time I picked myself up off the ground, the demon dog jumped up and down a handful of times as I watched through the small vertical spaces between the slats. He even chomped at the metal lock. I stood, horrified, rooted in place, as his aggression escalated. With a sharp crack of splintering

162

wood, one of the fence planks on the gate moved enough to open a gap. When the canine actually tried to eat the lock, the wood chipped away like there'd been a shark attack.

"Nice doggie, good boy, calm down, Satan."

That wasn't his name, but it fit.

I dusted off my backside and scurried around to the front of the house. There, I let myself in with the key. The alarm shrilled, and I pulled on the first latex glove. Glancing around for the red diode, I located the panel at the end of the entryway, and tapped in the code. After the house fell silent again, I worked my other hand into the second glove. For no good reason other than instinct, I reset the alarm and watched until the diode went from green to red. Once the ARMED ON PREMISES message registered across the digital display, I walked deeper into the house.

When choosing the unguided tour through someone else's home, one can never take too many precautions.

I flipped on the first light switch and allowed my gaze to wander over the living room. I'd been in this area before, at the Labor Day party, on my way to a guest bathroom on the first floor. It was nicely appointed, but it seemed clear to me from all the trendy faux finishes on the walls and on larger pieces of furniture that the Pfeiffers had used a decorator. Other than a few heirlooms from the previous century that didn't fit in with the rest of the décor, the place seemed chilly and devoid of personality.

Being too careful never hurt now that I had the run of the house. Hey, I saw the movie *Psycho* and it scarred me for life. I looked in the downstairs bedroom, behind the shower curtain in the private bathroom, inside the laundry room, and breezed through the kitchen. Just for fun, I opened the refrigerator to see if I could identify anything in it.

Cheesecake? Don't mind if I do.

After all, Gordon was bunking over at Byron's, Paislee was bunking in a drawer at the morgue, and the dog, Czar—I finally remembered his name—shouldn't have sugar. I looked around for a roll of paper towels, ripped off a length, and chose one of the pre-cut slices from the assortment. My personal favorite is strawberry.

I stood with my backside propped against the kitchen counter and snacked away while the dog stood at the back door, spreading the gossip around the neighborhood. I yelled at him once or twice to stop barking, before mentally penning an "F" on his canine report card. After I finished the last bite of strawberry cheesecake, I crumpled the paper towel, pressed my foot against the trash can lever, and waited for the top to pop open and swallow my garbage like a big, hungry mouth.

Next, I poked around upstairs, specifically in the master bedroom. It seemed strange to view the room from the inside, when I'd only previously seen it through a long lens from my place in the treehouse. But from my position in the doorway, I took in the room in a glance. Battenburg lace bedspread. A pair of vintage night stands. Wooden headboard with a tropical flare, as if it'd come from Pier 1, or Bombay Company, or a similar chain. Nice dresser, but it didn't really tie in with the rest of the pieces in either age or style. To be frank, it was a perfect metaphor—sort of a marriage between his-and-hers, where neither looked particularly good, especially when paired together.

I walked up to the first night stand and slid open the drawer.

This was clearly Gordon's side of the bed, as evidenced by the .38 caliber revolver, which magically appeared when I pushed aside a small notebook, a couple of pens, fingernail clippers, and a pair of eyeglasses with lenses as thick as Coke bottles. Just for fun, I got the gun in my grip, and turned toward the mirrored dresser to check myself out. Then I affected the classic FBI Weaver stance, and inwardly pronounced myself both menacing and hot.

Dainty Prescott: crack shot.

Fun over, I put the gun back and documented the contents of the drawer with my camera phone. Then I went to Paislee's side of the bed and photographed the contents of her night stand: travel maps, monogrammed stationery, an expensive French pen with a set of unopened replacement ink cartridges, a Bible—

Bible?

That threw me a curve. Once I discovered she cheated on her husband with my boyfriend, I never thought of Paislee Pfeiffer as anything other than a Jezebel home-wrecker and floozy. I picked up the Bible, flipped a couple of pages, and saw from the inscription in the front that it'd been a gift from the church to commemorate her baptism. Then I clasped it by its spine, flipped it over, and fanned through the leaves in an effort to find any small pieces of paper sandwiched between pages.

A small notebook dropped to the floor. I picked it up and eyed it with cold scrutiny. It took several seconds to identify what I held in my hands—*Paislee's little black book.*

And it contained a list of her playmates—men's names and phone numbers. And she'd rated them with stars the way men rated women in similar little black books. She'd logged in dates, times, motels and hotels, residential addresses, and more. And let's face it—Paislee Pfeiffer'd been a busy lady.

I'd just clicked the first photograph of the first page of the playbook, when I hunched over in concentration, zeroed in on the second shot, and waited for the image-finder to focus. But the click I heard didn't come from my thumb pressing the button on my camera phone.

Primal instinct hauled me up short. What was that noise?

The dormant alarm went off.

Not the high-pitched warning whine that activated when I first entered the house through the front door, but, rather, a molar-grinding, goblin-shrieking, ten-decibels-'til-deafness, bleating that echoed throughout the Pfeiffer's house.

My heart leapt to its throat. Experiencing a kind of delayed reaction, the sudden onslaught of noise had plunged me so deep in the throes of denial that, for a second, I stood, thunderstruck, and thought my ears played a trick on me. Then the cogs in my brain got a fresh shot of WD-40, and the slow-motion feeling disappeared in an instant.

The muscles along my neck tensed until I almost blacked out from the shock. Then I experienced a gut-cramping moment. The alarm fell deathly silent, with only the hang time from its shrill left to linger in the air.

I flinched at the sound of a voice.

It took all of ten seconds for my heart to jump-start itself, and my head to realize someone had entered the house—make that *two someones*—and my body to thaw out and get moving.

Voices filtered up from downstairs, a male and a female. I didn't recognize the man's, except to say that it wasn't Gordon's. My heart beat double-time as I caught snippets of their conversation.

"Who's here?" the unknown male shouted with a terrible intensity.

He instructed the female to wait by the front door while he searched the house for intruders. The air around me went ice cold. I slipped into panic mode.

Survivor instinct made me silence the ringtone on my phone.

Trapped like an animal, my only way out seemed to be through a second-story window, where I could drop into the backyard with the Beauceron. Because, I'm *Dainty Prescott, Super-Hero,* with super-powers like rubber ankles, and the ability to heal bones quickly, and that's just how I roll, right?

Well, *pardonez moi*, but I'd received bite marks in the leg of my Camoes, and fang marks in the spongy heel of the boots I wore the last time I tried to slip past this hell hound. I opened the window and was treated to a view of Czar licking his privates.

I found myself locked in an internal struggle, and could almost feel my personality split.

I should just go downstairs and make my presence known.

Are you crazy? You don't even know who these people are.

I could just explain why I'm here, show them the key, and ask what they're doing.

Yes, and they could be burglars who groove your head with a tire iron.

All out of choices, I pulled off the Battenburg lace coverlet, and knotted one corner around the footboard to anchor it in place. I'd done something similar at Hotel Malamuerte in Mexico—that wasn't its real name, but I thought *Hotel Flophouse* didn't lose anything in the translation since Ciudad Juárez's version of a five-star hotel was a step-and-a-half above uninhabitable. Down there, I'd made a plan and plotted an escape route in the event someone broke into Amanda's and my room—and when I'd finished tying the sheet off, I tossed the other end of it out the window.

I repeated the process in the Pfeiffer's bedroom. The only difference between the two situations was when I tried this at Hotel Malamuerte, people weren't breathing down my neck while I simultaneously prepared for my getaway. Well, not the only difference . . . I intended to go over the balcony in Mexico; I only intended to make it look like I went out the Pfeiffer's second-story window—especially when the next time I glanced out the window, I saw Czar grooming himself, pulling out tufts of fur like a cheap mattress coming apart.

Footfalls landed heavily on the stairs.

Part of me believed that making it look like I'd fled through the window would be enough to distract them. Intuition and desperation told me otherwise. In a last-ditch effort geared toward my self-preservation, I flung the bedside lamp out the opening, dropped to my knees, and scrambled beneath the bed as it crashed to the ground.

I watched in horror behind the king-sized bed skirt as a man's shoes came into view.

Outside, the dog went into a tailspin. The woman screamed that someone was in the backyard. As I watched the man's shoes recede toward the door, the cell phone vibrated in my hand. Whatever the caller had to say could wait.

Footfalls pounded the floor. The glass lanai slid along its tract and banged to a stop.

The woman yelled, "He's out here."

Out of the blue, I experienced a light-bulb moment—this house had a secondary exterior staircase that was virtually un-noticeable from the street because of the large pine tree concealing it—a spiral staircase I used at that very moment. Since I knew the amount of noise I'd make clomping down the stair treads, I hoisted one leg over the handrail and rode it to the ground. With the privacy fence between me and the interlopers, I took off down the road as the telephone rang inside Gordon's house.

I've had a bit of experience with security companies, and if you set off your house alarm, you're going to get a phone call from the service provider. First, they want to know if everything is all right. Next, they ask for your password. If you can't come up with the right one, the next thing you'll see is a cop in your face.

I had no plans to hang around long enough for the police to identify these people. And when I circled the block and came back around to the place I'd parked Gran's car—three doors down and across the street from the Pfeiffers—apparently the intruders didn't plan to wait around, either.

When I finally reached the sanctuary of Gran's Cadillac—believe me, I never expected to use the words "sanctuary" and "Gran's Cadillac" in the same sentence—I realized I still had the ringtone on my cell phone silenced as soon as I felt it purr.

Inside the car, after a couple of quick pulls, my latex gloves came off with a snap. I crushed them into my pocket, unmuted the wireless, checked the display screen, and saw that two texts and two voicemails had come in. I checked the one from Teensy first. She'd texted to inform me she's not speaking to me at the moment. I gathered, from the gist of the message, that she consulted a self-styled psychic who told her our relationship is surrounded by bad mojo brought on by my dark aura, and to stay away from me for the next few weeks. I'm not sure whether to hug her for keeping her distance, or slap her for being a complete *goob*.

The other text came in from an unknown number. As I sat behind the wheel, waiting to see if the cops would show up at Gordon's house, I sent a return text asking who I was communicating with. By way of an answer, I got a list of everywhere I'd been over the past two days. I fought off blind panic and only talked myself down off the stalker-ledge because I'm a professional, and because my boss was counting on me to get the job done.

I'd planned to wait to see if the police responded to the alarm. This would tell me one of two things: If law enforcement responded, then the people who showed up at the Pfeiffer house didn't belong there because they obviously didn't know the password; but if cops didn't respond to the alarm call, then whoever entered that house knew the alarm code and the password. Either way, I should really think about getting an organ donor card.

Finally, I checked the new phone message, only to hear from

a screaming-Mimi who accused me of sleeping with her husband, and threatened to send her people to take care of me. I contemplated that this had something to do with bludgeoning me into a blonde smear. I'd never heard of her husband. Then I listened to the second call telling me to disregard, that she'd dialed the wrong number.

After waiting fifteen minutes, I concluded that the police hadn't been called by the alarm company, and decided it was safe to leave. No way would I return to that house to get Paislee's little black book without Mr. Pfeiffer, even though I sensed those people were long gone. And yet, I wanted my job at the station back.

Seated behind the wheel, I gave myself a pep talk to screw up my courage: All I'd have to do is put on my gloves, go back in, turn off the alarm, run upstairs, and retrieve the book. Once I turned it over to Gordon and explained the heroic measures necessary to retrieve it, then he'd have to give me my job back, right?

Plus, there was cheesecake in the refrigerator, and maybe strawberry wasn't my favorite after all. Blueberry? I could use a slice of blueberry heaven.

I fired up the engine and pulled forward until I rolled up even with Gordon's house. Every second counted. Everything went according to my plan until I reached the top of the stairs. Every hair on my arms stood straight up. The window had been closed, and the bed covers had been piled on the bed. The drawer to the night stand had also been closed. When I opened it, pulled out the Bible, turned it over, and fanned out the pages, the little black book was gone.

My pulse thudded in my throat.

Had they taken it? Or in my haste to divert their attention, had I dropped it, or taken it under the bed with me?

I got on my knees and dropped down on all fours. Lifted the

bed skirt and stuck my head under the bed. The carpet was clear of debris, and I positioned myself to get up. But as I pulled my head out from under the bed, I glimpsed a shadow that stopped me in my tracks.

My heartbeat shifted into overdrive. I stayed perfectly still, trying to detect other sounds over the force of my own breathing. The air-conditioner compressor kicked on and a whoosh of air washed over the space above me. I slowly rose on all fours until my head came even with the top of the mattress.

"*Police, freeze.* Don't move."

The command struck like a harpoon to the brain. A hard-looking man in a black Fort Worth police uniform pointed his gun at me.

"Don't shoot, I'm unarmed." My voice went ultrasonic. I drew my hands up over my eyes. Excuses flowed out in a hyperventilating rush. "It's not what you think; I have permission to be here." But the latex gloves on my hands suggested otherwise, and it didn't take long for him to string a scenario together.

"Stay on your knees." He moved around the foot of the bed. Anger pinched the corners of his mouth.

Two things dawned on me: first, that he'd trundled up the spiral staircase without me hearing, and entered through the door I'd left unlocked; second, that I was in deep kimchee and might not be able to talk my way out of this. Outside, the dog tuned up and turned into the town crier, so I figured the officer had backup, and that his partner had tried to enter through the gate.

I had to get Gordon on the phone so he could vouch for me, but the gun barrel looked like a huge cannon, and I didn't even want to flinch—never mind pull out my cell phone.

"Put your hands on top of your head and thread your fingers together."

He hooked one handcuff on my wrist and ratcheted it on

tight, and then did the other one. His fingers dug into my arm, painfully, as he hoisted me up onto my feet.

"You're her, aren't you?" he said in all his sarcastic superiority.

I figured he must've recognized me from the news, but I still had to ask, "Her, who?" Because for all I knew, he could be my stalker, and that telephone text that'd come in earlier with the blocked phone number could've originated from one of the private lines down at the PD.

And the text recounted everything I'd been doing for the past two days, and let's face it—here he was, Officer Johnny-on-the-spot.

"You're the *Cat Burglar of Monticello.*" He gave an almost imperceptible nod.

"*What?*" I shrieked the word. I knew Monticello by heart. It was a ritzy area next to the even ritzier neighborhood of Rivercrest, where I'd grown up.

"You're her. The cat burglar who enters wealthy people's houses and steals their jewels." He stared at me with a degree of censure. "Well, sticky-fingers, you're under arrest. Guess you got tripped up this time, didn't you? You work for the alarm company? Is that how you got the code? But you didn't have the password, didja now?" He kept nodding as he said this as if by doing so, capturing me would secure his nomination for Officer of the Year.

Heavy footfalls trundled up the exterior staircase. He yelled, "In here, Bill, I've got her in custody."

"I'm not the cat girl—cat burglar—whatever. I've never broken into a house in my life except for my own . . ." Then it dawned on me why attorneys tell their clients to lawyer up. Rather than explain the time I broke the window on the back door of my family's Rivercrest mansion, when I went inside to get Teensy's hidden stash of money so I could fly down to

Mexico and bring her home after her harrowing ordeal—with her permission I might add—I stopped explaining.

Still, he called in to the dispatcher on his handheld radio, and stated that he'd arrested the "Cat Burglar of Monticello." I didn't realize the significance of this transmission until his partner locked the upstairs door, toggled the deadbolt, and marched me down the primary staircase and out the front door as two additional officers filed inside to have a look around. That's the moment I completely lost it. One of the competing TV station's ENG vehicles, or electronic news-gathering vans, had probably heard this over the police scanner, and parked across the street from Gordon's house. A reporter bailed out with his photographer in tow and started shooting video.

Mortified, I turned my head away from the camera.

The yard swam in front of me. I'd been running on an adrenaline high, and now that it wore off, pain set in where the officer had gripped my arm. My damp hair shellacked itself against my neck and face. After what I'd been through the past three months, I felt immune to indignity. But nothing compared to the shame this so-called arrest would bring on my family.

"Please take me back into the house. I can explain, and we can get my boss on the telephone—"

I didn't recall the rest of that conversation, only that whatever I'd said, nobody believed anyway.

Desperate not to be trotted out in front of reporters from our rival station, I didn't waste the opportunity to bargain, and invoked the name of Jim Bruckman. "I'm his girlfriend. Please. Please call him. Then we can call my boss."

"Who's your boss?" asked my arresting officer.

"Gordon Pfeiffer. He's the station manager at WBFD-TV. If you'll just reach into my pocket, I have a key to the front door." My pleas fell on deaf ears. These officers all wore the same blank, scary expressions on their faces. Terrified, I burst into tears. "Please. Call Jim Bruckman. He'll tell you."

CHAPTER SEVENTEEN

Nobody listened. No one cared what I had to say.

From the moment Officer Hot Dog slapped the 'cuffs on, I was treated like a common criminal, and paraded across the yard to the patrol car for all of the gawking neighbors to see. I'd never had any sympathy for people who tried to hide their faces from TV cameras when they were arrested for their crimes. But I hadn't done anything, and let's face it, I'm not just anybody. I'm Dainty Prescott; and if I couldn't be considered innocent until proven guilty, I could still hope I looked as good as when I broadcasted the news. Then a gut-wrenching thought came over me. Gordon had three zero-tolerance rules, and his voice echoed in my ears:

"The cardinal rule of journalism is to cover the news; you don't become part of it. Never become part of the story. It's the quickest way out the door.

"Don't break the law. Don't do anything that'll end up in a body cavity search.

"And, get everything pre-approved. I'm not paying off any law-suits."

I hadn't just become part of the story, I *was* the story. And to make matters worse, the competition had scooped us.

The officers opened the back door to the patrol car's caged area, and once again, I experienced a moment of déjà vu. The one and only time I traveled in the caged area of a squad car, I curled up like a cocktail shrimp and sank against the door with my drippy nose and hot breath fogging the window while Bruckman drove me downtown to see a judge because I refused to sign his little traffic citation. I didn't like the ride back then, and I didn't expect to like it now.

"I get carsick if I ride in the back," I pleaded.

Their response came in the form of an authoritative clunk of a door slamming shut. Once again, I found myself inhaling other people's rancid puke and urine, and figured I'd add mine soon enough.

Beyond the window glass, the reporter interviewed my arresting officer. As soon as the reporter's eyes shifted to me, I turned my face away from the camera. Being as this wasn't my first rodeo with patrol car cages and being handcuffed behind my back, I mentally offered thanks to Saint Genesius. The Prescotts aren't Catholic; I learned about the patron saint of dance from years of having studied ballet. After all those years of gymnastics, tap, and ballet, it didn't take long to contort my cuffed hands beneath my derrière and wriggle them out in front of me.

I dug for my cell phone, where I kept the number to Gordon's wireless on speed dial. When it cycled into voicemail, I said, "It's Dainty. Meet me down at the police station. Someone broke into your house." Next, I called the TV station. Unfortunately, I got Rochelle on the line.

Rochelle undergoes a constant inner struggle between good and evil. She always answers the telephone with a chipper *WBFD, may I help you?* but doesn't really mean it. Her modus operandi is to disconnect callers, and I expected her to do it to me as she's done in the past. I'd seen her in operation hundreds of times, mostly when the pace picked up around the station, and all the phone lines glowed yellow. She'd answer with put-on sweetness, then disconnect the caller and put the same line on *hold*.

She answered on the first ring, and I blurted out who it was before she finished announcing the station's call letters in her disingenuous greeting.

"Rochelle, for the love of God, I need help. It's me—Dainty."

"Dainty who?"

I could almost hear her thoughts: *My, my, what's that Dainty Prescott up to now?*

"Rochelle, please." I drawled out her name until it sounded like a squeaky hinge. "It's Dainty Prescott. Please—I need to speak to Gordon."

She used her lilting public relations voice, but her real message said, *Up your leg.* "Mr. Pfeiffer isn't available to take your call at the moment. May I give him a message?"

"Rochelle—I'm begging you. I was working on this Paislee thing, and someone broke into his house." I looked out the window of the patrol car and noticed the officer and reporter wrapping things up. "If he's not there, give me Byron's number."

"Nobody gets Byron's number. And I didn't say Gordon wasn't here. I said he isn't available to take your call," she said, unassailably indifferent.

"I'll give you my pearl bracelet."

"Already have one."

"Pearl necklace."

"No."

"Pearl ring." I thought quickly. "Wax your car. Complete detailing."

"Nope."

"Clean your house for free." Irritation turned to desperation. The other officers had cleared out of the house, when the arresting officer took a detour, walked up to Gordon's front porch, and stuck a card between the door and molding before heading back to the cruiser.

"How many times?"

"Once."

177

"Five." Rochelle drove a hard bargain.

"Three."

"Windows, too?" When I knuckled under, she said, "One moment please; I'll put you through."

The transfer clicked over and Gordon came on the line about the same time the policeman had another short conversation with the reporter before walking away for good.

"Gordon, it's Dainty Prescott. Someone broke in while I was at your house. I found something but I had to leave it behind. When I went back, the cops came and arrested me. They're taking me to jail. I need your help."

"Meet you there in a half hour."

"Come now," I said, panic-stricken, and not wanting to spend one more second than necessary at the FWPD bed-and-breakfast. "One of the rival stations heard the call over the scanner and shot video of me being taken into custody. If you can't get them to pull the video—"

The officer opened the driver's door.

"—my arrest will air on their Six-and-Ten." My voice dissolved to a whisper. "They think I'm the Cat Burglar of Monticello."

When we arrived at the police station, Officer YoYo, who'd undergone at least three mood swings during our short time together, paraded me through the building like he'd captured me off the "Ten Most Wanted" posters. Anyone bothering to look my way gave me empty, emotionless stares. Inoculated against embarrassment, I realized my humiliating experience wasn't even a fraction of a semicolon in the history of the Fort Worth Police Department.

I asked, once again, to see Bruckman. When I was told no, once again, I wished for divine intervention so that the man I loved would come sauntering out of his office. But once I was actually seated in the interrogation room—they could put their own spin on it and call it an interview room all they wanted, but let's face it, the only thing lacking to complete this interrogation was a single, overhead, incandescent light bulb and a billy club—it was clear that Bruckman was not going to appear. When the investigating officer turned me over to the custody of the detective assigned to the Monticello cat burglar's case, my life took a distinct turn.

"I'm Detective Stanton, and I'll be going over the events that occurred earlier today—would you like something to drink?"

There wasn't enough water in this entire building to slake my thirst, but I wasn't about to fall for this man's offer. I'd seen my share of forensics programs on the late-night channel where thugs that refused to give up their DNA were then invited to have a beverage "on the house," only to find later that as soon as the can went into the trash, it was ferried to the lab for DNA testing. I did a panicky review of my options because such a trick could also bring my freedom.

He said, "Why are you making those whimpering sounds?"

"I'm not your cat burglar. I'm not a burglar at all."

"No?" His mouth tipped at the corners. "Then who are you?"

Thoughts vibrated off the top of my head. "I'm Jim Bruckman's girlfriend, and if you'd just get him in here, I can explain this entire misunderstanding from start to finish."

His face creased into a broad smile. "That so?"

Before I could explain that I had permission to be in Gordon's house, the door swung open and Jim Bruckman entered the room. I sucked air. Then Gordon followed him in.

"Get your shit and let's get out of here," Gordon said.

Detective Stanton looked surprised.

Bruckman said, "It's true what she said—she's no cat burglar. This is her boss, Gordon Pfeiffer. He asked her to check on his house." He cut his eyes to me, and said, "You have a house key?"

"In my pocket."

"May I?" he asked Detective Stanton, and after a curt nod of approval, Bruckman unlocked my handcuffs, and I fished in my pocket for Gordon's house key.

A few more minutes, and the so-called interview was over. After I was told that I was free to go, I grabbed Gordon's sleeve.

"Can you stop that video from airing?"

"I put in a phone call. We'll just have to see. Need a ride?"

"I'll drive her back." The voice came from behind and to my right.

Bruckman.

And that's how I came to be in Jim Bruckman's office, seated in front of his desk, trying to keep from curling my fingers into the front of his shirt and hauling him closer. Even better, the hungry look in his eyes told me he felt the same way.

"Got all your stuff?" he said.

I nodded.

"Where's your car?"

"Back at Gordon's house. Actually, it's Gran's car."

Bruckman hooted. "You're no burglar, and you never will be. C'mon, let's go."

As soon as he offered me his hand, I launched out of the chair and threw my arms around him. But when I tilted my face up to his for a kiss, his fingers dug into my arms enough to make me hunch involuntarily, and he pushed me away.

"Jimbo, are you—?"

My eyelids fluttered in astonishment. While my vision was most of the time cast to the floor, and I never actually stared her right in the face, I recognized the problem immediately. The woman poking her head through the door in time to cheat me out of Jim Bruckman's kiss looked a whole lot like the ex-girlfriend, turned friend, turned current girlfriend.

Now that my reputation as the Cat Burglar of Monticello had unmasked me as Dainty Prescott, substitute news anchor, Bruckman didn't seem to have a problem with returning me to the scene of the pseudo-crime.

We were seated in Bruckman's unmarked patrol car before either of us spoke again. I'd been reviewing the awkward situation in my head, recalling how pretty my competition was with her long brown hair and crystal blue doe eyes. I reminded myself of the crestfallen look on her face when she caught Bruckman and me in a tight embrace; of being torn between wanting to hold him tighter so she'd know I wouldn't give up that easily, while simultaneously wanting to ask her to reveal her eyeliner technique so I could copy the way she made her dark fringe of lashes enhance the wideness of her eyes.

"Who is she to you?" I asked, with a pout of defensiveness.

"It's complicated, Dainty." He slid me a sideways glance. "We had an understanding about you gallivanting off to Mexico. You left, and I moved on."

A regrettable act that keeps creeping back to me late at night.

When he ticked off Babette's virtues, I desperately tried to muster enough energy to call a halt to these disclosures. Instead, I choked on my own spit and fell into a coughing fit.

"You don't have to convince me of her worthiness to date you." My emotions were still raw with the shock of being confronted with Bruckman's feelings for her, and I estimated my bottom lip protruded a good two inches. "Sounds more like you're trying to convince yourself." My words caught him off guard.

"I can't say I don't occasionally slip up and mention you in conversation."

My skin tingled. "Are you saying there's no chance for us to get back together?"

He gave me a one-shouldered shrug. If he intended to discourage me, it had the opposite effect since I didn't get an outright *No*. Until then, all was fair in love and war.

For the first time all day, I leaned against my seat back, calm as a three-toed sloth, opting for the damsel-in-distress approach—only, in my case, it was real. I told him about the letters that'd been sent to the station, and described how they'd escalated from kudos to threats. I'd been carrying them around in my car, along with the shoebox filled with doll parts, and I asked if he'd go over them with me and see whether or not it was high-time to file a police report.

As we rolled up to Gordon's house, I asked Bruckman if he'd wait while I got the letters from the car, so we could take them inside the house and go over them.

Bruckman laughed without humor. "Really, Dainty? You drove here in your grandmother's car to pull a caper, and parked in front of the house? Some cat burglar you are."

"I did not park in front of the house."

He gave me one of those skeptical, raised-eyebrow, *You must be in denial because your car's in front of the house* looks, which prompted me to explain that I'd parked three doors down when pulling my caper.

After I keyed us in through the front door, I flipped on the living room light. The chandelier brightened the room and got the attention of the dog. He bounded over to the lanai and tried to peer inside, smearing his leather doggie snout against the glass, and leaving traces of oily nose prints and shoestring drool all over the door, as he tried to see if we belonged there. I realized this wouldn't work, and suggested we move to the formal dining room, where our presence wouldn't agitate the dog.

Bruckman said, "You know if you're handling those letters,

you're just going to get more fingerprints on them."

"Way ahead of you." I pulled them out of the accordion file I'd been carrying them around in, and showed him that I'd separated each letter from its envelope, stored each one in its own plastic sleeve, and arranged them in chronological order according to postmark date.

"What about the box? You shouldn't be handling that, either."

I'd been carrying the box around in a brown paper sack, but I reached in my pocket, pulled out my latex gloves, and dangled them in front of him.

"You may not be the Cat Burglar of Monticello . . . more like cat burglar in training . . . but I'll be the first to admit you're starting to think like a real detective."

While I sat in silence and gazed into our happy memories, he slid on the gloves and reviewed each item with care. "Did you photograph these?"

"Should I have?"

"The first thing we do is photograph everything. Then we cut the glued area on the envelope flap and send it to the lab to process for DNA."

"How long does that take?"

"Longer than you probably have."

My heart stalled. I sensed I'd gotten myself into a bad situation, but now, Jim Bruckman, ace detective, had confirmed it. It occurred to me that, if I was dealing with a ticking time bomb, I didn't want to waste a single moment of my life without the man sitting next to me. After he gathered up the evidence and returned it to the file, we got up from the table, moved out of the fading light, and headed toward the door. We reached for the handle at the same time. His hand covered mine, launching a sexual rocket through my entire body. When he made no effort to move it, I threw myself at him.

I really can't explain what happened next, except to point out that I at least had the common decency to remake the downstairs guest bedroom with fresh sheets. But afterward, in a tangle of hair, while I deposited the rumpled sheets in the laundry hamper, I realized how much our spontaneous tryst had turned into an awkward moment for Bruckman, too.

"I'll fill out the report for you, but I'm turning it over to another detective. It'd be a conflict of interest for me to work this case . . ." I moved in close and took his hand while he continued to explain how he'd make copies for himself so he could still keep his thumb on the pulse of the investigation.

At this point, it didn't matter. My whole life narrowed into one single focal point. I knew, without a doubt, that my relationship with Bruckman was more than just one set of glands calling out to another. I loved this man. And if I made it through this stalker nightmare, I intended to marry him.

CHAPTER EIGHTEEN

After I reset the alarm, locked up, and left Gordon's house, I decided to drive back to Gran's house so I could shower and change clothes before returning to the FWPD to see how far Bruckman had gotten with the "Tim" letters. I wanted to look my best in the scant hope he'd want me back as his girlfriend. I had an uphill battle, I knew, because I'd seen his old girlfriend and had my face rubbed in her beauty. And even though I'm pretty, too, apparently Bruckman can't overlook my willful streak, and the loyalty I have for my family that he interprets as stubbornness, no matter how misplaced that loyalty was with Teensy.

When I wheeled the turquoise tornado onto Gran's street, I slowed enough for the electronic sensor on the big iron gate to read the proximity signal, or air waves, or whatever it's called and however it works. I drove slowly. The gate yawned open and then closed as soon as I cleared it. I rolled down the red brick driveway, and wound around to the back of the house. The pavilion next to the swimming pool where Teensy'd been parking her car was empty, so my sister's car was probably still at the dealership getting the dents banged out; but Amanda's was parked behind the carriage house. This was only the second time I'd seen this vehicle; it had been too dark to pay much attention to it before dawn this morning. But now I could see why Gran made Amanda park it on the far side of the carriage house, where none of the people in neighboring estates had to look at it.

The car, a Chevy Vega, circa seventies, had once been painted dog-vomit beige as evidenced by the paint directly behind the front bumper. Now it only had primer on its shell, as if someone had restoration in mind before giving up on it. When I pulled Gran's car beneath the pavilion, Amanda was standing beside her vehicle. I walked over and said hello about the same time I noticed the flat tire. According to Amanda, sometime between the time she purchased the car the day before, and left Crazy Gianni's for her first run of the day, she'd picked up a nail.

Long story short, Amanda said Teensy'd called Crazy Gianni's Pizza and Pasta, which is one of those places that offers "thirty-minute pizza" or it's free, and is located in a strip center about a mile from Gran's. In an effort to throw a little business Amanda's way, Teensy placed an order; now that Amanda'd delivered that order, she had one delivery left to complete.

That's when she asked me to drive her to the last customer's house so she could make the final pizza delivery.

"I have things to do," I said sullenly, and then ticked them off, *One, two, three*. "Shower and change clothes. Check on a report. Return to the TV station. And there's more. I have a job, you know."

"Come on, diva. I don't want to lose out on my tip money."

"That's the part you're worried about?" Then it dawned on Amanda that the *thirty-minutes-or-free* pizza idea was a super-great deal for the person who stood to get the free pizza, except that someone had to pay Crazy Gianni for it—which meant Amanda. Her head almost rolled off her neck in disappointment. Dark eyes pinned me. No matter how hard I tried to ignore her, Amanda's strong presence stayed with me like a stubborn foot fungus, or a bad case of herpes. *I can only assume.*

When I could no longer stand the pinched, accusatory expression, I caved. "I'll help you out this one time, as long as you never ask me again."

Amanda grabbed six pizzas, stacked them in the back seat of Gran's car, and climbed into the passenger seat. She read the address off the sales ticket on the side of the insulated plastic sleeve that covered the cardboard boxes, and while I generally knew the area, when we turned onto the proper street and I started counting down the block numbers, property values dropped at an alarming rate. In the game of urban survival, this place topped the *Don't go there* category.

I curbed the car in front of an apartment complex.

"Are you kidding me? We're in the ghetto. You made me drive you to the ghetto."

Amanda ignored the rant. "Come on, diva, help me carry these in. We'll get the money and get the hell out."

Grudgingly, I grabbed three boxes while Amanda took the other three. The entire apartment complex had been sealed off by a ten-foot-tall privacy fence, so we walked the perimeter until we found a gate.

I read the small metal sign: *No one under eighteen admitted.* "What's this? An apartment complex for swingers?" Said nastily.

"What it *is*, is a hundred and twenty dollars plus tax for the pizzas, and probably thirty bucks for me in delivery charges and tips. So zip it and let's just get it done."

Amanda pressed what appeared to be a standard doorbell button, and when a voice came over the intercom telling us to state our business, Amanda announced, "Pizza delivery."

A buzzer went off. The lock audibly disconnected, and we opened the gate and walked inside.

The first thing I noticed in the center of the courtyard was the excessive ratio of naked men to naked women hanging out by the swimming pool. Suddenly, in a universe of mysteries, the phrase "every swingin' dick" made perfect sense. Only then did I realize we were delivering pizzas to a nudist colony.

I kept my eyes firmly averted and looked around for the office. Then a blustery old man with incredible shrinking gonads yelled, "Nobody comes in here with clothes on."

I thought he was making a joke until he started our way.

"Amanda, you'd better fix this." Then I remembered I had a brand-new taser in my purse, and my anxiety lifted.

"Over here."

We glanced in the general vicinity of the resounding tenor and saw a nude male beckoning us toward a corner apartment with a small, rectangular placard on the door. I assumed this was the office. Despite my reluctance to be in such a place, I forged through. *Head down, keep walking.* We delivered the pizzas, Amanda got her money, and we headed back to Gran's house.

"I have an idea." Back inside the car, Amanda counted out the pizza money, plus forty-three dollars in delivery and tips. She said, "It's been awhile since we did anything together. Let's go back to Crazy Gianni's, I'll turn in the money, and we'll see if there are more deliveries."

"Great idea," I said, but I made sure the expression on my face said *Absolutely not.* "Has it occurred to you that every time we do anything together, somebody ends up getting hurt—and by *somebody* I mean me?"

"Come on, diva. I need the money. El Paso County Sheriff's Office is going to lock me up."

I owed Amanda my life—well, mine and my ungrateful sister's—so I found myself contemplating helping out with a few more deliveries. Thank goodness my phone rang.

Since I hoped this had something to do with me needing to be anywhere but here with Amanda, I thumbed on the cell phone without looking at the number.

The voice at the other end of the airwaves was robotic and taunting and muffled, as if the person had used a towel over the mouthpiece to further disguise his identity. "You didn't follow instructions. I warned you of consequences. You're a very willful girl. Don't let it happen again. This is your last warning."

The phone went dead in my hand.

I looked over at Amanda, who regarded me with concern. "I can't. I have to take care of a big mess."

My mind raced with possibilities. Bruckman had called me willful. Had used that exact term to explain why we couldn't be together. I felt like I was going crazy for having suspected him, even for a few seconds, but my mind shifted into "high alert" mode, and I wondered: *Is this the day the person who wrote the crazy letters will attack me?*

When I walked into Gran's house, I found her in the front parlor talking to a couple of dangerous looking men who appeared to be in their forties. Activity faltered when I entered. I knew they were detectives even before each stood and extended a hand for her to shake, causing the fabric on their jackets to shift and expose their gold badges. Neither seemed particularly hostile, but I'd been around Bruckman long enough to know that the nicest detective down at the FWPD also had the highest number of confessions, and the best clearance rate.

So, lesson learned: There's a reason why good cop, bad cop works.

Paused in the rotunda, with my mouth gaping, I clung to the banister and felt my face go through a series of unwelcome contortions. They were either here about the man Gran shot, or following up after CPS on that ugly indecent exposure complaint, or they'd come to arrest me for unpaid, photo-enforced, red light tickets. Carnal panic went through my stomach. I simply could *not* be carted off to jail twice in one day. Frozen in place, I ran through a mental checklist of my recent crimes while I waited to see which one of us miscreants they planned to haul down to the hoosegow.

My eyes shifted to Amanda. Judging by her sick expression, we shared a simultaneous thought: me, for the tickets; her, for that little restitution problem that she'd neglected to take care of.

Gran led them out of the parlor, to the front door. "Well, of course I feel so silly now, for calling in about the neighbor across the street. But she'd been staring at me for three straight days and I thought she had it in for me. How was I to know she wasn't alive?"

When she saw me standing next to the staircase with a white-knuckled grip on the banister, she said, "Oh, Dainty, you're home," and made introductions. "Gentlemen, this is my grand-daughter, the television star."

"Broadcast journalist." My voice cracked. I felt as if I were behind the eight ball, and made no move to shake hands. When your arm's extended, it's easy to get spun around and hand-cuffed. I should know. I'm practically an expert on the matter. "I read the news for WBFD-TV."

One of them made idle chit-chat about the rival TV stations in the Metroplex. He said, "I always watch Channel Fifteen for the weather. It's supposed to be unseasonably hot tomorrow. They said to get out between six and ten in the morning if you need to do any running around."

"That's why I watch WBFD. They know their audience and would never dream of saying get up by ten A.M.," I said.

Neither made a move to peel my fingers off the mahogany railing. Since I'd already learned my lesson about invoking my right to counsel, I considered remaining mute. While I tried to psyche myself up for an overnight in jail, one of them asked for my autograph, and seemed confused by my speechlessness.

Then Gran placed her fingertips on my arm. "Wonderful news—remember the man I shot the other night?"

Again, I found it ironic that phrases like "wonderful news" and "the man I shot" could be successfully paired together in the same sentence.

My eyes widened. We'd come this far without having to talk to the Grand Jury, so I telepathically signaled her to *Put a sock in it.* But did she? No, she did not. My grandmother spilled her guts.

"These nice men came to see me about that shooting on Harry Hines the night I picked you up from Love Field." I tried to head her off at the pass by sending her eye-encrypted messages, and grotesque facial contortions, but her mouth just continued to run like an old, blue-haired Chatty Cathy doll without the string coming out of her neck. "Turns out he's the serial rapist they've been looking for. Doesn't that make the most delightful story?"

For a second, the room blurred. "I think we need to beef up our security system." I mentioned this while feverishly contemplating my fate.

"Don't mind her," Amanda came to my defense. "Her midlife crisis has started early. She wants to set up cameras around the house, barricade the doors, black out all the windows, and prepare bug-out bags for everybody here in case we suddenly have to pick up and leave. I wouldn't be surprised if she's been buffing up on gun culture, germ warfare, militia mentality, and survivalist conspiracy theory bullshit."

Still unable to release my grip on the railing, and, not completely satisfied that this wasn't a cop trick, I gave Amanda a blank stare for goading the police.

But the cops told Amanda I had a good point. Which only made me feel worse now that I had acquired a stalker.

Chapter Nineteen

On Wednesdays, Gordon holds weekly briefings where the news team assembles in the conference room to bat around ideas for Gordon to either accept or veto. But because a couple of people were going to be out of the office, midweek, he moved the regular nine o'clock Wednesday meeting to two o'clock Monday afternoon.

When I arrived at the station, the man living behind the wall who likes to take his underwear off the clotheseline wearing nothing but his sandals was outdoors, gathering his laundry to bring it inside. I felt blessed to have arrived at the exact same time his arms were so full of air-dried clothes that they hung down over his private parts. Then he saw me walking across the parking lot and dropped the bundle to wave, reminding me, once again, why there's a wall to keep them away from us.

This particular Monday afternoon meeting was standing room only. In a room full of adults and only a handful of babies, the babies will always engage with each other instead of the adults. And for this reason, I scanned the room, looking for my own kind—people my age with entry-level jobs, or interns, like I used to be. The two new female interns from Southern Methodist University stood so close to each other they appeared to be velcroed together. But the male SMU intern had apparently disenfranchised himself from the coeds, and stood near Steve Lennox, who was supposed to co-anchor the noon broadcast with Aspen Wicklow. Then I remembered there were actually four interns, and recalled Teensy telling me how last week, after the meeting, Gordon called one of them into his office and reprimanded her for constantly texting her friends while on the job. When she did it again, Gordon fired her via text. Now that I figured out it was the blonde, let's just say the music stopped, and she didn't have a chair.

I tried to skirt the SMU idiot, er, intern, whose note suggested I shower, but she stepped in my path. In her soft Southern drawl, she whispered conspiratorially. "Just so you know, I'm on to you. You were trying to intimidate me, weren't you?"

Intimidate her?— I couldn't remember ever talking to her. Squinting in confusion, I shook my head.

In a soft, low voice, she admonished me. "Mr. Pfeiffer's not scary. He's just a big ol' bear."

"Yeah. *Bipolar bear.*" As soon as I said it I got an involuntary giggle of *What the hellness.* Probably because I'd just diagnosed my boss with a mental illness, but if you really studied these people like Jane Goodall in *Gorillas in the Mist* you'd know I was right. Tig Welder's the narscissist; Rochelle has multiple personalities; Misty Knight's schizophrenic; Steve Lennox is a borderline personality; Chopper Deke's a sex fiend; Gordon's bipolar—or maybe he's just stressed out because of all the big decisions he has to make on a daily basis, not to mention having a dead wife—and Stinger Baldwin's normal when compared to his mother, Rochelle Le Duc. But that's supposed to be a secret. That Rochelle's his mother, not that he's normal. Normal here, you stick out like a sore thumb.

The SMU intern accused me of trying to sidetrack her from cozying up to the boss. The only thing necessary to complete my impression of this stuck-up fashionista with less candlepower than the night janitor was a yapping bitch of a Yorkie that wore its hair exactly like hers.

"You didn't want me to shine up to him." Snooty-nosed, she radiated confidence. "You're afraid I'll get your little entry level job, aren't you?"

"Yeah. You got me. Busted."

With a look of *faux* contrition riding on my face, I moved along in search of a chair, without muttering the words that were hot-wired to my tongue: *By all means, shine up to him, you silly cow. He's been in a filthy mood for a month. When you come down off your high horse, I might even help you carry your little box of crap out to your sports car when you get the boot.*

At these staff meetings, the news anchors—or, "blow-dries," as Rochelle calls them—formed a separate clique. They always gossiped among themselves while the photographers tried to drum up interest from the interns, and the topic du jour at this particular gathering seemed to center around the dead body stashed in the break room, and whether it was or was not Gordon's wife.

As usual, Tig Welder sat, marinating in cloying cologne, at one end of the table, while Stinger Baldwin, his rival for stories, raises, and hot babes, sat at the opposite end of the table and shot Tig dirty looks. And I was so sleep deprived I thought I might be dead. Otherwise, why else would I take the empty seat next to Chopper Deke, listening to him comment on the three extra pounds I gained from drinking too much soda pop, just so I wouldn't have to stand through the entire meeting?

As I settled back in my chair, I took a hard look around the room. In my mind, everyone was a suspect until they weren't a suspect. It just wasn't right to take someone's life and turn it upside down. Then I decided I was paranoid. And then I decided stalkers win if you get paranoid.

Rumblings of Aspen Wicklow's whereabouts, and her fate, made the rounds until Gordon and Rochelle walked in, all put together and professional. Then everyone turned to hear what the boss had to say.

"Do we have meat?" Gordon asked of the room at large.

Before he got his answer, the door banged open and Teensy rushed in.

Well whaddaya know? Teensy Prescott has a pulse, is awake, and apparently didn't hit any jackpots at the Indian casino over the weekend, so I'm guessing she decided to amuse herself by making my life a living hell and showing up here.

She'd dressed like an undertaker's haunted hearse, with black eyeliner penciled on so thick it looked like a little toy car had burned rubber across her eyelids. Her fragrance smelled like casket pillows. I decided her new vampire-at-a-blood-bank look, which encouraged disapproving stares from my colleagues, must be a fad. Last week, Teensy was into Rastafarian hair and hats with feather plumes.

My sister singsonged, "Sorry. *Mea culpa.* My bad. Did I miss anything?"

Gordon torqued his jaw. Rochelle stiffened. Everyone else sat, bug-eyed, waiting to see what happened next.

Stinger Baldwin raised his hand. "We have meat, boss. It's called 'False Arrest.' "

Until now, I hadn't really noticed that Stinger, who's normally a fashion plate, looked like somebody tipped over a port-a-potty with him inside. Seems he'd been slammed against his car, thrown to the ground, and arrested for outstanding warrants from 1979. Stinger was born in 1983.

"I want to investigate the police." While Stinger laid out his interview idea for the upcoming "sweeps," Teensy passed a couple of my colleagues and air-kissed their cheeks with a *mwah, mwah* on her way to an empty seat.

My jaw dropped open at her brazenness. Seconds ticked by before I gradually became aware that I looked like a mouth-breather. I tightened my jaw until my bee-stung lips thinned into a thread. Teensy acted as if she'd called the meeting herself. It was enough to make me grind my molars. Then, to make matters worse, instead of standing with the low-level employees, she took the empty seat next to Misty Knight, our meteorologist—the empty seat where Aspen Wicklow always sat.

One by one, each member of the WBFD team shared what they were working on. When Misty's turn rolled around, she shrugged off her pole-axed expression and announced her plan to stop in at the county health clinic before they closed at the end of the day. That left several of us furrowing our brows, as in *Why's our meteorologist going to the county health clinic?* Gordon and I must've shared simultaneous thoughts because, while I remained quiet, he echoed my sentiments by asking why she picked the staff meeting to regale everyone with details of her personal life.

He reminded her that the station airs a Wednesday show called "Ask Lindsey," and suggested that maybe Misty should be taking this up with Lindsey—who also missed the meeting.

Then I wondered if Misty had contracted one of those childhood diseases from those elementary school kids who showed up on a recent field trip with their teacher to learn more about the weather. In retrospect, even that field trip seemed weird, because what'd those little kids need to know about the weather other than *Should I put on my coat?* or, *Should I not wear my gloves?* or, *Should our family get one of those SUVs with the performance radials and the wiper on the back windshield?* or, *Does Porsche make one of those? And, if so, how can I get one?* Then I remembered that Misty thought one of the brats had chicken pox, but it turned out to be measles. And that made me wonder if she was hatching a workers' compensation claim against the station for making her be around annoying school children.

Then Gordon wanted to know what this had to do with what Misty was working on.

She said, "I found out that no good, hockey playing, son-of-a-bitch was screwing around on me, so I'm going to get tested for HIV."

Teensy did a conspiratorial lean-in and patted Misty on the knee. "Think positive."

I noticed my colleagues watching me. They all shared similar facial expressions—awkward looks and scowls that I interpreted to mean, *Do something. She's* your *sister.*

What'd they expect me to do? Immobilize her with a death ray?

Then it was Teensy's turn. I knew she wasn't working on anything so I wasn't worried about what goofball craziness she might reveal to the group. But apparently, I should've been worried, because instead of passing her turn, my sister announced that she'd been thinking we ought to do a six-part series about how hard it was for working mothers to find decent child care—only from the babysitter's perspective.

I did a heavy eye roll about the same time Gordon said, "I think that's an excellent idea," and wanted an example.

A spooky sound effect popped out before I could squelch it.

While Teensy babbled, I flashed back to the conversation I had with my mother at the hospital when Teensy was born, revolving around my jealousy over the new baby, and losing my place as the center of attention. No matter how my mother tried to get me to adjust to the new baby and take on the big sister role, I wasn't having any of it, until she took me into her confidence:

"I think we should just throw this baby in the trash. What do you think, princess? Should we throw the baby in the trash and get us a new one? No? Oh, wait—did you want her?"

And then, *"It's a big job, Dainty, taking care of a new baby. Sure you're up to it?"*

"Uh-huh."

"Then it's settled. I'll give her to you and you can take care of her and love her and watch out for her. Won't that be wonderful? Here you go. Hold out your hands. She's your baby now."

And later, *"What'll you name your new baby, Dainty?"*

"Teensy. 'Cause she's so tiny."

Slapped into reality by the promise I'd made my mother, I mentally formulated the next entry for my journal:

Dear Diary,

If I could go back twenty-one years ago, to my two-year-old past self, I'd smack the fire out of her, and tell her that she does not need to watch out for her sister, and protect her all the live-long day. Holy freaking Geez. It will take you forever to get your damned job back. Serves you right. Signed: Your bloated, crying, begging, asshat, wannabe anchor self.

I came out of my trance in time to hear Teensy telling this roomful of talent, ". . . and so that's why my last employer thought I watched gay porn."

Rochelle cleared her throat menacingly.

Gordon, who'd had a chance to digest this idea, grumbled that while her point was fairly interesting and bore looking into, possibly by a mental health care professional, it wasn't relevant to the meeting. "Who's next?"

All eyes turned to me in a collective shift. Those who'd been nervously glancing at their watches now double-dog-dared me to open my mouth.

"Pass."

"Fine," Gordon said, "let's talk about Christmas." And then he all but insisted that we get into the holiday spirit by hanging cheap plastic, Chinese-made decorations and Christmas lights all around the station, and wearing stupid little red and green bells that'd been stitched onto wool felt bracelets. We'd barely gotten through Thanksgiving, and thrown that horrible open house, and now he expected everyone to jingle their bells. Holy freaking cow, none of us would be able to slip into the ladies room without calling attention to ourselves like a team of Clydesdales.

I didn't get it. I wanted to yell out to my co-workers, *Can somebody answer me this?* Gordon's wife ran around on him, he filed for divorce, and the dead wife rolled out of the freaking closet in the break room, and now he's the prime suspect on the cops' hit parade; and yet he's in the Christmas spirit. Me, I'm so run-down some mornings I can barely pour myself a glass of orange juice.

But not Teensy. Chipper, perky, Teensy came up with the best idea of all. And instead of keeping it to herself, she raised her hand, waved it around, and fidgeted in her chair like she had Tourette's, or developed Saint Vitus Dance. Gordon and Rochelle pretended to ignore her.

"I have a super-great idea," Teensy bubbled. "Dainty and I have this super-cool houseguest—"

I alerted like a drug dog and stopped tweeting about how lame this meeting had gotten.

"—and she's a pygmy. Yuh-huh." Her head bobbed like a float on a lure. "Really. A real, honest-to-goodness pygmy with a capital 'P.' We should get her up here and pay her to play like she's one of Santa's elves."

I shook my head and cleared away the idea of Amanda working at the station like a feather duster on a cobweb.

Did she just say "play like"? What is she—six?

"And then the cameramen—"

Photographers.

"—could film her—"

They shoot video.

"—passing out candy at the next open house."

Rochelle became the "heavy." She said, "And how do you

propose that we pay her?"

"Oh, that's not a problem," Teensy effervesced. Since everyone knew how tight funds were around here, the entire roomful of people looked at her as if a barbed tail had suddenly worked its way out of the seat of her black slacks. "You can pay her out of my salary."

In a voice tight with controlled fury, I said, "You're being paid?"

Teensy clapped a hand over her mouth. "Oops. My bad." She flashed Gordon and Rochelle a look of practiced innocence. "Was I not supposed to let anyone know you're paying me?"

My mind hearkened back to *Murder on the Orient Express*— a Hercule Poirot movie I'd seen a long time ago with my mother, wherein everyone on the train to London from Istanbul became a murder suspect. Well, sorry to say that I briefly considered passing out steak knives to everyone in attendance. But a person can only take so much, and that's why Texas has a "crime of passion" defense.

Back to the meeting.

I pulled out my cell phone and tried to zone out by typing out a tweet.

Finally, Traffic Monitor Joey's turn came. Joey had actually quit six weeks before when the brand of pants he wore couldn't stand up to the pucker-power it took to survive the midair shenanigans Chopper Deke pulled during the morning traffic report, just to hear him scream. But Joey quickly found that the job market was pretty tight for indolent folks wanting to be paid without actually having to work hard. He only stayed away a week before returning on his knees, begging Gordon for his job back.

All eyes moved to Joey in one collective shift. I hadn't expected the atmosphere to be charged with such hostility, but we'd grown sick of the meeting and sick of each other and nobody wanted anybody dragging things out any longer than necessary. So we bombarded him with sinister looks, and simultaneous telepathic messages to *Shut the hell up.*

Apparently our bad vibes landed like darts, because the traffic report guy answered "Pass"; but when Gordon asked if anybody had anything else they wanted to talk about, Traffic Monitor Joey piped up that his cat died. Rumblings of "I'm sorry" traveled throughout the room, proving that his co-workers weren't complete jerks. But many of them were still bitter that they had to fill in for Joey after he left, and fly around the Metroplex with their sphincters slammed shut because of Chopper Deke. So, for clarification, while they no longer gave a rat about Joey, they did care about the cat. And that made his eyes glisten with tears.

I'm pretty sure Teensy's harrowing ordeal in Mexico brought out the killer instinct in her, because as soon as Joey's eyes rimmed red, Teensy developed a nervous laugh; then she started crying from laughing so hard, before she finally had the common decency to leave the room while everyone stared at me like I was the strangest exhibit in *Ripley's Believe It or Not!*

I finished my tweet about the lame meeting, and some random guy tweeted back that I should check out my bad-ass car. Did that mean I'd find another decapitated Barbie on the windshield? I double-checked my purse and made sure my taser was still inside it.

Mercifully, Gordon adjourned the meeting. I exited the conference room to the sight of my co-workers ricocheting off each other trying to get out. Then Chopper Deke squeezed past me and suggested under his breath that I stitch a couple of jingle bracelets to my ass and breasts. He really needed a girlfriend. I wondered how he'd kept from developing a crippling case of Carpel Tunnel. What a pig.

But on a positive note, things seemed back to normal around here.

CHAPTER TWENTY

Before I left the station and headed out to see how Bruckman was coming along with the letters, Gordon called me into his office. When I told him I'd be there in five minutes, he told me I'd be there "right now."

"I need to download a copy of a picture I took at your house. It's on my phone."

"It can wait."

"The copy's for you. *From your house.* I figured we could talk about it after you took a look at it."

"Well, why didn't you say so?" He left me standing in the corridor.

I went to my office to download the two photos of the little black book I'd found secreted away in Paislee's Bible, and after I printed off color copies, I took them to Gordon's office. The vertical blinds were twisted open a sliver, and by the time I passed Rochelle's empty desk—the desk with the phone with all of the lights put on hold and the petite woman standing nearby looking as mousy and worn out as the housedress she had on—I could see my boss sitting in the swivel chair with his back turned away from me. This time, he had the telephone receiver pressed to his ear so he was talking to a real person instead of ranting to the walls, but as soon as I quietly cracked open the door, the gentle shift in air must've alerted him to my presence. He swung around in his chair to face me standing in the doorway.

"What the hell's going on?" He said this to me as he banged

the telephone back in its cradle.

I recapped my adventure as I handed over the printed copies. Just for good measure, I called up the photos on my phone.

"The second one's not very clear," he said.

"Yeah." I barely suppressed a sigh. "That happens when you don't have a panic room to hide from burglars, and you have to scramble under the bed." Caustic humor bolstered my courage. "By the way, I hope you weren't attached to the lamp on your wife's side of the bed. I broke it."

He pulled out his wallet and counted out twenty one-hundred-dollar bills. Then he took one back to cover the cost of the lamp. After he handed over the money, his hand went for the desk drawer. My stomach sank. He pulled out another letter and handed it across the blotter.

"You need to be careful, Prescott. I could hire you a full-time bodyguard, but the fact of the matter is if somebody wants you bad enough, they're going to get you. So you have to be diligent. It could be anybody. They may not stop at sending letters. I'm telling you to pay attention to your surroundings, understand? And let's say you're at the mall and you're walking to the parking lot by yourself; get the security guard to walk you to your car, all right?"

These were all good points. Trouble is, I only heard about half of what he said, kind of like bopping along with a Lady Gaga tune, and then the radio station plays music by an artist you dislike, so you change channels. And somewhere in the middle of Gordon's pep talk, I stopped liking what I was hearing.

Back to the letter.

Tim wanted me to wear a low-cut blouse so he could check out my cleavage "to see if they're real." And he wanted me to leave a pair of my underwear in Gran's mailbox. If I didn't do what he said, the next communiqué I received from him would describe my murder in grisly, gory detail. I sucked air.

He knows where I live.

My chin corrugated. I bit my lower lip in the scant hope that the tear trying to sluice down my right cheek would retreat. My shaky voice sounded almost as warbly as Gran's when I spoke. "This is like a horror movie. You know he's out there but you don't know where he's at, so you're always looking over your shoulder."

But Gordon provided a different take on the matter. "It doesn't necessarily have to be a man."

I glanced up absentmindedly. I must've misheard. "What?"

" 'Tim' may not be a man. What I'm saying is don't let your guard down."

My immediate fear was physical harm. "Are you holding out on me? Because if you are, you should just tell me."

"I'm just saying don't be complacent and think it's a man just because he signed a man's name."

This new bombshell effectively ended my attempt to think for myself. "Do you think his real name is Tim?"

He gave me an exasperated headshake. "Would you sign your real name if you were threatening someone? He's a coward. If, in fact, we're dealing with a 'he.' "

I needed to keep my focus on my job. The collateral damage was just too great not to.

"One other thing," Gordon said, "just so you know, while I was down at the PD, I filed a missing persons report on Wicklow. Her parents are useless in this situation. Her father has Alzheimer's and claims he doesn't have a daughter, and her mother has a closed-head injury with short-term memory loss and keeps forgetting to file a report. Nobody's seen or heard from her. Not even her insignificant other, Sheriff Granger. So I did it. I'd appreciate it if you'd fill in for her on the ten o'clock news. You don't have to if you don't want to. But I'm short of people and

I'd rather not be forced to rely your sister."

I sensed that we shared a simultaneous thought—*Whack-a-doodle-doo.*

"I'll do it."

"She's nuts, by the way. And I'm going on record that I'm not forcing you to do this. You're doing it of your own free will. I can pull you from the lineup 'til this blows over, and that might put an end to the matter. The reason I'm telling you this is because of the station's exposure. I don't want the liability."

"I said I'd do it." I didn't have much of a choice. I could've refused, and then my career would be trashed, but I'd still have a long run as a celebutante.

I put the letter in my purse and rose to leave. True, my stalker was a coward. And while I hadn't quite formulated a plan, I had an idea how to deal with cowards.

"I'm sick of being a father figure to all of the emotional cripples around here. Maybe you should run this by your daddy. See what he thinks. Get his take on the matter. If he doesn't want you to keep filling in, I'll understand."

I squared my shoulders. "I make my own decisions. And for what it's worth, I think you make a great father figure."

"You're just saying that because you're sweet on me." He gave me an *Aw shucks* grin. Which was kind of endearing, really, because I'd pretty much seen his range of emotions since I'd started working here and didn't think he could pull off *Aw shucks.*

I gave him a heavy eye roll.

Then Gordon yelled as I walked out the door. "You still owe me an entire cheesecake. Don't think I don't know it was you."

After I walked out the front door, I stood under the portico and pretended to fumble for my keys. But what I really did was scan the area and took note of what was happening on other side of the wall. Halfway across the parking lot, I saw a disappearing flash. The glint of metal coming off Gran's hood happened so fast that I mistook it for a heat mirage from the sun. I cast furtive glances all around and even did a quick eye scan past the wall. Mr. Bilburn stood statue-still beside a raised flower bed, looking like a giant, hulking black version of *le Petit Julien,* the famous Brussels landmark of a naked little boy urinating into a fountain. He saw me—frozen in my tracks, and gaping—and waved. Once my startle reflex relaxed and my jaw snapped shut, I felt an incredible sense of relief that the groin-high object he held in his hand turned out to be a trickling garden hose— which had not been my first thought.

I returned an unenthusiastic wave.

Footfalls behind me pounded the pavement. Back on high alert, I whipped around. The mousy woman in the threadbare housedress who'd been standing next to Rochelle's empty desk ran toward me, full bore.

Gordon's comment that my stalker didn't have to be a man resonated with me. My chest pounded. The hair on my neck stood up. A lance of terror went through my heart. I admit it, I screamed bloody murder.

Without warning, she dropped to the pavement and thrashed violently against the asphalt until she became a slobbery, drooling mess with her eyes rolled up into her head. Chopper Deke flew out the front door to my rescue. Rochelle followed him out on her broom, grim-faced. Gordon trailed Rochelle. His eyes executed orders from afar.

And that's about the time Chopper Deke grabbed the taser out of my hand and took it away from me.

Gordon stopped in his tracks and pulled out his cell phone, which I soon found out meant he'd placed a call to Byron. When I asked Rochelle why he'd stop to call Byron at a time like this, I learned Byron held the dual role of not only being

Gordon's best friend, but also legal counsel for WBFD-TV; and that it was routine procedure when the talent twisted off for Gordon to set up a "go-see" with him—in this case, so I could explain why I'd caused two metal fishhooks, positive and negative poles of extreme high voltage, to taze a lady's nervous system for no good reason when she'd only come to the station to get my autograph for her kid.

In a mental review of my conduct, I'd had the sort of response someone confronted by an attack dog might have. On the brink of tears, I watched as Chopper Deke and Rochelle lifted the woman to her feet. Each took hold of an arm to steady her while my eyes telescoped back into their sockets.

In my struggle to keep my voice calm, I kept repeating "I'm so sorry," in a stage whisper, and chanted it like a mantra. I rummaged through my purse and found my notebook, flipped to a fresh page, and scrawled out my signature. Then I walked over to the lady and noticed her standard-issue brown eyes, and the letter "P" emblazoned on her collar, and asked her child's name. She told me it was Bennie, and then I asked if it was for his birthday. She nodded, and I wrote *Happy birthday, Bennie* above my autograph. I pulled out one of the hundred-dollar bills from the money that Gordon had given me and handed it over with my autograph.

"Tell your son it's from me." This wasn't an altogether altruistic move on my part, I know, but he probably wanted toys and she probably couldn't afford to buy him any, so I considered it damage control. And the hundred dollars would help, and maybe she wouldn't hate me so much that she sued me.

She croaked out a *Thank you*, and I peeled off another hundred and handed it over. "I'm so sorry I made you ruin your dress." True enough, it had grime on it where she'd ground herself against the pavement. Then she started to cry, which made me cry, and pretty soon, we were hugging each other, and bawling into each other's necks—not only because of this awful experience, but also roaring out our grief for all of the other times we'd held in our tears—and I felt so bad for her, but I no longer expected her to sue me. I mean, if you were poor, could you sue someone your son liked after the object of his adoration made it possible for you to buy the little rascal toys for his birthday? I peeled off another hundred-dollar bill and told her to take Bennie to the snow leopard exhibit at the zoo—on me— and to be sure to buy treats at the concession stand, because that's what I always liked when I was a kid.

I looked up in time to see a big penis truck with a grill guard on the front, backing out of a parking space. I recognized Dr. Wright behind the wheel, waving as he drove out of the lot. I assumed he'd driven in at some point to see Teensy, and wished he'd encourage her to find employment in her chosen field, since I saw no psychological benefit in working with a relative.

I drew in a sharp intake of air.

What a brilliant idea.

New plan. Now all I had to do was get Dr. Wright to see my side and convince Teensy to quit.

Gordon came back outside with a bottled water for the lady I tazed—I hadn't even realized he'd left during the commotion— yet brought nothing for me, thank you, even though, *Hello,* I'd been traumatized, too. As I played leap-frog with the shade, he patted her shoulder and spoke soothing words while looking at me slitty-eyed. When the lady gave him an enthusiastic nod, one with the potential for whiplash, he quietly signaled me to leave, so I got into Gran's car while they led Bennie's mother back inside the building, presumably for Gordon to continue the schmooze-fest.

On my way to the frontage road, I caught a red light. My eyes flickered to the rearview mirror. As I looked around to see if anyone had followed me, the metallic glint hit my eye again.

This time, it was so bright I flinched. A gold-colored object had been taped to Gran's windshield wiper. For no good reason, I remembered ancient public service television commercials about what to do if you found a blasting cap around a construction site. The light turned green and I pulled ahead. But this time, instead of taking the on-ramp to the freeway, I pulled over to the curb, jammed the gear shift into park, and got out for a closer inspection.

It wasn't a blasting cap.

It was a bullet.

On the off chance Bruckman could lift fingerprints off the tape, I decided to leave it alone. When I came within a mile of the PD, I called and asked him to meet me on Taylor Street, on the west side of police HQ. He was already waiting for me at the corner when I pulled up.

He took one look at the bullet, pronounced it "a copper-jacketed hollow point," and stretched his fingers into a pair of latex gloves. After carefully sliding the taped bullet off of the wiper, he dropped it into a small brown paper bag and headed back upstairs while I hunted for a parking space.

Bruckman shares an office with other detectives in an open-concept room with a bunch of government-issue desks in it. Everyone has their own telephone, and it seemed that the lines were all bleating at the same time.

When I asked if he'd had a chance to look at the letters, he told me he'd made his own copies before turning them over to the detective in charge of my case, and had already read through them. Then he explained the fingerprint procedure in-depth.

"Detective Leland will probably spray it with ninhydrin, which will turn any fingerprints on the paper purple. He can also use acetone, which might actually be better. Regardless, it's a long chain of steps that would probably bore you to death.

But we'll get the prints unless he wore gloves. And everyone else's, too."

Crestfallen, my chin dropped to my chest. I saw the latest letter protruding from my purse, and handed it over in a plastic protector. To save him the trouble, I told him what the letter said.

"He wants me to show him 'the girls'—" I thumbed at my chest "—and to leave a pair of panties in Gran's mailbox. So I'm pretty sure he knows where I'm staying." Then I had an epiphany. "Maybe I should stay with you?"

Three hours ago, he couldn't keep his hands off me. Now, he acted like I'd broken into his country home and boiled his bunny. I'm beginning to think men are like shadows. You run toward them, they run away from you. You run away from them, they run toward you.

He hemmed and hawed, and finally came out with, "That might be disruptive."

A female voice stopped me from asking why.

"Jimmy, they were out of—"

The seductive-looking brunette bounced into his office with two fast-food sacks, a couple of canned sodas, and a chest big enough to mount a frontal assault. Her mouth gaped at the sight of me. Eyes shined ghostly blue beneath the fluorescent lighting.

And that pretty much brought into perspective the reason why my presence at Bruckman's house might be disruptive.

Ever the gentleman, Bruckman stood. Instead of becoming flustered, he exercised an almost super-professional demeanor, flicking his eyes back and forth between us like a quick game of ping-pong.

"This is Babette."

My insides turned into one big emotional and hormonal battleground.

Her pouty lips were smeared crimson. She stood in stricken silence, gripping the grease-stained paper bags, as the ramifications of my presence sank in. Her mouth trembled; her eyes glistened. She paled, finally seeing the detour her afternoon had taken. Then she recovered, as if a magic wand had been waved, releasing her from her trance.

"Jim's girlfriend," she added by way of introduction, still frozen in the doorway in her estrogen-churning, second-skin excuse for pants, and a determined expression hardening on her pale marble face. "You're the girl from the news. It's a pleasure to meet you." Her eyes dipped to the grease-stained sacks. "I'd shake hands if mine weren't full."

We exchanged brittle smiles.

"Dainty Prescott. It's nice to meet you, too." But it wasn't nice. I felt sick to my stomach, as if my guts had fallen out and I should be gathering them up and shoving them back inside.

Babette handed over their late lunch, or early dinner, whatever.

Then Bruckman spoke to her in a brandy-smooth voice. "Would you excuse us? We need to finish our business. Go ahead and start without me." Babette looked as hurt as I felt when he moved toward the door and dismissed her with his eyes.

As he closed it behind him to shut her out, I was thinking *Hold 'em or fold 'em,* just like the song, and pictured her having a psychotic break. I know I would have.

"Don't look at me that way, Dainty. I warned you if you took that second trip to Mexico, we were done. You left, and we were over. I took solace in Babette. She'd lost her husband; I lost the love of my life. It was a natural progression."

He said "were." *Not* "are." *Should I read anything into that?*

My mind cast back to earlier in the afternoon, when my lips felt as if they were disintegrating when his met mine. So, while physically, I was sitting across the desk from Bruckman, in my head, I was stripping off passion-rumpled sheets in Gordon's guest bedroom and hiding the evidence in the laundry chute.

"And now?"

"Dainty, do you really want to pull at that thread?"

"I have to know."

He gave a slow headshake. "I don't know." He picked up the brown paper evidence sack with the bullet inside. "As for this, I can see fingerprints on the tape. Detective Leland will probably freeze it so he can peel the tape off without compromising the fingerprints. Then he'll likely dust and photograph them and we'll submit them to AFIS." He meant they'd run them through the national database known as the Automated Fingerprint Identification System, or AFIS for short. "Someone will get back with you if they get any results."

He seemed almost clinical in his delivery.

"Yes, well, I have to go now." I moved uneasily under his intent regard, and paused at the same door he'd shown Babette out of, feeling as if I'd received notice of a death in the family. In a way, I had.

As soon as my hand touched the doorknob, he was at my side, calling my name.

"I love you," he mouthed without sound, and I melted from the stubborn gleam in his sexy, smoldering eyes.

CHAPTER TWENTY-ONE

Since I still had to do the *News at Ten* broadcast, I drove to the station and phoned home instead of returning to Gran's after meeting with Bruckman. I wanted to speak to someone who still appreciated everything I'd done for them, so when Teensy answered, "Prescott residence," I disguised my voice, and asked for Amanda C. Moreof.

Oops, Freudian slip.

"Amanda Vásquez, *por favor.*"

"Who's calling?"

"Inspector Garza with Border Patrol."

Teensy hissed, "Bullshit. It's you."

I abandoned my fake Mexican accent. "Cursing is so un-Rubanbleu, Teensy. I hope you get kicked out for swearing."

"I've heard you say the same thing. And, believe me; if I get kicked out, I'm taking you with me. Are you calling from jail?"

I yanked the phone from my ear and stared at it. Seriously, my sister'd lost it. Then it occurred to me that the rival news station aired an early news report and that Gordon probably couldn't stop them from airing the footage of me being led off to the calaboose in the caged area of a patrol car. "Why would you ask that?"

"Because I just heard on the news that Sweetie's Cupcakes got robbed. Oh, wait—they took money, not cupcakes. Never mind, forget I mentioned it," she said snottily. "By the way, I consulted my Celtic runes, and we're not even supposed to be talking."

"You are such a cow. Make that a mad cow."

"You're the cow. Or, rather, you're *la vaca, señorita* Garza. Or, is it *señora*? Oh, that's right—you can't be a *señora;* you're not married. You're not even engaged."

"Neither are you."

"No? Well then what's this big, fat diamond on my left hand?"

I gasped. Then I lit into her. "Teensy, you haven't known that man long enough to be engaged to him."

"Not that it's any of your business, but I am. So . . . *ha.*" I heard the rustle of fabric as she bosomed the phone, and yelled for Amanda.

Amanda took her sweet time taking my call, and when she did, she answered in a low voice, as if she had no idea how she could've been found at the Prescott mansion, and didn't suppose any good could come of being tracked down.

"Amanda, I want you to call Crazy Gianni's and order a pizza for me. All meat, except I don't want pepperoni. And no anchovies. And no vegetables. And I want thin crust, not thick, because then it's all doughy, and I want it crisp on the bottom. Don't forget the little red pepper packets and parmesan cheese."

"Where are you?"

"At the TV station. And I want you to deliver it here."

"You're outside the delivery area."

"No, see, what you do is: You order the pizza, pretend you're me, and—" I applied a bit of Teensy-speak from the afternoon meeting "—play like you're delivering it to Gran's address, only deliver it here. I'll totally make it worth your while."

"How?"

"I'll tip you and pay the delivery charge."

"I'll use up more than that in gas, diva."

"Will you do it if I can get more people to order pizzas?"

"I'm not stupid. You've got an ulterior motive."

I hated to admit it but she was right. I called back in fifteen minutes with an order for four large pizzas. Amanda showed up within the hour in her dilapidated Chevy and made twelve dollars in tips and delivery charges, plus the fifteen I tipped her. She was counting out her money as I followed her into the parking lot.

Except for concentrated pockets of light from a couple of mercury vapor lights, the farther away from WBFD's front door you traveled, the darker and more menacing the parking lot got, including the neighborhood across the wall where poor people tended not to burn their outside lights. Shadows cast by the overhang of tree branches gave the night a spooky feel, made worse by the shrill laugh track of a sitcom filtering out through the screen door of one of the creepy residents.

"I was thinking you could do me a favor." I shot furtive glances all around.

She whipped around to face me. "I knew you weren't doing this to help me. What do you want?"

I gave her a bland smile and tried to keep my voice light and convincing. "I just want you to drive me by somebody's house so I can scope it out."

Her eyes slewed over to Gran's car. "Drive yourself."

I explained that I couldn't. That Gran's car was way too memorable for me to be pulling a reconnaissance mission in it.

"And this piece of junk isn't?"

"Nobody will know it's us if we use your car," I said. She sarcastically passed a dramatic hand along her brow, as if flinging away her worries, so I upped the ante. "I'll pay for your gas."

"Damned right, you will." She held her hand out, palm up, in demand.

"I only have a hundred. Can you make change?"

"Sure." Amanda gave me the tip and delivery money and snatched the hundred from my grasp.

First we drove to Babette's. It relieved my anxiety to see that Bruckman's truck wasn't in her driveway. Then we drove to Bruckman's and observed a black Thunderbird next to his truck. I took this to be Babette's car, and shut my eyes, assaulted by a vision of Bruckman and Babette in bed together. My stomach flipped.

"Did you get what you wanted?" Amanda said as I sunk into my seat and allowed myself to be lulled by the drone of the tires.

I mimed a smile. "No. But, like the great philosopher Jagger, I got what I needed."

After Amanda dropped me off at the station, and I went inside to prepare for the *News at Ten* report, I stopped by my mailbox—which isn't a real mailbox, but more of a cubby hole—and found a handwritten note from Rochelle telling me to pick up a brown envelope on her desk. I took it to my office, sat behind my desk, and kicked off my shoes before opening it. It contained a Christmas card in a red envelope, along with a note from Gordon that read: *It's time to get the police involved. If you don't, I will.*

Since bad things were supposed to occur in threes, I didn't see how opening the card could make things any worse . . . until I read it.

Among other atrocities, Tim wrote that he wanted to rape me. Psychologically, it felt like he already had. I got the creepy feeling he might be outside, lying in wait for me, even though I knew the gate would keep out unauthorized people.

Note to Self: You're assuming the person who wants to kill you doesn't have a key card to the building.

Self to Note: Shut the hell up.

I called Detective Leland and left a voicemail suggesting Mr. Bilburn might be behind this, since I'd seen him staring at me earlier in the day. Making that phone call didn't exactly raise my comfort level, but it did make me feel more proactive. But what I really wanted was to run away.

Then I looked up and saw Amanda framed in the doorway. "I thought you left."

"Hey, diva, I figured since I was already here, I'd study you in your natural habitat; maybe stick around and watch you do the—what's wrong?" She moved into the room, taking tentative steps toward one of the guest chairs.

I told her about the letters that had come in threatening my life. But instead of sympathizing, she took the opposite approach.

"Well you know what you've gotta do, right?" When I gave her an uninvitingly blank look, she said, "You've gotta fight back."

"How do I fight the invisible man? It's like trying to grasp smoke." I massaged my temples to fight off the headache building inside. "I wish Gordon were here so I could ask him what to do."

But Amanda shook her head. "You know what to do. You knew what to do in Mexico, and you know what to do here. I'll admit, you were green as a gourd, but instinct and intuition will get you by—now go do it. Trust your instincts."

Out of the blue, it hit me—I knew exactly what to do. Not only did I plan to blatantly disregard Tim's demands, I intended to call him out on it. No way would I show my cleavage on-air. Like Gran says, "Showing off your ta-tas anywhere but behind closed doors is not Rubanbleu approved." Plus, on the off-chance Gran tuned in to our broadcast, I didn't want to hear her rant.

I'm a seventh-generation Texan; my Texas roots go back to

when Texas was a Republic, and I know my history. In the remaining moments before the live broadcast, I got on the Internet and pulled up a photograph of the Gonzales flag—the very flag that a small band of Texans fashioned during the Texas Revolution back in the 1830s as a message to the Mexicans who demanded the Texans return their cannon. After printing out a copy, I took it with me into the studio.

Fifteen minutes after I'd picked up my news copy and seated myself behind the anchor's desk, the floor crew swarmed in, and the audio department made sure the mikes were working. As I gave my notes a final once-over, a strange sense of calm enveloped me. Soon, the floor director signaled me which camera to look at, and told the people in the studio to "stand by" as we came back live from the commercial.

The news went off without a hitch.

With a minute left to run, I let viewers know that we always appreciate their cards and letters. "And in a special message to 'Tim' tonight, Tim, if you're watching, you need to buff up on your Texas history, pal, and in particular, the message in the Gonzales flag—"

I held up the photocopy and watched on the monitor as the camera zoomed in for a close-up:

Come And Take It.

"—because this message is for you. It's not gonna happen, buddy . . . not gonna happen."

Then the musical finale came on; I caught the *That's a wrap signal* out of the corner of my eye, pulled off my mike, and headed back to my office. For a few minutes, I sat behind my desk and stared at the phone as if it were a huge growth that needed removing.

Amanda looked on with concern.

A couple of lights lit up, and the intercom came on. "Dainty, pick up line two."

With a shaky hand, I lifted the phone to my ear. At the other end of the line, the caller's voice was robotic and menacing.

He described his plan to stalk, rape, and strangle me with my pantyhose. Then he went on to describe my murder in gory detail. I didn't have to assume it was Tim—I knew it. By the time he played out his fantasy on the phone, I realized that his true motive was to try to make a really strong woman afraid.

Then it was my turn to speak.

"You don't have to sneak around to find me—I'm right here at the TV station. It's easy to find; I'll even give you the address. But know this: While you've been stalking me, I've had people watching you. I know where you live, what kind of vehicle you drive, and where you go during the day and night. The police report's been filed, and they're going to find you. So be afraid. Be very afraid. Because when they pick you up, we're going to be there with a camera crew, zooming in for a close-up of your sad and pathetic face. And everyone in the Metroplex will know what a vicious little coward you are when we air it on the news. Want me? Come and get me, you bastard." Not even the great Sphinx could keep a straight face if he had to serve up that lie.

Amanda sat wide-eyed. Not that it mattered. I think the click I heard at the other end of the line was Tim hanging up when I called him a coward.

"Nice job, diva. He'll probably kill you now. Not to mention you probably just put me, and your sister, and your grandmother in harm's way. Otherwise, that's pretty much what I would've said."

What Amanda didn't understand is that I'd grown tired of being afraid. Tired of flinching at men who looked at me the wrong way. Tired of being scared of my own shadow. I couldn't afford to jump the gun and break a kindly old grandfather's nose, or taze another innocent bystander. Now, I not only welcomed a showdown, I ached for it.

Amanda and I stepped out into the crisp night air. I drew in a deep inhale and tilted my face up to the overcast sky. A full moon shined like a lustrous pearl.

Out in the parking lot, I found another decapitated Barbie head stuck on my windshield wiper. An accurate timeline would be impossible to narrow down since I didn't look the car over when I left the police station. I didn't check, because nobody would mess with your car around a police station, right? But at this point, everyone except me was a suspect, including any officer on any police department within our broadcasting area. Even my psychotic, envious sister who wanted to beat me out of my job, and could use a mental health intervention, was a suspect.

Amanda said, "I know what you're going through. Today, this person followed me around in the grocery store, and I thought he was going to hurt me. He yelled at me because I couldn't tell him how to find the hemorrhoid cream. It got even worse when another guy interfered. I realized he was working with a partner when they tag-teamed me. His accomplice turned out to be the store manager. The douche bag fired me for not knowing the inventory. Think about it, diva. I got fired for providing lousy customer service, and I don't even work there."

"Are you making fun of me?"

"Little bit."

Amanda followed me home in her car, but I didn't feel safe for either of us until we drove through Gran's formidable gate. No sooner had I arrived home and sauntered through the front door than Gran started raising hell in general. It's a wonder the neighbors didn't complain—the woman sounded like bagpipers tuning up on a Scottish highland before battle.

"I turned on the news in time to see a live report about the increase in crime in Fort Worth, and what do I see?"

I clenched my teeth and half-closed my eyes. Our rival station must've aired the footage of me after all. I'd probably be getting a letter from The Rubanbleu in the next few days. At the very least, I'd get invited to appear before the board of directors.

But then Gran said, "One minute in, my drunken granddaughter appears behind the news reporter, buck naked, and dancing. It's a good thing we've got that Hobby law because they let her go when she sobered up. Idiot." Then she turned on me. "Why can't you do something about her?"

"What would you have me do? She's a grown-up."

"Honestly, Dainty, you're no help. No help at all."

"What's this thing about Teensy getting an engagement ring?"

"She's a fool. By the way I've decided to take a cruise. While I'm gone, get the glass man out here to fix the cracked pane in the kitchen door. Your idiot sister tried to make a rocket by mixing cola and those high-powered mints. It worked."

Then Gran flounced off to bed in her billowing silk kimono, leaving Amanda and me to fend for ourselves in the kitchen. After we split a peanut butter and jelly sandwich—grape on Amanda's half, strawberry on mine—we went upstairs to turn in. While giving Amanda first crack at the guest bathroom on the second floor, I lay saucer-eyed on the bed for a few minutes and took a load off my aching feet. When Amanda returned without makeup and towel-drying her hair, I went downstairs and showered. After I came back to my room and got ready for bed, Amanda had fallen asleep and was snoring like a buzz saw. As an afterthought, I checked my email.

Messages from my two best friends popped up in my inbox; I ignored all the others for the time being.

Venice wrote that Africa was so primitive she only had access to the Internet once a week, but that she hoped I was *"having as good a time"* as she was, *"ha-ha."* A second email purporting to be from her claimed she'd been mugged, and her passport, driver's license, and traveler's checks had been stolen and asked me *"please to click the link provided to wire money."* Since I read the emails from top to bottom, I decided the earlier message was spam and deleted it.

The email from Salem, my fiery redheaded friend and a debutante of The Rubanbleu, said she and her boyfriend were having a great time in Ruidoso, skiing, but would be boarding an outbound flight to Denver where the snow was better. Then I got to read complaints about how sore she was from skiing, and how sorry she was for taking Tandy Westlake and her boyfriend with them, but they had those two free tickets, and nobody actually expected me to make it back alive from Mexico . . .

Welcome to the crowd.

It was enough to make me grind my molars. Then I considered the irony of having to motor around town in Gran's embarrassing vehicle while there was a perfectly good hot pink Smart Car, trapped and unused, in Salem's parents' garage, and I did a slow burn all over again. But the next part of her email really bothered me. She wrote:

"I really didn't appreciate you sending me this video. What made you think I'd want to see a close-up of your boobs? Are you trying to tell me you've switched teams? I sincerely hope you're not crushing on me, Dainty, because while I love you as a friend, I don't 'love you-love you.' And where is this dump you're dancing in? It's disgusting and filthy and looks like it's already been condemned. If you needed money that bad, you should've just asked. Is this in Mexico? Did you get kidnapped and sold to one of those white slavery outfits again? Because if not, how desperate and stupid do you have to be to post it on YouTube, where ladies of The Rubanbleu might stumble across it? Have you lost your ever-lovin' mind? Hope you don't get kicked out. Better hope this doesn't go viral."

Scrolling down the body of the email, I found the IP address where it had purportedly been sent from me. Only I hadn't sent anything to anybody. But there it was, pulsing like an open sore . . . my email address, along with a message to "Check out this link."

My heart raced. I clicked on the link and my mouth went slack.

There I was—or what appeared to me—grinding my crotch into a stripper pole, while disgusting old geezers who wouldn't have been able to get it up with a crane and guy-wires sat glassy-eyed in the audience, covered in drool. It wasn't my body, just my head—my décolletage is much better looking than that—and my hair was styled the way I do it for the news.

Besides, that stripper had a gut on her. Definitely not *moi*. I printed out Salem's email and set it aside.

For no reason other than instinct, I ran my name through a search engine.

The website purporting to be mine turned out to be a real eye-opener. According to *"Dainty Dishes,"* I'm a slut who likes to meet men *"any time, any place."* The pictures of my face had been pirated from my social media profile, and photo-shopped onto pictures of naked women, or altered to make it look like I was involved in porn.

And there, you have it, I thought. *If God didn't mean for rich girls to dance on tables, He wouldn't have created busboys to clear off the dishes.*

Tears scorched my eyeballs. I printed out a color copy of the home page and set it aside.

Clearly, a vile and vicious person had created a duplicate profile and pretended to be me. I even found a second "page" on the same social media site that my pictures were stolen from. This venomous snake had "friended" all of my friends and sent hateful messages to them from my fake profile. Consequently, all of my friends posted nasty things on my page.

I printed a color copy of both social media pages and mentally thanked God that the hacker hadn't been able to get past the WBFD firewall and desecrate my TV profile. Then, I tried to delete the fake profile, but whoever created it used a different password. The only reason I didn't delete the profile I created for myself is because I figured that by keeping it open, the police might be able to develop something useful from it. Before I exited both sites, I sent a complaint to the social media site's customer service, but knew it'd be awhile before I could get a response.

My enemy remained elusive. I didn't feel safe. When would this person reveal himself? I suspected Tim was behind this, and that he'd become bitter and resentful, with a sense of entitlement.

I knew very little about computers, but what I did know had to do with the hunt for IP, or Internet Provider, addresses. IP addresses were like fingerprints for computers. If nothing else, the police could subpoena the owner of the IP address to find the person behind this attempt to humiliate me and ruin my reputation.

Before I logged off, I checked my inbox one more time.

Sure enough, I had a message from Tim.

By calling for a showdown, I'd gotten one.

When I opened the message, it read: *Go ahead and call the cops. See if I care. Maybe the reason you haven't caught me is because I am one.*

CHAPTER TWENTY-TWO

The day dawned with a brilliant sunrise. The overnight deluge of rain that Misty Knight failed to predict had subsided, and the sun burst through the low-hanging clouds.

I dragged myself out of bed on a yawn, realizing that this would've been Aspen Wicklow's day off. Since I hadn't heard from Gordon, and since I'd become world-weary over this squabble with Teensy, I decided to take Dr. Wright up on his offer for family counseling. Maybe he was right, and I could help my sister work through her post-traumatic stress. Or psychosis. Or schizoaffective disorder. Whatever. At least find out her diagnosis, and figure out how to get meds and make her take them.

As I scampered downstairs, I noticed Teensy's door was closed and assumed that she was still asleep, only to find Amanda sitting in the breakfast nook with her arms braced, giving my sister the evil eye as Teensy chattered away.

Apparently, I'd walked in on the tail end of the conversation.

Teensy said, "Gran's mean because the other night I wasn't hungry, and so I hadn't finished my dinner. And then Gran said I needed to eat everything on my plate because there were children starving in Africa, and I said 'Name one,' and she slapped me."

Beyond the back door, Gran was enjoying a steaming cup of coffee out on the terrace, where she could look out at the pool, despite threatening thunderclouds that hung overhead.

Then Teensy gave me a dismissive head toss, and switched subjects, specifically regaling us with the knowledge that she'd always had a burning desire to try culinary school.

As previously mentioned, Teensy's no chef. So while Amanda's untouched rubbery-looking egg did the breast stroke in the excessive amount of grease on her plate, and the last of the toast-stack was rimmed in shades of charcoal, the oven decided to lock itself in the middle of cooking bacon.

"Good morning, lovelies," I announced to the room at large. I smiled at Amanda, gave Gran a little finger wave, and shifted my eyes to my sister. "And then, course, there's Teensy."

Amanda acknowledged me with a brusque jut of the chin; Teensy, dressed in a riot of color, continued to ignore me.

"What's up?" Curiosity got the better of me. "Let's see the ring."

"I took it off before I went to bed and haven't put it back on yet."

Teensy, who takes photos of nearly everything, would've taken one with her camera phone to text to all her friends, so I said, "Pics, or it didn't happen."

"Pics, or it didn't happen," she said mockingly.

I headed to the pantry for cereal, only to discover that my sister had swilled down the last of the milk. So I went back inside the pantry to exchange the cereal box for the box of granola bars, and those were gone, too. Frustrated, I stepped out into the kitchen and looked at Amanda, who, after staying here for one week, had developed the power to read my mind.

"Pizza? Crazy Gianni's? All meat, no anchovies, no vegetables, thin crust—did I get it right?"

"No pepperoni. And don't forget the little packets of crushed red pepper and parmesan."

"I'm on it." Amanda gave me a little finger salute and left the room.

When she returned, she had on her ball cap with the Crazy Gianni's Pizza and Pasta logo on it, and the keys to her car in her hand. My sister and I were still playing the "Quiet Game" with each other when Amanda headed out the door. As soon as a plume of gray exhaust boiled out of her car's tailpipe, I turned to Teensy for explanations.

Maybe I didn't handle it as well as I could've when I opened a dialogue with *What the hell's wrong with you?* but it got my point across. When she faced off with me, I saw that she'd shaved off her eyebrows and had drawn them back on with a Sharpie. I liked her much better this way because she actually seemed interested in what I said, for a change.

In my twenty-three years, I, Dainty Prescott, have come to accept three tenets: One, the best way to hide something is in plain sight; two, no matter how smart, or pretty, or talented you are, there will always be someone smarter, prettier, or more talented than you; and three, your boyfriend is bisexual if he looks at pictures of naked men and sends them love letters.

Today, I decided to examine the first tenet. Someone knew me well enough to follow me, find out where I lived, and harass me. And that meant that I had to accept that my stalker might be someone close to me. Setting aside family, I needed to consider others who had access to me, or access to someone close to me. For this reason, I asked Teensy for Dr. Wright's business address.

She immediately became defensive. "Why do you want it?"

"Because, unless he's rolling in money and can afford to turn away new clients, I thought I'd throw a little business his way." I neglected to tell her the new client was me.

She disappeared into another part of the house. When she returned, she presented me with his business card. I studied his address, hell-bent on paying him a visit if he could work me in later in the morning. As I walked out the back door to join

Gran on the terrace, the screen slapped shut behind me. There, I planned to wait until Amanda returned with my pizza.

When I pulled up a chair, I noticed Gran staring off into space. When I asked what was so interesting, she pointed down the lane to Old Man Spencer, declaring his love for her by sticking his hand inside his shirt and palpating it like a beating heart in a bad music video.

"Silly old fool," she said through a smile. Glittery blue eyes thinned into slits. Distress puckered her lips. "That doctor's an idiot for dating your sister."

My blue-haired grandmother, whom I've never before seen when she wasn't put together, or dressed to the nines, had neglected to wear clothes under her kimono. When she leaned in to refill her coffee cup, the flap of her robe caught on one of the wrought iron bistro table's little curlicues. She inadvertently flashed her wrinkled, gelatinous, sagging right breast as Old Man Spencer pirouetted around the grounds of his house. At least I thought it was accidental, but then again, I'm living with crazy people. I instantly wanted that memory erased, yet came to the heady realization that my Victorian grandmother might've been egging him on.

I shuddered. "Think I'll get a glass of juice; please excuse me."

When Amanda returned, I paid for the pizza and gave her a generous tip, along with the delivery charge. Then I invited her to share it with me. I wanted her to know I appreciated her coming by the station and following me home.

I took a heartfelt moment to study her in earnest. "I really do appreciate you, Amanda." Her eyes thinned into slits. "No, it's true. I sincerely care about you. And I care what happens to you." Between bites of pizza, she relaxed. "If you were a vegetable, I'd still care about you."

"If you were a vegetable, I'd chop you up and sauté you in a skillet."

On some level, I believed her. Since we'd known each other, I admit I hadn't treated her with the respect she deserved. And on that note, thinking she might enjoy going to an arts benefit event as friends, I expected her to jump at the invitation.

"Not if I have to drive us there, diva."

"Your car's not that bad. At least it runs, and you own it, which is more than I can say for myself."

"Not today." She lowered her voice to a whisper. "I don't have a valid driver's license. I went in to renew it and was told to come back dressed as a man. They told me to remove the makeup, too. So I need to pick a time when Gran and Teensy aren't here—that would be this afternoon. Otherwise, they'll find out I'm a guy and make me leave."

"Take care of the license. I mean it, Amanda. I have enough on my plate to deal with. Seriously. You think them finding out you're a man will make Gran show you the door? Well, I can assure you, an overnight in jail will have the same effect."

Teensy prissed in and grabbed up Dr. Wright's business card. "You can't have it. Jot down the information, and be quick about it."

I complied with her demands and watched her flounce out of the room as I downed a glass of grapefruit juice. I drank grapefruit juice since the orange juice container had about two swallows left in it. No need to discuss who'd been swigging directly out of the carton since a Post-it stuck on the side bore the message, *I spit in this.*

Before I left the house, I penned my own Post-it and stuck it against the plastic-ware bowl that held a head of lettuce so Teensy'd be sure to see it. The note read: *Dear Teensy, You're such a sloppy, incorrigible, slovenly mess. What makes you think you can use the last clean towel without doing a load of towels? You're so self-*

ish and self-centered you probably make out with yourself. By the way, I spit on something of yours in the refrigerator. Good luck with that.

I said *ta-ta* to Amanda, grabbed my purse, along with the Internet file I compiled to show Detective Leland, and headed out the door. The first thing I did when I fired up Gran's car was to check the gas gauge, which still read Empty. Then I backed the Cadillac out of the carriage house and wound around the brick driveway until I came to the gate.

And that's where I rolled to a stop.

A gang of dangerous-looking Latina 'hood rats had parked their lowrider at the mouth of the drive, effectively blocking my way past the wrought iron gate. I stepped out of the car to see what all the hoopla was about, and got a lot of castigating Spanish from these brown-skinned barbarians. When I pushed my hair behind my ears, my fingers trembled. It would appear that my arrival had set off fireworks.

I'm not accustomed to having angry mobs coming after me, so it just made sense that these recidivists mistook me for Teensy.

Over the next few minutes, I learned that my sister had allegedly posted inflammatory comments about illegal immigration on one of those public forum websites. Now, these uncultured savages were spoiling for a fight. They hung onto the gate and shoved their upraised fists through the bars, shouting for my sister to come out and fight them. Besides the incitefully riotous posts Teensy left on the website, she'd stupidly furnished her real name and address, inviting anyone who didn't agree with her post to "come shut me up if you think you're ballsy enough."

Unlike the new-and-improved Teensy, it's not in my nature to go around picking fights. I'm not used to dealing with cutthroats. So I did the best I could under the circumstances.

I explained that we'd just learned that Teensy had been murdered, and asked them to respect the family's privacy.

Triumphant with rumblings that it served her right, they slunk back to their car, an older model sedan with plenty of room to pile six or seven bangers into it. I imagined how they'd look wearing stripes, and hoped my sleeves weren't ringed in perspiration. Oddly enough, everything went fine except for that pesky little problem of trying to breathe. Then one of them—presumably the leader—hung back.

She liked Gran's car and wanted to know if it was for sale; then *Ooh'd* and *Aah'd* about how cool it'd be to cruise around town in it. I fibbed that the car had all kinds of problems, especially with engine, which I knew to be a big ticket item if you had to pay a mechanic. Which I knew wasn't true, but the last thing I wanted to do was get crosswise with these people, and I hoped a couple of "Fs" on the Caddy's report card would deter her from coming back to steal Gran's wheels. I told her it belonged to my great uncle Harold, who lived in El Paso, and I'd ask him after the funeral if he wanted to sell it. She wrote her name and telephone number down on a scrap of paper and asked me to give it to him, and then drove her *"cholas"* back to the 'hood.

If that little recidivist comes back, I plan to tell her the tragic story about how poor great uncle Harold drove the Cadillac off a bridge after he got into a fight with a Nazi helicopter—a wasp—and lost, and that her dream car was sitting at the bottom of Lake Ray Hubbard.

I credit my two trips to Mexico for being able to think on my feet.

Chapter Twenty-Three

I pulled into the parking lot in front of Dr. Wright's building and knew instantly why Teensy had been seduced by the location. The strip center had been built around plenty of mature trees and embodied several retail areas, including high-end boutiques, a Michelin-star restaurant that had recently been written up in *The Dallas Morning News,* and a bank. I found the suite number for Dr. Wright's office as soon as I rounded the corner. I entered a glassed-in lobby and located the directory, and since I must've missed his name the first time, I reviewed each listing from the beginning, in the event he'd given his psychology practice a name to confuse the public—such as *Head Games,* or *The Great Depression,* or *Bipolar Bear*—or some other pithy, all-encompassing description for his business—instead of using his own name.

While I pored over the directory, Dr. Wright came shooting out of the real estate office down the hall. He must've spotted me through the plate glass window because he intercepted me before I could locate his office. After exchanging pleasantries, I explained that I'd considered his offer for a free session, and had decided to do it if it would help Teensy.

He showed me to an office adjacent to the realtor's, and as he unlocked the door and flipped on the lights, I noticed several secretaries from the real estate agency giving me the stink eye. These pretty girls caused me to wonder if Teensy felt the least bit insecure because her boyfriend—correction, fiancé—worked next door to these big-busted, big-haired Texas beauties.

I also noticed the plastic *For Lease* sign taped to the glass storefront, with a phone number printed underneath.

He apparently caught me staring because he gave the sign a dismissive wave. "Oh, that. I keep forgetting to take it down."

We walked inside and he apologized for the size of the small waiting room, where a single cream-colored vinyl couch, a couple of vinyl chairs, and a few potted plants sprinkled around the room took up most of the open space. The place also featured the typical pass-through window with sliding glass panels where a receptionist should've been seated. No receptionist.

To his credit, the latest copy of *People Magazine* lay on a small side table next to the door.

"There's nobody else here?" I asked.

He laughed without humor. "My girl, Shannon, is off, but it's a light schedule today. I was trying to see if one of the ladies next door knew of anyone I could call in to sub—that's what I was doing when you came in."

"Why not Teensy?" Teensy could hold a phone to her head. Matter of fact, there were plenty of folks who thought she actually had one growing out of her ear.

He shook his head. "I can't do that to her. She's fragile. And some of these people are, well, to be perfectly frank . . . crazy."

And she's not?

I gave him a pointed look.

He led me into an inner office that also had Spartan furnishings, and two doors: one that appeared to be a closet and another that was slightly ajar enough to be able to discern that it was a bathroom. Diplomas and framed certificates hung on the walls, but I didn't see any file cabinets or books on the shelves. When I remarked on it, he explained that he shared the cost of a moving van with another doctor in the same strip

234

center, and the movers had to unload the neighbor's furniture first.

I shifted my eyes to his desktop, where a familiar pair of lace panties lay near the edge. He quickly swept them into a drawer. I knew they were mine because they were French cut and expensive, and did a slow burn with the dawning realization that Teensy had been wearing my things. Knowing they were French didn't make this discovery any less disgusting.

He invited me to sit, and motioned me into a chair. For the first ten minutes, we exchanged mindless chit-chat. Then, once again, he asked about my deepest, darkest fear. I said if I had to pick one, it'd be finding out the Bingo's Frozen Custard drive-through had gone out of business. He pronounced my attitude "cagey" and asked me again.

My greatest fear? Losing another member of my family. It's just me and Teensy and Gran and Daddy, now; and even though they've turned into lunatics, they're my lunatics.

For reasons even I don't understand, I didn't disclose this to Dr. Wright. Right now, this Tim thing had me so paranoid that I'd developed trust issues. Well, maybe not with Amanda. Which seemed odd under the circumstances, since I've known her all of two months. But the Mexico experience cemented our bond—like soldiers bound together by trench warfare during WWII, or being one of only two tunnel rats in the same platoon in Vietnam. We'd been through a lot together, and even though we weren't best friends, we might be BFFs—best friends forever.

"What's your sister's deepest, darkest fear?"

He delivered this in a way that I mistook for compassion. And since my trust level had dropped to zero, the person whose decisions I trusted the least were my own.

Like I said, I'd become paranoid.

So my mind started spinning off on its own volition, and I wondered if Dr. Wright would ever turn on Teensy. Lord knew, she could be annoying. I myself wanted to slap her silly. But if I gave him confidential information and he used it against my sister—like that guy over in the UK who jumped out of the closet and scared his girlfriend so badly she dropped dead of a heart attack—well, I'd never forgive myself.

I turned the tables on him. "Do you love my sister?"

He let out a humorless chuckle. "She's too unstable."

This jarred me. Then he got up from behind his desk and excused himself into the bathroom. Because I could hear everything going on behind that non-soundproof door, I rose and strolled over to the wall to read his diplomas and licenses as a matter of decorum.

Mitchell I. Wright.

I squinted. Or was the initial a *T*?

Bachelor of Science degree from Baylor University.

Licensed in family . . . *wait—what?*

Counciling?

That riveted my attention, and not in a good way. My eyes nearly bungee jumped out of their sockets. Something dead up the creek. These licenses purported to be issued by different institutions. But while the certificates differed in the typeset used, as well as the shade and grade of paper they were printed on, their common denominator was the word *Counciling* instead of *Counseling.*

I experienced a real *a-ha* moment.

Water splashed in the lavatory.

Mitchell T. Wright was a fraud.

My first thought was a logical one—*Tim.*

Of course he knew where I lived—he'd been inside the family home.

My breathing went shallow. Probably made those diplomas and certificates on his home computer. My heart raced. My hands felt damp and clammy. I glimpsed the twist of the door handle opening and froze in place. The trick was to open the doorknob slowly and hope he didn't notice.

"Whatcha doin'?" he asked.

I could almost pinpoint the exact moment killer instinct flashed in his eyes.

Run for your life.

I felt a thrill of terror. With a smile so forced I felt my jaw go numb, I grabbed the knob to the door leading into the waiting room. I sensed the advancing blur the second he lunged. With anger rolling off him in waves, he came after me. I let out a pathetic scream, but he clapped a hand over my mouth and forced my back against the door.

Thoughts of survival fragmented inside my head. I felt the heat of stale coffee breath against my ear.

"Don't leave," he said in a deep, roughly textured voice. "Listen to me. I don't love your sister. She's a whack-job. It's you I want."

Repelled by the touch of his hands roaming my body, I struggled to break free. He kissed me, hard and insistent, until I thought my gag reflex would kick in. He was bigger and stronger than me, and in this awkward position, I didn't possess the upper-body strength to defeat him. I couldn't knee him in the snow-globes either. My throat tightened. My eyes burned. I remembered in grisly detail what he'd said he was going to do to me: stalk me, rape me, strangle me with my pantyhose, and I needed to make sure that didn't happen.

In a desperate ploy for freedom, I relaxed.

"I'm going to remove my hand, Dainty. Don't scream." See-ing my almost imperceptible head bob, his face hardened into immobility. "I mean it. Don't. Scream."

He had a scary look in his eyes when took his hand off my mouth. His other hand remained against my throat.

I took deep breaths until I got a dizzying rush. And when I

finally spoke, I tried to keep the thickening dismay out of my voice. "You gave Teensy an engagement ring."

He flat-out denied this. Which left me to believe Teensy must've bought the ring herself.

I stood perfectly still and unblinking, as if by doing so, I could lull him into a false sense of security. "Could we sit and talk about this?" And then for no good reason, I added, "Pretty please with sugar on it?" and flashed him a beauty pageant smile.

When he hesitated, I tried a different approach.

"I should call off Teensy—" I slid my hand in my purse "—because when I left the house, she said she'd be here directly. We can't let her know about . . . us."

He backed away enough to give me breathing room.

Instead of pulling out my cell phone, I pulled out my taser and zapped him in the ba-doobies. As he writhed on the floor and emitted a groan of convulsive agony, slinging spittle and shoestring drool onto the carpet, I picked up the heaviest thing on his desk—a bronze of Sigmund Freud—and wielded it overhead.

"Stop thrashing or I'll do it again." In this strange new role reversal, I spoke in an authoritative and almost unrecognizable voice. "I'm asking the questions now, understand?"

He flopped around a few more times before the seizure-like movements abated.

"How'd you come to know my sister?"

"Saw her on TV."

"And me?"

"Same." He panted out his answer in short bursts. "When Border Patrol . . . caught you and that . . . midget sneaking across the border."

For the record, Amanda and I didn't "sneak across the border," but now didn't seem to be the time to set the record straight. I needed answers, and needed them fast.

"Where'd you meet my sister?" The cell phone on his belt shrilled. "Don't answer it. Answer my question."

"Grocery store."

I imagined him seeing her bandaged head and striking up a conversation with her; then gaining her confidence by representing himself as a doctor. Outrage heated my cheeks. He'd gone through my sister to get to me.

"What's your real name? And don't lie or I'll get those women in here." I jutted my chin in the direction of the heifers in the real estate office. I glanced at the prongs from the taser, still fish-hooked near his groin. "I feel like I'm picking low-hanging fruit here. But if you don't answer in the next five seconds, I intend to do this again."

His eyes watered. "George. Please don't do it—George Welch."

"What do you do, George Welch?"

"Realtor." Limp-handed, he thumbed toward the office down the hall.

Like magic, several more puzzle pieces fell into place.

"Let me see if I get this right. Every time I get the right answer, you don't get zapped. You saw me and my sister on TV, and decided you wanted to meet me?" He nodded. "And in order to do that, you came up with a plan to trick my sister by pretending you were a doctor and offering her free counseling so you could find out more about me?" Another nod. "And then—I want to be careful here, because I'd hate to wrongfully shock you, so if I'm getting a little off base, then feel free to chime in with the correct information, okay?" Fear swam in his eyes. "So you're a realtor with an empty office for lease—" I said this slowly as I pieced together his scam "—and you made a bunch of diplomas and certificates, and gave yourself a fake identity."

"Please don't shock me again."

"Then why don't you tell me the rest?"

He was crying now, screeching like a tree full of howler monkeys. Mucus dripped out of his nose, and from the down-turned corners of his mouth. But he pulled himself together enough for me to find out that he'd been following me. Like the day he showed up for the open house, and found me stranded on the side of the road when Gran's car ran out of gas. And the day he drove into the parking lot and waited for me to come out of the building so he could talk to me, but saw the neighbor lady thrashing around on the ground.

"Did you send me letters?"

"No."

I shot him a menacing glare, wagging the taser at him for good measure. I no longer recognized the sound of my own lethal, cruel voice. "I'll ask you once more—and don't lie to me—did you send me letters?"

"No—please—don't do that."

I took a step toward his desk, where I'd seen him sweep my panties into a drawer, and realized that by doing so, I was no longer in a position to crack the statue over his head if he moved. "If you so much as flinch," I warned in a hectoring voice, but I didn't have to finish the threat. Appropriately cowed, he almost seemed like a marionette, with me as the puppeteer.

Keeping my eye fixed firmly on his every move, I put down the bronze, fished until I felt the silk and lace fabric, and dangled them out by one finger.

"Where'd you get these?" I expected him to tell me my sister left them behind. But when he answered, I felt a block of ice where my heart should've been.

"Your bedroom."

"You were in my bedroom?"

"Just for a minute. I swear that's all I took out of the hamper. I just wanted to . . . smell you."

"Do I look like a Barbie doll to you? You want to take off my head and tear off my limbs," I declared in the face of his confession. I felt myself slipping out of control. "Let's just clean the whole fish here, shall we? How many times have you done this before?"

"Never."

Hostility crackled all around me. I hit him with a second charge. He let out a piercing scream. This time, his bowels emptied. In seconds, the room filled with a vile stench. I waited for him to stop thrashing and come out of his stupor.

As he lay curled up on the carpet, sobbing himself into hyperventilation, I repeated my question. "How many other victims?"

"A few."

"You're going to have to do better than that. Ten? Twenty?"

"Five. Maybe six. I can't remember." He seemed on the verge of a coronary, and the words got stuck in his throat.

"Give me names." With my free hand, I switched on the voice recorder on my cell phone and waited. Apparently, I'm intimidating when I'm posturing. I put the phone on the desk, and picked up the statue again and brandished it. "Out with it."

He spit out names of women like Teensy, who he'd taken advantage of. I didn't get six names, but the four that I did get should be plenty.

"You were going to kill me, weren't you?"

He was sobbing again, and groaned out a prolonged *No*.

I gave him a piece of advice. "If you ever come near me or my sister, I'll kill you. Is that clear?"

He bobbed his head with such enthusiasm it's a wonder he didn't get whiplash.

"I'm going to hand you the phone now. You're going to call my sister and put a DNR on the relationship. You know what a DNR is, right? *Do not resuscitate*. Break it off for good. If I get

the idea you're offering her so much as one ounce of encourage-
ment, I swear, I'll hit this switch so many times it'll turn those
grapes into raisins, got it?"

He assured me he understood. I dialed Teensy's number and
tossed him my phone.

"Teensy, it's Doc. Remember when I told you 'Love is a
drug'? Well, your prescription's up." A pause. "Don't ever call
me again. I mean it. You're unstable, and probably dangerous."

I nodded approval. But I knew my sister's stubborn streak.
Teensy was like a booger you couldn't thump off. I sent him an
eye-encrypted message to add more.

"If you ever come near me again, I'll have you arrested, y'
hear?" He pleaded with me through his eyes.

"Tell her she's fat, and that you don't like fat broads," I hissed.

He repeated this word for word.

With a twirl of the finger, I signaled him to *Wrap it up*, which
really didn't turn out to be necessary. According to him,
she'd disconnected as soon as he said "fat." And when
he repeated verbatim what she said, it was completely
"Rubanbleu-unapproved."

After I left George Welch in a crumpled heap, I flew out the
door, to the parking lot, feeling the raindrops like tiny wet kisses
on my face.

I never noticed the angry woman approaching me in the parking lot until I was already behind the wheel with the door
locked. With condemnation written all over her face, she ham-
mered her fist against the window. I nearly stroked-out from
fright.

"You stole my husband." Her words hit me full force.
Startled, if not flat-out petrified, I pretty much just stared. She
must've mistaken me for Teensy because she started screaming
at the top of her lungs. "You're having an affair with my

husband, George. Don't even try to deny it, bitch."

I blasted the horn until she grabbed her ears. As I locked gazes with this dowdy, unsophisticated woman, I pantomimed *Hush* by putting a finger to my lips.

Her eyes misted. I lowered the window an inch or so, and agreed to speak to her as long as she remained calm. She didn't just calm down; she deflated. I've never understood why spurned women get angry at "the other woman." They should be taking their fury out on the man who cheated on them.

"If you mean George Welch, the realtor, he's been stalking me by proxy for several months." When I realized she probably didn't have enough candle power to know what that meant, I told her he'd broken into my room and stolen my panties. I also might've suggested he liked to try on women's lingerie, but I could've hallucinated that part. Then I recommended she count her bras and high heels, and let nature take its course.

"You probably ought to go home and get him a clean pair of slacks," I said. "I think he had an accident." When she arched a confused eyebrow, I added, "He smells like an outhouse."

Mrs. Welch looked pretty rough—the kind of woman you wouldn't want to meet in a dark alley—and when she receded in my rearview mirror with her mouth pinched, and looking a bit puckish, I felt sure she'd give him a comeuppance that was every bit as good as mine, or better.

As soon as I hit the highway, I contacted one of the Dallas detectives who'd come to see Gran. I didn't remember which one I was talking to, but I explained how I'd recently tangled with a rapist, and could supply the names of at least four victims. When I gave him George Welch's name, he said, "Jiminy Christmas," and set me an appointment for nine the following morning.

Chapter Twenty-Four

I admit it, street theater is *so* déclassé, but *Hello,* I'd just experienced one of the worst days of my life. I told myself things couldn't get any worse. I was wrong.

After I recapped my scary experience with George Welch for the Dallas police detectives, I got a phone message from Gordon asking me to go by his house and feed Czar. He was back down at the PD again and suspected investigators might be in the process of getting a search warrant for his home.

As for the dog, he said I could toss food over the fence if I was afraid to go into the house and put chow out through the back door. But then he added that he'd be eternally grateful and make it worth my while if I'd go back inside and make absolutely certain that little black book hadn't fallen into a crevice.

"How eternally grateful?"

"I'll pay you."

"I want my job back. The one you promised me. My externship. I want it back."

"We'll talk. Call me when you're done."

The offer went beyond temptation. I arrived at *Château Pfeiffer* a few minutes before noon. The first thing I did when I entered the house was open the refrigerator. No cheesecake. Then I went to the garage to see where they kept the bag of dog food. Paislee's Jaguar was gone, and so was Gordon's SUV. That made me stop to wonder . . . where'd she park her car?

Not at the TV station, that's for sure. So how'd she ended up in a broom closet in the break room?

About six weeks before, Gordon had hired me to find out who she was seeing, and I ended up giving him photographs I'd shot of his wife entering Tig Welder's house. To me, Tig seemed the most likely murder suspect, but that could've been because I just flat didn't like him. And, much as I wanted to, I still couldn't rule out Gordon—apparently, neither could the police if they'd invited him back for a second interview.

A shiver went up my spine. Even though I had permission to be inside the house, I could already feel my shirt tacking itself to my back. I'd need freon nerves to climb those stairs and search that bedroom for a little black book that I knew wasn't there. But let's face it, I was no longer subsidized by my father—oh, who am I kidding? I was broke—and Gordon would either pay me with money or give me my job back. Either way, it'd be win-win for *moi*.

Upstairs, I got on my hands and knees and looked beneath the bed skirt. What I saw made me feel like I was living in a parallel universe. A day ago, this bed had been uncluttered underneath, with a clear vantage point over to the top of the landing. But today, at high noon, I found a pair of expensive women's shoes. I looked at the maker's mark on the leather insole and saw the name *"Berlanga,"* with *"Hecho en España"* printed beneath it.

Blood pounded in my ears.

I had the skin-crawling feeling I wasn't alone.

Pulled from my search by instinct, triggered by the breaths of an intruder, or the sweep of air from an open door, I snatched up the high heels and came out from under the bed with one in each hand. The heels, alone, could put out an eye, and me, defenseless, with my purse at the foot of the bed.

"Shit." The word exploded from a soprano's mouth.

I drew in a sharp intake of air, then clapped a hand over my mouth to squelch it. This was the first real indication I'd had of sharing the house with an unknown person. I heard the scuffing of sensible shoes against the marble floor, then silence shuddered up to the ceiling.

As I did a quick lean-in, past the dresser and down the stairs, I saw a woman with her back to me, and took in her presence, in stages. She'd dressed in a shock of color that had to be sewn together in lines of pure haute couture. At the sight of her cherry red, shoulder-length hair, I thought I'd found Aspen Wicklow. But this made absolutely no sense. What would Aspen be doing at Gordon's? My mind flashed back to the missing persons report Gordon supposedly filed at the police department. But why would he bother if they were close enough friends for her to have his house key? Rapid-fire scenarios crossed my mind . . . all of them uncharitable, starting with Gordon's dead wife.

I dropped the heels on the bed and snatched up my bag. Reached inside and grabbed my cell phone. Snapped a photo of the woman with her back to me.

I heard a barely audible *click* as the mechanism engaged, but I might as well have fired off a starter pistol.

She suddenly stiffened, then reached for the cutlery block, grabbed a handle, and whipped around brandishing a butcher knife.

"Paislee?" Oops—I might've said that out loud.

Stricken, she spoke to me through the arched opening of the kitchen pass-through. "Who are you? And what're you doing in my house?"

My stomach went hollow.

Sure enough, I stared into the Bambi-eyes of Paislee Pfeiffer. The hair should've been dark brown, almost black, but the sea-green eyes and the voice were the same.

"Paislee? Oh my lord. You're alive." I said this on a whoosh of air.

"Who are you?" She snipped off her words like nail clippers. "I'm calling the cops."

"I'm Dainty. The intern from TCU. I met you here at the Labor Day party."

She smiled an unpleasant smile. "So you're having an affair with my husband?"

For the next twenty seconds I operated in that same parallel universe, back in the Pfeiffer's treehouse, watching this woman through binoculars as she performed CPR on my ex-boyfriend Drex's, genitalia.

"Lord, no." Then, my shock at seeing her wore off and I went mad cow on her. "You're one to talk. You stole my boyfriend."

"Are you crazy? I'm married."

"Damned right you're married, so you shouldn't have been screwing around with everybody and their dog. Do you realize how many lives you ruined?"

"Well, I never!" Flashes of anger glinted off her pupils. Having her virtue maligned offended her. She stared, burning a hole in me with her laser-like eyes as she came out from behind the pass-through, still holding the knife. I held my ground at the top of the landing. "How dare you talk to me that way? I'm having my husband fire you."

"*Ha.*" The word exploded like a cannon blast. "Your husband's divorcing you."

"Gordon would never leave me. He loves me." She wound up in a normal tone of voice. "I'm calling the police."

I took my first step toward her, descending the stairway with my hand barely touching the banister. "I have permission from Gordon to be here." Then I took another step, and a *très, très,* bad thing happened.

Instead of picking up the telephone twenty feet away, she

moved toward the alarm panel and set it off.

"We'll just see about this," Paislee said, whereupon we stood our ground in our respective places: Paislee, in the front foyer where she could keep an eye on me; me, seated near the top of the landing with my fingers wrapped around the taser in case she got any funny ideas; and the dog, outside, resting rigid next to the flower bed, tense and alert and waiting to burst through the lanai like the point man on a DEA no-knock warrant.

"Now what?" My demeanor went even frostier.

"We wait for the cops to get here. I'm having you arrested for breaking and entering."

"There's no such thing as breaking and entering in Texas. It's burglary. You watch too much TV." Then I wanted to slap myself for helping her.

"Fine. I'm having you arrested for burglary," she said with quiet insistence.

"Fine. Then maybe we'll get to the bottom of this *Who killed Paislee Pfeiffer?* thing." I had no idea what might happen, but I knew that I had to put an end to this ongoing imbroglio with the Fort Worth police. "We thought you were dead."

"Why would you think I was dead?" she snapped, all angry and confused and slamming her dyed-red eyebrows together.

"Well, for one thing, you rolled out of the broom closet."

This disclosure confused her even more. "Are you calling me a witch? Because if you are, Gordon's firing you for sure, missy."

I recapped events from the last few days. When I came to the cringeworthy part of the story—the death-warmed-over smell in the break room—I saw the change in her demeanor as she absorbed my words.

Faint sirens wailed in the distance. I knew the police were only blocks away, and didn't like to think of doing an overnighter in jail while Gordon sorted out the mess.

And if Paislee wasn't dead, then who was?

She moved toward me, considering me at the foot of the stairs, her pale sea-green eyes dazzling me beneath the fringe of dark lashes.

I knew if the police didn't believe me, they'd haul me downtown and Paislee might leave. It'd be days—or longer—before I could prove my innocence.

The sirens shrilled louder.

I said, "I'm calling Gordon." And I did. The call cycled to voicemail. I left a short message for him to call, and then texted him: *Your wife is alive. I know because she pulled a knife on me.*

Then I sat back and waited.

"I like your dress. Where'd you get it?"

"Spain."

My heart started doing the rapid-beat thing as I began to understand my miscalculation. "When were you in Spain?" She didn't answer. I remembered that Paislee's sister left Czar with Paislee because she was doing a photo shoot in Spain. Then I remembered either Gordon or Rochelle telling me the sisters were twins. I'm all for blinders when the need arises, but this wasn't one of those times. I suddenly realized it wasn't Paislee who'd slept with Drex, and Tig, and who knew who else?

Once or twice during my internship last semester, I'd heard Gordon remark how bored his wife was sitting around the house. He said she complained about never getting to go anywhere fun, while her sister jetted all over the world on photo shoots. Rochelle suggested he talk her into taking a class at the community college, and I think Gordon tried, but that fell on deaf ears. He even came into the office one day saying how much better things would be if he could take the time off to fly to Europe with her—maybe that'd settle her down for a while. But a vacation wasn't in the cards for him. Not only had Gordon become something of a boozer, he was also a workaholic.

If Gordon thought the woman on the viewing screen in the

morgue was his wife, then it must've been Paislee's sister. Nothing like the shock of scandal to clear my head . . .

I felt a thrill—a very bad sign.

"I just figured it out." But I was thinking, *How slow am I?*

Sirens died out in front of the house. I talked fast. "You talked your sister into trading places with you, didn't you? You took her photo shoot in Spain and left her here with her dog and your husband. But what you didn't know is that your sister— what's her name?"

"Penslee."

"Right. Penslee. While your sister was here pretending to be you, she ran around stirring up trouble, sleeping with people Gordon knew, and even some he didn't know. And all the time she did this while pretending to be you. I guess she figured if she made him angry and stayed away, he wouldn't figure out y'all had exchanged places. One of the men she slept with was my boyfriend, Drex. Remember him from the Labor Day picnic? You were wearing a green and white flowered print sundress, cut low in the front, and he couldn't take his eyes off you."

Her eyes went wide. Realization dawned, and I could only hope it was because this confirmed that I'd been an invited guest in her home.

A heavy knock sounded on the door, the kind of knock that jostles the hinges and rattles the glass. The cops had arrived and I was about to "beat the rap, but not the ride" as they say. Again. I felt my words working their way to the surface until I bit out, "You broke Gordon's heart."

Footsteps thundered up the exterior spiral staircase. Then they stopped. I glanced over my shoulder and saw FWPD through the glass panel in the door.

Okay, I cracked.

"Would you mind calling them off, please? Someone murdered your sister. Your husband thinks you're dead. He viewed her body on the video screen at the morgue. I'll tell you everything I know. I'm not seeing your husband, I work for him. Call off the cops and we'll talk." *Pretty please?* "Help them find who killed Penslee."

The knock at the front door grew louder. The officer out on the landing shouted, "She's up here." To me, he yelled, "Open up." When I turned around to let him in, he muttered, "Aw, crap—you again?"

CHAPTER TWENTY-FIVE

Paislee Pfeiffer and I both ended up down at the police station, but only one of us rode in a patrol car. Care to guess which one? Not me.

Parking places are slim pickings down around the PD because the Fort Worth Police Department sits across from the Tarrant County Justice Center, and is catty-cornered from the Tarrant County Jail. So you have people who are about to be thrown in the slammer in one building, people who've already been thrown in the slammer in another building, and people who've been thrown in the slammer who are trying to get out in yet another building. Not to mention all the "baby mamas," in all states of sobriety outside the jail, who were trying to communicate through the use of incomprehensible hand signals with their worthless "baby daddys," who may or may not have been able to see them behind the window slits and wire mesh in the salmon-colored brick walls. So let's just agree that the parking situation is backed up tighter than my fictitious great uncle Harold's colon and leave it at that.

While Paislee Pfeiffer got the third degree from detectives, Gordon took one shocked look at his wife and complained of chest pains. When last I saw him, paramedics hauled him out of the station on a clacking gurney.

I stopped off at Bruckman's office first. He told me he was working a lead but wasn't sure yet, so he was keeping his opinions to himself. He asked me to come back in a half hour, after he made a few phone calls.

As I headed for the door, he said, "I broke up with Babette."

I felt a shiver run up me and stop in a place where it shouldn't have stopped. My heart banged against my ribs trying to get out. I wanted to launch myself into his arms. My muscles had somehow short-circuited the message to come back in a half hour and I stood, anchored in place, instead of leaving. I drew in a long breath before speaking, and then for no good reason, cut myself off. If Bruckman wanted to get back together, it needed to come from him. I'd already thrown myself at him too many times lately.

He said, "What's wrong? I thought you'd be happy."

Not only did his announcement catch me by surprise, but one of his colleagues walked in and set a brown envelope on his desk. I didn't quite know what to say now that we no longer had privacy, so I told him I wanted to buy a gun.

"A .38 caliber like the one you carry off duty."

I prepared to tell him about fake Dr. Wright and what happened earlier, when the other detective walked back out the door.

Without a preamble, he reached into his ankle holster and pulled out a Smith & Wesson Chief Special, popped open the cylinder, and handed it over. This five-shot revolver only had four bullets loaded in it. I hooked a fingernail under one, pulled it out, and turned it over. Sure enough, Bruckman carried copper-jacketed hollow points.

"Why only four rounds?" My heart beat fast. "Where's the fifth bullet?" My voice dissolved to a whisper. I instantly knew why he'd only chambered four rounds, and I wished my tongue didn't have a hair trigger, and that the words hadn't shot out of my mouth. Now, all I could think of was getting out of his office.

"What are you talking about?" Bruckman's wheat-colored

brows slammed together in confusion.

A call came in and Bruckman took it. While he spoke to the caller, he waggled his fingers for me to give him back his snub nose. When he looked at the open cylinder, his stare curdled my blood. Then he snapped the cylinder shut and returned the S&W to his leg holster. As he listened to the voice on the other end of the line, he muffled the receiver and mouthed, "Don't leave."

But I was thinking maybe I'd been wrong. That George Welch was just a pervert who got his jollies conquering pretty women; and Teensy had turned into a jealous witch; and that neither had a thing to do with my stalker. But I wasn't about to stick around when it dawned on me that Bruckman could've been the one who stuck that bullet under my windshield.

He said, "I'll take care of it," and then clicked over to the other line. "Bruckman." After a few seconds of lag time, he said, "Hey beautiful, are you free for an early dinner? I'll pick you up at work around four o'clock."

I experienced a polar shift.

Instinct told me he was talking to Babette, and I figured I must've just witnessed the shortest breakup in history. Instead of wasting my time with a world-class cheaterpants, I headed down the hall to find Detective Leland.

When Detective Leland saw me in the doorway, he invited me inside.

"Sit," he said, grim-faced, in his usual deadpan baritone, and patted the air downward with his palm.

I filled him in on the video that'd popped up on the Internet, as well as the "Dainty Dishes" website and the fake social network page. He wanted to see the video, of course, and watched it while I sat cringing.

"Well, it's definitely your face, but that's not your body. With all the porn out in the ether, there are a whole lot of women with prettier bodies to choose from. Seems to me, whoever did this not only wanted to humiliate you because of the porn aspect, but also wanted to embarrass you by superimposing your face on someone who didn't have a rockin' body."

Exactly.

Well, at least we were on the same page. I continued to feel adrift.

He said, "We identified several prints off a couple of the documents."

I'd half expected this, and figured he'd tell me they belonged to George Welch, AKA Dr. Wright, but to my horror, he told me they belonged to Teensy.

Teensy might be nuts, but in all fairness, she had access to the mail as an intern, and I told him so. But the bigger mystery was how he got Teensy's fingerprints for comparison. I knew she'd never been arrested, so there was no reason for her prints to appear in the AFIS database. And I didn't recall her saying whether she or anyone else from the TV station had given their prints voluntarily in order to rule themselves out as suspects in Paislee's so-called murder.

I took a stroll on the blunt side. "My sister's never been arrested, and she's never applied for any jobs where she'd have to give her fingerprints as a condition of employment. So how do you know they're hers?"

I sat speechless as he told me that Teensy furnished her fingerprints, along with other applicants, when she applied for a job at the police department a few weeks prior.

I hooted. "Teensy? A cop?" The *You're pulling my leg* factor kicked in. "No. Teensy planned to go into nursing."

"She applied for a position in the forensics lab."

"Teensy? Are you kidding me? Last week, she almost electrocuted herself with a hair crimper. I'd like somebody to explain how she's qualified to operate electrostatic lifting devices, and any other expensive equipment you people have on hand. Seriously—make note of that. We're talking *Disaster waiting to happen.* You heard it here first."

He didn't say anything right away, which only heightened my anxiety.

"Unbelievable." I flicked invisible sweat from my brow, expelled a relieved sigh, and tried to look on the bright side. "For a minute, I thought you were going to tell me she had an arrest record." I mentioned this with a nervous giggle. "Which we know isn't true, because she's . . . well, she's a Prescott. We're debutantes. We're in The Rubanbleu." I gave him an aristocratic sniff. He should've been able to tell by looking at us that jail and the Prescott sisters would be an imperfect fit for The Rubanbleu.

His smile flatlined. "You don't know your sister as well as you think you do." He thumbed in the direction of the county lockup. "She's in jail right now."

"That's impossible. I just saw her this morning."

"We get a printout every day. Her name's on it. I saw it a few minutes ago." As I sat, pole-axed, Leland did a quick lean-in. "Look, I've been wanting to talk to her about this but she keeps blowing me off. I'd like to eliminate her as a suspect, because, as you say, she had the occasional mailroom duty, so there could be a perfectly legitimate excuse for her fingerprints being on these documents."

"My sister's gone berserk lately, but she's no stalker and she didn't write these letters."

He shook his head. "She's not under arrest for that. Yet."

I told him about Teensy's boyfriend, and how he attacked me earlier. I suggested Detective Leland network with the Dallas PD detective handling the case. After I finished telling him about my experience, I wanted to see my sister and get to the bottom of this, since Detective Leland practically had me convinced that George Welch and Teensy were acting in concert together to get my job, and perhaps Teensy had asked him to scare me out of the TV station and out of the broadcast journalism field altogether.

Chapter Twenty-Six

Since visiting hours at the Tarrant County Jail wouldn't take place for several hours, Detective Leland escorted me over to lockup and made arrangements with the watch commander for me to see my sister. I was told I'd have twenty minutes to talk to her, and not one second more, so I secured my purse in one of the safety lockers, and went through security in order for them to make sure I wasn't a terrorist smuggling in a stinger missile. This isn't my first rodeo with metal detectors, but I had to go through twice because I'd neglected to remove my shoes, and the metal shank inserted between the sole and the insole set off the buzzer.

Five minutes later, I ended up on the other side of a Plexiglass window, perched on an uncomfortable metal stool, with a phone receiver pressed to my ear. A blur of orange cloth swept past the unoccupied partition next to mine, and then a jailer escorted Teensy to the stool on the other side of me. Once the guard stepped out of sight, she picked up the telephone receiver mounted on the wall beside her.

Words rushed out in breathless, abbreviated strokes. "Oh my lord, Dainty, I'm so glad you're here." She said this in a hushed whisper, as if we were being recorded, or the jailer remained within earshot, but beyond my view. In the midst surrounding the *What the hellness* of this situation, she seemed appreciative that I'd come to see her.

"What the hell's wrong with you? What have you done?"

She put a finger to her lips and shushed me. "Calm down. Everything's fine . . . perfect."

I glanced around, frantic. "You're in jail, Teensy. You got yourself arrested and embarrassed the family, and for all I know, as soon as this hits the papers, you'll be kicked out of The Rubanbleu."

"None of it matters."

Since when did membership in The Rubanbleu not matter? But my sister seemed relatively unaffected by her surroundings, as if she'd discovered how to live, rent free, with all of her meals cooked for her on a daily basis.

"What asinine thing did you do to get yourself here?"

"Don't worry. It was nothing."

I found the cavalier attitude off-putting. Then I thought back to fourteen, unpaid, photo-enforced red-light tickets that were still marinating in a brown envelope in my bedroom, and considered maybe Teensy had accumulated a few on her own.

"Cops don't just go around jerking people up and throwing them in the slammer. What the devil did you do?"

"I bought weed. The dealer was an undercover cop."

"Oh my god." The next part, I said to the ceiling. "My sister's a drug addict."

"Stop it. I need to talk to you. Pay attention, Dainty. It isn't anything like that."

"I don't even know you anymore." I brushed back a strand of hair from my forehead and stared at the person on the other side of the glass. She acted more like the Teensy I'd grown up with than the borderline sociopath I'd been putting up with for more than a week. "Are you a drug addict?"

"I don't have a drug problem. Please don't cry, Dainty. If you cry, I'll cry. If you'll just simmer down I'll tell you everything." She inclined her head past the short partition and vectored the guard's location. "We don't have a lot of time so I need you to be quiet and just listen. This was the one and only time I've ever bought weed."

"You're such an idiot."

"No—" she shook her head in all seriousness "—I'm not. I'm the smart one, remember?" She winked. "I never intended to steal your job. You're the pretty one. The one who's meant to sit in front of a camera. I need to be a lawyer, or a medical doctor. And I'm sorry for all the mean things I said and did over the past week. I love you. You're my sister. And you're the most important person in the world to me."

"So all those mean things you said . . . ?" My brain tingled. I thought I might be losing my mind.

She shrugged and gave me a wan smile. "I didn't mean any of them."

"And that crazy stuff you pulled at the office meeting . . . and those bizarre clothes . . . and the pink hair?"

"It had to be done—for you, and Daddy, and Gran."

Tears blistered my eyes. But the mention of Daddy bolstered my confidence in her ability to get bailed out quickly. In his absence, I spoke for him, and put the most positive spin on her situation. "He'll get you a bondsman. He'll hire the best attorney money can buy to get the charges dropped. In a few years, we'll get your record expunged. It'll be like this never happened."

She shook her head. "I don't want out."

"But, why?" So far, none of this registered with me. Most people who get locked up in jail are climbing the walls to get out. Not Teensy. You'd think she just learned she could live here with free room and board for up to two years.

She moved in close, until we were inches from each other, separated only by a clear plastic shield. Her voice dropped in inverse proportion to her proximity to the glass. When we were little kids, and the adults gathered in Gran's informal living area, Teensy and I were excused to allow the grown-ups converse in private. But they overlooked the fact that the room had a mezzanine with secret doors and fake walls, so while the adults were discussing topics too mature for Teensy and me to understand, she and I were honing our lip-reading skills. I sensed my sister was about to do that now, and what she mouthed chilled me to my core.

"I'm three cells down from Nerissa." With the two-way telephone receiver still pressed to her ear, she mouthed, "Can you keep a secret?"

I nodded, continuing to lip-read.

"I've come here to kill her."

For a few seconds, I sat speechless, trying to piece together what I'd just heard. "Are you engaged?"

She shook her head.

"Is Dr. Wright your boyfriend?"

Another head shake.

"Do you even know who he is?"

She nodded. "Well, sure. He's my therapist."

"I don't understand. Why would you act like a psycho and make all that stuff up?"

"Insanity defense. He can testify that I'm crazy. I'm not responsible for my crimes if I'm mentally ill." She nodded knowingly, and then winked again.

I was seated across from an evil genius. My sister had hatched a plan that took frontier justice to an art form.

"You can't go through with this. Your 'Dr. Wright's' a fraud. He's not a real doctor." I could read the disbelief in her face. She thought I'd made it up. That I was lying to discourage her from making a huge mistake. "It's true, Teensy. I went to see him."

She shook her head, and it nearly killed me to tell her the rest of it.

'He saw me on the *News at Ten* broadcast when Amanda and crossed the border to get back into the United States. He said it was love at first sight for him, and he thought he could get to me through you. You're the one who needed help. So he posed as a psychologist and offered you free therapy."

She nodded, trancelike.

"There's nobody to bolster your insanity claim, Teensy. If you insist on doing it now that you know this, I have to tell Daddy. I have to save you from yourself."

"Don't. I worked this out while you were gone, and I already laid the groundwork to get this far. Nerissa murdered our mother, and tried to kill Daddy. She deserves what she gets." Then she drew her finger across her throat in a long cello stroke to indicate a grisly ending. And, just so there was no mistake, she mouthed, "Death."

I'd have to tell, of course. As much as I wanted justice for my mother, and Daddy, I couldn't let her go through with her plan. I couldn't let her ruin her life.

Now that I knew the reason for her bizarre behavior I spoke into the receiver and asked the burning question. "Teensy, I have to know the truth. Are you behind the letters?"

"What letters?" She seemed genuinely puzzled.

"Did you send me stalker letters?" When she shook her head, I became more insistent. "Because the police found your fingerprints on a couple of envelopes."

"Easy to explain—Rochelle asked me to distribute the mail."

As the guard moved in to take my sister back to her cell, Teensy pressed her little finger to the glass. "Pinkie swear."

I lined up my pinkie even with hers, and touched mine to the glass.

She mouthed, *I love you,* as the jailer took her away, and that's when I thought, *Holy cow, I'm going to hell.*

★ ★ ★ ★ ★

After I retrieved my purse from the safety locker, I tried to c
Daddy on my cell phone, but couldn't get a signal until I walke
out of the jail. Upon leaving the building, I still didn't feel like
I'd gotten one step closer to identifying my stalker, and if I had
to go much longer without knowing, I'd be the one who ended
up in a padded room at Club Med. I considered Teensy's
behavior in the time I'd been home, and didn't like to think
about what went on during the two weeks I hunted down our
stepmother.

I do recall Amanda mentioning how Teensy confessed that
the last time she went out, she woke up naked, duct-taped to
the exterior wall of a microbrewery in Deep Ellum, with no
memory of how she got there. I wrote it off as just another way
for my sister to try to impress Amanda, so Amanda would think
Teensy was more fun to hang out with than me. Which, we all
knew, she was not.

When I concluded that Amanda might be the sanest person
in my social circle, well, I found the notion to be pretty daunting.

CHAPTER TWENTY-SEVEN

While I stood on the sidewalk in front of the jail, Bruckman pulled up next to me in the unmarked patrol car and lowered the passenger window.

"Get in." When I tried to ignore him, he said, "I'm not going out with Babette tonight. I told you we were done, and I meant it."

I waited for the traffic signal to change, refusing to make eye contact while he continued to talk.

"Get in, Dainty. I think I've figured out who's behind this."

I shot him a look of utter disgust. His head should've disintegrated, but no, he just kept talking.

"Get in. I have to make a stop first."

The driver behind him tapped the horn. The light had turned green but I stayed put. Bruckman made no effort to go through the intersection, and, instead, proceeded to inconvenience the long line of drivers stacked up behind him.

With a dismissive flick of the wrist, I said, "Just go, Bruckman. Leave me alone."

"What are you mad at? I told you I broke up with her."

The driver in the car behind him laid on the horn. Bruckman jammed his cruiser in park, jumped out, and stormed over to the driver's window with his badge held aloft. I seized the opportunity to get away. Once I reached the other side of the street, I heard the squeal of tires and the roar of an engine behind me. Instead of keeping to the sidewalk, I ducked into a

multi-story garage and picked up my pace, happy that Br
couldn't drive through the railroad-crossing control
without a key card.

But I'd underestimated his ability to get what he wante
because the next sound I heard was the scream of his tires as he
curbed the vehicle. Footfalls thundered behind me, echoing
through the open area of the above-ground garage. I moved
ahead at a trot, hearing the click of my heels and the swish of
traffic behind me.

He yelled, "Police. Stop her," to a couple of winos sharing a
bottle on the opposite corner.

My eyes searched the sidewalk beyond them, but when the
men fanned out and staggered toward me with their arms
outstretched, I had no choice but to halt in my tracks. One had
a face like a dried-up riverbed, and they both had swamp fumes
radiating off their scum-infused clothing. When considering the
lesser of the evils, I had to go with Bruckman.

He called off his newly deputized, smelly accomplices, and
they went back to working on solutions to the national deficit.

I whipped around to face him. "What do you want?"

"Geez, Dainty, what the hell's the matter with you?"
Cornflower blue eyes thinned into slits.

"Well, I'm afraid that's going to require a list." Said nastily. I
gave him an eye roll that threatened to jump out of my head,
spin across the concrete floor, and out into traffic.

"Dainty, listen to me. I think I know who your stalker is, but
I need to make a stop first. Go with me."

"Why? So you can strangle me with my pantyhose?"

"What?" The surprise in his voice carried a bit of hang time
before the reverberating din of traffic absorbed it. "Oh, now
that's not going to help, is it?" He shot me an equally cutting
look.

But I wasn't having any of this. "You told me you broke up

r. And then you asked her out to dinner. What're you
to do, take me along?" I said in a raw voice.

ᴀe brought his hands down on my shoulders, stilling me.
ᴀll me a lovesick baby, but my emotions flared as I stood there
ᴀuming.

"I'm doing this for you. Don't you care?"

"Let's just say if you could work the term 'rat's ass' in there,
you'd have it."

The winos barked out a couple of laughs. Then one turned
and projectile-vomited on the other one's shoes. On the street
where Bruckman abandoned his vehicle, we heard tires scream
against the asphalt, and the sound of metal-on-metal behind it.

Uh-oh, that sounded expensive.

I turned to see if Bruckman's unit had been struck, but it
turned out to be the driver of the car behind his, trying to avoid
ramming the unmarked patrol car's bumper. Instead, he got his
own bumper rammed by the driver of the car behind him.

Watch out for the guy behind the guy in front of you.

Right out in front of the police station, I might add.

I don't actually remember what he said that took the fight
out of me, and made me give up and trudge back to the
unmarked car with him like a convicted felon. I sat in the front
seat while Bruckman made sure everyone at the accident scene
was okay, and then radioed for a traffic cop to come to the
scene and investigate the accident. Once the traffic investigator
arrived, he took photos, measured skid marks, and diagrammed
the collision, allowing Bruckman and me to leave the scene.

After we were well beyond the downtown traffic and out on
Airport Freeway heading east toward Dallas, I asked where we
were going.

"To tell you the truth, it didn't add up until an hour ago,
when you asked to see my backup pistol. Every day since I've
been a cop, anytime I've carried that Smith, I've popped open

the cylinder and made sure it was loaded with five rounds
going on duty. I did this out of habit, to make certain no
messed with my weapon. Every morning but this morning."

"What does that have to do with my stalker unless you.
him?"

His expression hardened. "I'm going to let that go for right
now." He took a calming breath. "I checked every morning
except this morning, because this morning I broke up with Babette."

In my fascinating journey to clarity, I still didn't see where
this was going. I checked the time on my watch and reminded
him, with unmistakable sarcasm, of the four o'clock dinner date
with Babette.

He said, "I'm sorry you had to hear that but I didn't expect
her to call, and I didn't expect you to be standing there when
she did. I had no intention of taking her to dinner. I just wanted
to make sure she waited at her office for me instead of going
home."

"If you broke up with her, why do you care if she goes home?"

"A hunch. I have a key to her house and I don't want her
showing up when I'm there."

For a moment, I thought maybe he intended to pick up a few
personal items he'd left there when they were trying to make it
work as a couple. But the closer we came to her house, the
creepier I felt.

The words I'd been wanting to ask finally worked their way
to the surface, until I bit out, "What? Did you move in with
her?"

"No."

"I see. She moved in with you." I shook my head in disbelief.

"She didn't move in with me. But she's been staying there
almost a week because she's having her kitchen redone and the
house is a mess. At least that was her excuse. We'll see."

y do you even care?"

et me do my job. Let me play out my hunch."

found this galling, and we drove the next few miles in silence th me snubbing Bruckman, and Bruckman checking his watch at varying intervals.

His cell phone bleated. According to my watch, it was ten past four. Babette probably wondered what took so long.

"Aren't you going to answer that?" I wanted to snatch it up and answer, so she could hear my voice. I debated . . . couldn't happen.

"No. Not yet." He tightened his jaw.

The ringtone stopped, but a few minutes later, his phone went off again.

This time, he locked gazes before answering. "Dainty, I know the way you are. Do not, under any circumstances, pull any of your dumb stunts, or whatever you women do to mark your territory or put your claws out and let your rival know you've got the upper hand."

Moi? By way of illustration, I touched a hand to my chest and feigned an offended expression.

"I'm not kidding. Do not say a freaking word to let her know you're with me—understand?"

"You're scaring me."

"I'm a little worried myself." He thumbed on the phone before it cycled to voicemail, and Bruckman's one-sided part of the conversation played out in the front seat of unmarked cruiser. "Bruckman. Sorry. Yes, I knew it was you—you have your own ringtone. I couldn't catch the phone in time. Because the traffic's backed up, that's why. Babette, don't start. Look, there's a wreck up ahead and the traffic's down to one lane. I'll get there as fast as I can. Maybe ten minutes. Just sit tight." Then he slid me a sidelong glance. "Me, too."

No need to mention what that meant. Insulted, I sniffed and

turned my face toward the window to show my disple. then re-fluffed my hair at the sight of my reflection.

Bruckman thumbed off the phone, laid it on the seat betwe us, and reached over and gripped my knee. "Don't read anythin into it."

"I never gave it another thought." We both knew that wasn't true.

"We have ten, maybe fifteen minutes tops before she calls again." His mouth hiked up at one corner, and I noticed the contrast of his skin and his cornflower blue eyes were made even more delicious by the blue in his shirt.

Driving on Airport Freeway was absolutely insane. Think bumper car hell where people drove like maniacs, and people in flatbed trucks or pickups never tied down their loads. Bruckman dodged boards from broken furniture that had spilled onto the highway, and trash and other debris that blew out of the back of lawn trucks.

When we rounded the last corner to Babette's, Bruckman asked if I had my cell phone, and then told me to wait in the car. He made the task he'd delegated to me seem important, trying to sell it to me as though I'd have to be his eyes and ears.

"She drives a black T-bird. If she drives up, call me immediately. Got that?"

"But you told her to wait ten minutes."

"What can I say, Dainty? Like you, she doesn't always listen." Then he gave me the visual once-over and pronounced me perfect. "But then you already know that." He walked away from the car and keyed open Babette's front door.

I glanced at my watch and started the ten-minute countdown, only we'd already burned up three minutes, so I spotted him six with a minute to spare.

My phone went off, notifying me of a new text message. Since the text returned to the area code for El Paso, I knew it

om Amanda, probably wanting to know if I wanted pizza
inner, and planning to hit me up for a big tip and gouge
on the delivery charges, even though it was already time for
er to get off work.

The text said she'd gotten her driver's license renewed, *sans*
makeup, but when she checked her rearview mirror on the way
out of the DPS parking lot, she got a rude awakening, and for
the next six years, she'd be known as the man with the black
eyeliner.

Then Amanda called my cell phone.

"Got your message about the eyeliner, but I'm on another
call. Ta-ta for now." I didn't have another call but she didn't
know that.

Distracted by the moment, I realized Bruckman had exceeded
the safety net by two minutes. I bailed out of the car and flung
myself through the front door. It opened to a prolonged squeak,
the kind heard in horror movies just before the serial killer
throws his next victim in the trunk and speeds off. Then the
door sucked shut behind me.

CHAPTER TWENTY-EIGHT

Babette's place had a decidedly eerie feel, with the living room drapes drawn and the TV blaring louder than the stereo. The afternoon sun slanted through the slit formed by the two curtain halves, striping the carpet yellow, like a no pass zone.

Frantic, I called out Bruckman's name.

"Back here—hurry."

I followed the sound of his voice, to a rear bedroom where I got the shock of my life. Aspen Wicklow, on the brink of tears, was tied to a chair, looking gaunt and dehydrated, with duct tape peeled back from her lips. An empty water glass lay at her feet, while Bruckman unsuccessfully sawed at her bindings with a paring knife, presumably from Babette's unimproved kitchen. The air around her was noxious with the smell of human waste and rotten food. To my horror, I saw my black cashmere coat on the floor, and knew instantly that Aspen must've borrowed it. I hadn't seen it since my first night back at the station. Unexpectedly, the puzzle pieces fell together and two words popped into mind: *Mistaken identity.*

I studied Aspen's face and witnessed the expression of someone who'd just realized that the debutante she didn't particularly like was not only the one who'd gotten her into this scrape, but was also the one who may have saved her life.

My heart beat so fast it echoed in my ears. Bruckman had managed to cut her duct-taped hands free, but not her ankles. Babette had used zip ties, probably pilfered from Bruckman's

gear, and they were harder to cut through. For no good
~on, I took Aspen's picture with my camera phone. When
~uckman pronounced it a good thing, I snapped a few more
~ver her protests.

Aspen placed her head in her palms, massaging an obvious
headache. In a moment of disorientation, she said, "I want my
mom."

Bruckman asked for a time check. We were five minutes past
the self-imposed limit. Completely unfazed, he said, "She'll be
on her way. I want you to take my car and drive it around the
corner." He dug in his pocket and handed me the keys.

"Don't leave me," Aspen cried.

"Nobody's leaving you, sweetie. You're going, too."

I said, "Can't you just call her and make sure she's still there?"

"She's not. It's her fifteen-minute rule." Then he explained
it. Babette didn't wait on anyone to keep a lunch or dinner
date. After fifteen minutes, she packed it in, and added you to
her "You're dead to me" list.

I took Bruckman's keys. He instructed me to back the car
into the driveway, and open the trunk while he carried WBFD-
TV's *News at Ten* anchor out of Babette's self-styled prison,
chair and all.

I did as I was told. As soon as I popped open the trunk,
Bruckman loaded Aspen into the opening. As I sped away with
the lid bouncing, I caught glimpses of Bruckman in the mirror,
walking back into the house. I drove one block over and rounded
the corner. Halfway down the block, I saw a man in a wife-
beater "T" working on a Harley in his garage.

I slammed on the brakes, jammed the car into park, bailed
out, and ran toward him. He barely had time to jump up with
his monkey wrench and get into position so he could knock my
lights out in the event he perceived me as a threat.

"I need your help. A knife. I need a knife." Dizzy with the

promise of protecting incriminating evidence, we unl▓
Aspen from the trunk.

The biker pulled a survival knife out of his boot, the k▓
with a sharp edge on one side of the blade, and a serrated edg▓
on the other. I told him not to damage the chair. Then I asked
for a paper sack to put Aspen's bindings into, like an honest-to-
goodness crime scene detective.

I grabbed Aspen's hands and gripped them until she winced
and focused on me. "I have to go back but I'll leave you my
phone. Call Sheriff Granger. We'll sort out the rest later. I have
to go back for Bruckman." To the biker, I said, "Call the cops,
and don't let anything happen to her." Then I grabbed the chair,
tossed it in the trunk, and slammed the lid.

When I rounded the corner, the air thickened. The black
T-bird was parked in the driveway. What I'd been through so far
had been a carnival of enjoyment compared to what happened
next.

Blood pounded in my ears.

I pushed into the house, to voices and hysteria. My muscles
had somehow short-circuited the trip wires to the common
sense lobe of my brain, and I moved forward instead of running
back to the car. With my frayed nerves sparking, I crept across
the room, staying beyond Babette's vantage point if she looked
down the corridor. The music had reached a deafening pitch,
and WBFD's *Live at Five* report blared on the TV, but as long
as Babette was raving, I could pinpoint her location.

As I closed in on the back bedroom, I caught words like
"mistake" and "together" and "our secret" and "kill."

Babette, who'd completely lost her composure, had turned
into a sniveling mess. "You weren't supposed to find out,
Jimmy." Then I saw the glint of metal, and thought *Gun.* "I can
take care of Aspen. If you just won't say anything to anyone
about this, I'll go away. I can't go to prison. I can't."

uldn't hear Bruckman's response, but when Babette spoke
, the tone and texture of her voice had changed. It no
ger sounded hypnotic and manipulative, nor whiny and
iildlike. She had full command of it, and I sensed only deadli-
ness in her presence.

My heart fluttered, and not in a good way.

Then I heard her laugh over something I wasn't privy to, and
I became more frightened than ever for Bruckman.

He said, "Put down the gun, Babette. Everything's going to
be fine." Which at least Bruckman and I knew meant not so
fine. Shrouded in mystery, the rest of their conversation sounded
pretty "Deep Throat" to me.

Enough of the melodrama.

This excessive, if not cloyingly psychotic, behavior had frayed
my last raw nerve.

I slipped up behind Babette. She and Bruckman eyed each
other like a couple of gunslingers. Then his eyes flickered to me,
and his expression changed.

The love of my life betrayed me with a look.

Babette whipped around two seconds too late. By that time,
I'd tazed her with a full charge.

After Bruckman subdued her, and she finally stopped thrashing, she sent me a knifelike glare meant to cut me dead.

In a roughly textured voice—his cop voice—he placed Babette under arrest, hoisted her to her feet, and led her out to
the unmarked patrol car in handcuffs before the first marked
unit ever rolled up.

CHAPTER TWENTY-NINE

While Bruckman wrote a report, I watched through the interview room's two-way mirror as Detective Leland interrogated Babette in his controlled, dispassionate tone. The detective wasn't that large in stature, but he had a formidable voice that made him seem like a giant.

I'd been correct in assuming the kidnap of Aspen Wicklow was a case of mistaken identity, because Babette confessed that she'd planned to eliminate the competition and do me in. She'd gotten a stomach full of Bruckman talking about how wonderful and brave and tenacious I was—okay, she didn't exactly use those words but I knew what she meant—and brooding over me while I was in Mexico hunting down Nerissa. Eventually, she'd come to the daunting conclusion that even though he'd erased me from his mind, he couldn't erase me from his heart. Consequently, she couldn't get me out of her thoughts.

As I stood at the two-way mirror and listened, Babette confessed that she owned a computer-geek business and had created the offensive profiles that purported to be mine. You'd think Bruckman might've mentioned her occupation to me, wouldn't you? But I guess I hadn't gotten around to telling him about the YouTube videos, and he didn't know to ask until he listened in on Babette's interrogation.

What didn't come out in Babette's confession, Aspen Wicklow filled in the blanks. As the two of us left the PD together later that night, Aspen described how she'd left her phone in

nagged my black cashmere coat on the hall tree, and
outside with the collar upturned to keep the biting
from reddening her face. In her best guess, Babette had
owed one of the night janitors in through the gate, and laid
wait for me. Once she mounted her attack, she'd put her
plan in motion and had no choice but to follow through. She
duct-taped Aspen's hands and forced her into the car, and the
next day during the open house, she returned during the hub-
bub to dispose of Aspen's car. We're both pretty sure once it sits
in one place long enough, the police will tag it as an abandoned
vehicle and run the plate and Aspen will get her ten-year-old
vehicle back.

Gordon had been right—just because the person who wrote
me all those horrible letters called himself "Tim" didn't mean
my stalker was a man.

Later, when we were at Bruckman's house, he pulled the
raunchy video up on his computer. I watched it with him for
several minutes but couldn't stomach any more. I told him to
take all the time he wanted, but that I was going to bed.

That's when he said, "I'm not done with you yet," and turned
to me with a sexy gleam in his eyes.

I hadn't been asleep for a half hour when Gordon called to
say he'd been released from the hospital—that the heart attack
they thought he had was indigestion from too much fatty barbeque brisket. I blame Byron for that, since he's a partner in
one of the more famous barbeque hangouts in Fort Worth, and
he's all the time hauling Gordon over there to eat for free.

As for Paislee, I had a short conversation with Gordon about
her. He didn't blame her for wanting to trade identities with
Penslee to taste the glamorous life of a model. But now that
she'd gotten it out of her system and wanted to be home, they're
going to work on their marriage since she thinks she'd like to be
a mom. I didn't want to burst his bubble and reveal the fly in

the ointment, but that's what happens when you own you~~r~~ detective agency and are just naturally inquisitive.

Something didn't set quite right with me about this wh~~o~~ Penslee-and-Drex thing. I didn't realize it until after I mentione~~d~~ Drex and the Labor Day party to Paislee at the house, that she really did have an affair with my boyfriend before Penslee ever came into the picture.

I figured this out once I checked the dates Drex was home from college against the calendar on my cell phone because he didn't spend that time with me even though friends later insisted they'd seen us huddled together in a few dark theaters here and there.

But I'm not going to say anything. The police are still investigating Penslee's murder, and I figure the part about Paislee and Drex will come out in due time. It's not for me to burst Gordon's bubble. In the meantime, in Rochelle's office pool, I've got my money on Tig Welder, and I'm looking forward to spending my winnings at a little B&B on the Gulf Coast when Tig's wearing stripes, and it turns out I won.

As for my externship, Gordon gave it back to me, full salary and all. And I get to do the *News at Ten* while Aspen and Sheriff Granger are off on that trip Byron not only authorized the station to pay for, but mandated they do so. He thought WBFD would actually come out ahead if they gave her a nice paid-for dream vacation instead of having to foot the bill for her therapy if she sued them. Between me and you, Aspen's not that type of person. She's more "live and let live," like *moi.* But I imagined when she and Granger weren't kissing each other, they were kissing the Blarney Stone and looking up her Irish relatives.

Believe it or not, I arrived home the next morning to find Teensy sitting at the breakfast table. Tear tracks stained her face, and when she looked up at me from a half-eaten bowl of cold cereal, I wanted to hug her.

. said, "Mandy left us."

gave her a blank look. To get my goat, she'd taken to calling
nanda "Mandy" like Amanda was her BFF—while we all
now that she's *my* BFF. Even so, I slid in across the table from
my sister to get the details.

Images of Amanda, dressed in drag, vibrated off the top of
my head. "Tell the truth—did Gran throw her out?"

Teensy shook her head. "Are you kidding? Gran likes her better than us. Go figure." She took a deep breath. "Amanda
missed her kids." She sniffled. "She said she'll be back, but I
don't think so. It's like taking a fish out of salt water, and trying
to make it live in fresh water, you know?"

I wanted to cry, too. She hadn't even said good-bye to me.

"You'll be happy to know I quit my job at WBFD, so you can
have your externship back." I didn't tell her Gordon already
gave it to me. She dabbed at her tears with her napkin and said,
"Chopper Deke texted me a picture of his junk." My eyes
widened, and she went on, "I'm not going to say anything to
Mr. Pfeiffer, though. I really like Chopper Deke. He saved my
life. If he wants to send me a picture of his junk, fine by me."

"Pics, or it didn't happen."

"Sorry, I deleted it." She brightened. "But I can show you
the picture I sent him of my junk if you like." She winked to
show she didn't mean it.

I told her I had to change clothes and get to the station in
time to do the noon broadcast. And I asked her what she wanted
for Christmas.

Her eyes glittered with tears. "Everything I want is right here
in this room."

Exactly.

I trudged up to my room to find that my bed had been made
with fresh sheets, and a note written in a surprisingly elegant
script had been left on my pillow.

Diva,

You white people aren't normal. This morning, Gran ask me if I wanted to chaperone her cruise with Old Man Spence. What's that about? I have no interest seeing wrinkled old codgers in swim trunks and bikinis. I delivered pizzas to his house the other day for his grandson's birthday and they were all sitting around the table wearing beanies. What's up with that?

Don't panic, I'll be back. I told Teensy I left because I missed my kids, but the truth is that I have a pesky little hearing which I now can take care of since I have the money to pay off my restitution, thanks to my menial and demeaning delivery job at Crazy Gianni's. Besides, I have to come back. You people need help. Not to mention I have a date with that guy at the nudist colony. Plus, I wouldn't miss Christmas with the white people for any amount of money. You never know who'll show up, right?

Love,

Amanda

P.S. Don't be so hard on Gran. She's kind of cool, and even when she's not, she's good for entertainment purposes. She's got her eye on a crocodile belt, by the way. She showed me when we went to Harkman Beemis the other day, and she told people I was her own personal elf. The sales clerk's holding the belt, so feel free to thank me. You're welcome.

P.P.S. I know what you're getting for Christmas because I heard your crazy grandmother talking to the Porsche guy. It's pink, your signature color, and she called a friend of a friend with a friend down at the capitol to make sure your DBUTNT license plates arrive in time. All I can say is you're getting scarves from me if there's anything left of my measly paycheck so you can ride around topless. I'm talking about your new

*ertible, diva; not your brief stint as a pole dancer on the
ernet. But don't spill the beans. Let them think you're
urprised.*

CHAPTER THIRTY

On the way to my job, I stopped at the little sweets boutique and bought a flat of Gran's favorite candy, and took it to the station. When I got out of the car, I saw Mr. Bilburn outside watering his pansies. The little boy who wanted my autograph was outside, too, playing with a couple of bright toy trucks that I'm pretty sure his mama bought him with the money I paid her so she wouldn't sue me. I called them over to the fence, and as they walked toward me, I ran back to the car and got an armful of candy boxes and lobbed them over the wall.

"From me, to you," I said, and hurried on in before the cold got to me.

I had about forty-five minutes to spare so I pulled out my journal and grabbed a pen.

Dear Diary,

The last two months have been so sad and unpleasant that I decided to re-boot the year, burn the calendar, and upgrade to next year's Version 2.0. Welcome to the slightly shortened version of my new year.

Now that things have calmed down around here, and the holidays have brought a lull in business for the Debutante Detective Agency, I've started my search for Chopper Deke's daughter. I hope, when the time comes, that this turns out to be a good reunion and that I don't uncover any horrible secrets: like that his daughter has a sketchy past; or she's serving time in the penitentiary; or she turns out to be a

digger wanting to fleece Chopper Deke of his entire savings. I
n't have a lot to go on at the moment, but I intend to give it my
best shot.

Nerissa's still locked up in the county jail, awaiting trial, and the
rumor around here is that her trial has been set for sometime next
year. Like everything else around here, we don't discuss the matter
because the whole sordid mess is so Rubanbleu-unapproved.

At the moment, we're preparing for Christmas at the Prescott
mansion, and when Teensy opens her presents from my blue-haired
grandmother, I'll try to hold it together and play like I don't miss the
new clothes Gran raided from my closet.

Daddy already said he's bringing Jillian Wicklow to have
Christmas dinner with us. Good news, though—if it turns into a
debacle like Thanksgiving, she has a closed-head injury with short-
term memory loss so she probably won't even remember what happened.

I can already visualize Bruckman and me taking my new car out
for a spin—top down and our blonde hair ruffling in the breeze. I
know what I'm getting from him, even though he doesn't know I
know. Nobody spilled the beans—I simply pretended to be comatose
when he wrapped a tape measure around my ring finger.

As for me, I already got the real Teensy back so I have everything
that I need. And as for Daddy, I've decided to forgive the two million
dollars he owes me. And if he doesn't forgive the $1,996,854.78 bill
he presented me for raising my "spoiled, pampered ass," then I can
always bill him double that amount for bringing my sister back from
Mexico.

Because around the Prescott compound, it just isn't Christmas unless somebody cries.

ABOUT THE AUTHOR

Sixth-generation Texan **Laurie Moore** received her B.A. from the University of Texas at Austin and entered a career in law enforcement in 1979. In 1992, she moved to Fort Worth and earned a degree from Texas Wesleyan University School of Law in 1995. She is currently in private practice in "Cowtown" and lives with her husband and a rude Welsh corgi. As a licensed, commissioned peace officer, she recently celebrated her 34th year in law enforcement.

Laurie is the author of *Constable's Run*, *Constable's Apprehension*, *Constable's Wedding*, *The Lady Godiva Murder*, *The Wild Orchid Society*, *Jury Rigged*, *Woman Strangled—News at Ten*, *Deb on Arrival—Live at Five*, *Couple Gunned Down—News at Ten*, and *Wanted Deb or Alive*. Contact Laurie through her website at www.LaurieMooreMysteries.com.